TEETOTALED

Also by Maia Chance

TEETOTALED

Maia Chance

MINOTAUR BOOKS
New York

TEETOTALED. Copyright © 2016 by Maia Chance. All rights reserved. Printed in the United States of America. For information, address St. Martin's Press, 175 Fifth Avenue, New York, N.Y. 10010.

www.minotaurbooks.com

LIBRARY OF CONGRESS CATALOGING-IN-PUBLICATION DATA

Names: Chance, Maia, author.
Title: Teetotaled / Maia Chance.
Description: First Edition. | New York: Minotaur Books, 2016. | Series: Discreet Retrieval Agency mysteries; 2
Identifiers: LCCN 2016016833 | ISBN 9781250072214 (hardback) | ISBN 9781466883598 (e-book)
Subjects: | BISAC: FICTION / Mystery & Detective / Historical. | FICTION / Mystery & Detective / Women Sleuths. | GSAFD: Mystery fiction.
Classification: LCC PS3603.H35593 T44 2016 | DDC 813/.6—dc23
LC record available at https://lccn.loc.gov/2016016833

Our books may be purchased in bulk for promotional, educational, or business use. Please contact your local bookseller or the Macmillan Corporate and Premium Sales Department at 1-800-221-7945, extension 5442, or by e-mail at MacmillanSpecialMarkets@macmillan.com.

First Edition: October 2016

10 9 8 7 6 5 4 3 2 1

For Somer.
We'll just have to arm wrestle over which
one of us gets to be Berta.

Everything in life that's any fun, as somebody wisely observed,
is either immoral, illegal, or fattening.

—P. G. WODEHOUSE

TEETOTALED

1

July 14, 1923

The afternoon Sophronia Whiddle offered us the diary job, it was so hot, you could've sizzled bacon on the sidewalk. Which wasn't a half-bad idea, come to think of it, except that I was out of funds for bacon. I'd been living on shredded wheat for days. All right, hours.

My detecting partner, Berta Lundgren, and I were reading at the kitchen table in our poky little Washington Square apartment, waiting for the telephone to ring. Stagnant city air puffed in from the window. My Pomeranian, Cedric, panted in front of an electric fan. I yawned, and turned a page of the latest issue of *Thrilling Romance*.

"Mrs. Woodby, would it be remiss of me to suggest that you spend your leisure hours reading edifying publications?" Berta asked in her stern Swedish accent. She held up her book. *Mexico City Mayhem*, by Frank B. Jones, Jr. The cover depicted a man in a fedora wrestling a sinister-looking fellow in some sort of Aztec temple.

"*That* is edifying?" I asked.

"Indeed. Thad Parker's advice for decrypting ancient hieroglyphics could benefit our detective agency. *Thrilling Romance* is merely, well, pulp."

"But Jake Cadwell, Wall Street tycoon, is about to propose marriage to innocent young Lucinda from the typing pool. It's all she's ever dreamed of."

"I do realize you are pining for the absent Ralph Oliver—"

"Pining? What absolute hooey."

"—but between you and me, Mrs. Woodby, if a man abruptly ceases to telephone, well, it is an indication that he has lost interest."

"I don't give a squirrel's acorn about what Ralph Oliver may or may not be interested in. Besides, he's on a job in Cuba."

"If you say so."

I gave *Thrilling Romance* a shake and resumed reading.

The clock ticked.

I looked up. "I happened to notice that *you* boing like a broken spring every time the telephone jingles."

"I am hopeful for detective work."

"Not hopeful that Jimmy the Ant wishes to squire you to the movie palace?"

"Mr. Ant must keep a low profile for a time."

"He's hiding from the Feds, you know."

Berta sent me a dirty look, patted her gray bun, and went back to her book.

Is this what had become of the newly hatched Discreet Retrieval Agency? Two sweaty, bickering ladies waiting for ginky fellows to telephone?

We needed work.

A knock at the apartment door launched me to the little entry foyer. Berta wasn't far behind. Cedric made a halfhearted yap but stayed in the kitchen. He had been lackluster lately because he was on strict kibble rations. If he didn't slim down in time for his photograph session in two weeks, the people at Spratt's Puppy Biscuits weren't going to use him in their advertising campaign. Cedric's career would be over before it began.

"You do not have shoes on, Mrs. Woodby," Berta said. "If it is a client—"

"Oh, they'll understand," I said, and opened the door. At first it seemed that no one was there. Just the stairwell, stinking of mildew and fried onions. Then I noticed the snub-nosed five-year-old boy.

"Oh, hello, Sam," I said. "What have you there?"

"Five cents, ma'am," Sam lisped. He held up a grubby nickel. "Ma said this is for finding Puffy."

"Thanks awfully, Sam, but why don't you keep your money? Tell your mother the job is on us. Puffy was only behind the water tank on the roof. He wasn't really lost."

"Okay, sure, thanks something fierce, Mrs. Woodby!" Sam pocketed the nickel and scampered up the stairs in the direction of his family's third-floor apartment.

I shut the door and turned.

Berta blocked the foyer doorway. "This simply will not do," she said.

"You're preaching to the choir."

"What has our commission been since we printed our business cards? Zilch."

"Don't remind me. I drank the last drop of whiskey last night. I'm now an unwilling teetotaler."

We drifted back to the kitchen.

In the past month, our fledgling agency had solved a total of five cases: disappearing milk bottles, nicked newspapers, two lost cats (including Puffy), and a spying endeavor involving the teenaged Martin Ulsky and his two-timing ways. The only payment we'd accepted was a set of Mrs. Bent's hand-knitted egg cozies. Which *were* pretty cute.

"The rent will be due again," Berta said.

"That's the trouble with rent."

"Perhaps we should take out a larger newspaper advertisement. I knew the one-and-a-half-inch square would not attract enough notice."

Another knock sounded on the door. Cedric didn't bother yapping this time.

Berta and I locked desperate eyes.

"For pity's sake, Mrs. Woodby, put on your shoes."

Once I'd stuffed my feet into a pair of T-straps, Berta opened the door.

"I had almost decided that I had the wrong address," a stout, elegant, middle-aged woman said. "But I see it is indeed you, Lola Woodby." Her eyes flicked to Berta. "And . . . your cook?"

"Mrs. Lundgren used to be my cook," I said. "How pleasant to see you, Mrs. Whiddle." Seeing Sophronia Whiddle was about as pleasant as an ingrown toenail. Sophronia was not only a New York grande dame, but my own mother's bosom friend, too. Mother, by the way, had no inkling that I'd gone into the gumshoe trade. I was supposed to be mourning my recently popped-off husband, Alfie. But since Alfie had left me high and dry, I was no longer a pampered, thirty-one-year-old Society Matron. I was a working lady. At least, I was trying to be a working lady.

Sophronia did a once-over of my wrinkly, last-season dress, my mussed dark brown bob, and my wide mouth and blue eyes that I hadn't spruced up with lipstick or mascara. I was conserving the last of my department store cosmetics.

"Might I come in?" Sophronia asked.

"Of course," I said.

Berta and I led Sophronia through to the sitting room. I slid magazines and dime novels under a sofa cushion. I hid the dregs of last night's highball behind knickknacks on the mantel. "Please, sit," I said.

Sophronia perched gingerly on the sofa as though she feared contracting a health concern. Which was indeed a faint possibility, given that this was Alfie's former love nest. Untold cavortings with chorus girls had occurred on that sofa.

Berta and I sat in the two chairs facing the sofa.

"What brings you here, Mrs. Whiddle?" I asked. "I wasn't aware that Mother knew of this address. Is it something to do with the Ladies' Opera Society?"

"Your mother knows nothing of this, and she never shall."

Oh, thank goodness.

Sophronia extracted a slip of newsprint from her handbag and unfolded it to reveal our advertisement. "'The Discreet Retrieval Agency'? 'No job too trivial'?"

"Oh. Right. Yes, that's us," I said. "You weren't surprised to see us, yet our names aren't on the advertisement. How did you know?"

"Does it matter? I have a job for you. I wish to keep the matter among the *right sort* of people, you see." Sophronia folded the paper and replaced it in her handbag. "You must retrieve my daughter Grace's diary."

"Can't you do that yourself?" I asked.

"No, no. Quite impossible. You see, Grace is a peculiar girl, an awkward wallflower, really, and although, alas, she is not terribly bright—she takes after her poor deceased father's family in that regard—she has, since the age of ten, been a passionate diarist. Scribbles in it incessantly, keeps the back-logs locked in a small safe in her bedroom. She has always guarded her diary with an unbecoming ferocity."

"Would you explain, Mrs. Whiddle?" Berta asked.

"Once when Grace was fourteen years old—she is nineteen now, you know—I was mildly concerned about her possible interest in a rather too forward grocer's delivery boy. I wished to look into her diary to discover if I had any reason to worry. Well, I attempted to take it from Grace while she was sleeping—she sleeps with it under her pillow—and she woke, raving and thrashing, and she bit me! It was terrifying, really."

"Why do you wish for us to retrieve this diary?" I asked.

"Grace is to be married in eight days—surely you are aware of this, Mrs. Woodby. It is to be the society wedding of the summer. I believe I sent you an invitation months ago."

"I'd plum forgotten," I said.

"Grace is to marry Gilbert Morris—you do know the Morrises?"

I nodded. Winfield Morris, Gilbert Morris's father, was not only a high-society fat cat but a New York state senator as well.

"Grace will not have another chance like this," Sophronia said. "She is plump, you see, and she requires glasses. I fear there may be things in her past, recorded in the diary, that could jeopardize her marriage."

"How do you propose that we retrieve the diary?" I asked.

"How? Well, I would assume that devising the how of the matter is your job, Mrs. Woodby."

True. "From your house?"

"No, no. From the health farm. Grace is booked in for the week."

"If your daughter is to be a bride," Berta said, "why is she visiting a health farm?"

"To slim," Sophronia said. "She will wear my own wedding gown, and the seamstress has already let it out to its utmost capacity. I told Grace it was up to her to do the rest."

"A nice strong girdle might do the trick," I said.

Berta said, "In my village in Sweden, the plump girls were the most popular. Men prefer girls who are liberal with butter."

Sophronia compressed her lipsticked mouth. "At any rate, while Grace is booked into Willow Acres Health Farm on Long Island— do you know it?"

I almost fell sideways in my chair. "No," I lied.

"But I understand that your brother-in-law, Dr. Chisholm Woodby, is the owner and head doctor," Sophronia said.

"Oh, *that* Willow Acres. Yes. I mean, no. I mean to say no, we simply can't accept the job."

"Of course we will accept the job," Berta said, cutting me a death glare.

I got up and went to the window. I had to look like I was noodling profoundly, even if there wasn't an ice cube's chance in Hell that I would say yes. "The job will be compromised," I said over my shoulder. "Not only are you, Mrs. Whiddle, my own mother's friend, but Dr. Woodby would not be keen on me checking into his farm. We aren't precisely pals."

"We are a discreet agency, Mrs. Whiddle," Berta said loudly, "and as such, we select our cases with great care. . . ."

"Yes, of course," Sophronia said. "You must discuss it in privacy. I'll just go and fix my hat in the powder room."

"Down the hallway on the right," I said.

Berta and I waited until we heard the bathroom door shut.

"Are you mad, Mrs. Woodby?" Berta whispered. "We must take this job. We are nearly broke."

"If my mother finds out about our agency, she'll be angrier than a wet cat and she'll do everything in her power to put an end to it. She will say I'm ruining the family's social standing and Father's Wall Street connections. That I'm crushing Andy's and Lillian's"— these were my siblings—"chances of being invited to play tennis with Vanderbilts and Rockefellers and, oh, I don't know, the King of England. And she'd be *correct*."

"Your mother will find out about our agency sooner or later."

"Golly, I hope not. It's grisly enough that I'm making a mess of my own life without bringing down my entire family. Anyway, Berta, what about Chisholm? If we go to his health farm, we'll be at his mercy. I wonder what he does to his patients at that farm. I'd bet a million bucks that health bread has something to do with it."

"Health bread?" Berta hesitated. "Well, it will only be for a day or two, surely."

"There's no guarantee of that."

"If we are to make a go of this agency, we must do our utmost. Are you willing to do your utmost, Mrs. Woodby?"

Berta was right: I had to take the plunge. Say toodle-pip to my old life and take my future by the horns.

"Well?" Sophronia said, coming back into the sitting room. "If you don't wish to accept the job, there is another agency that—"

"We'll do it," I said.

"I might rely upon your utmost discretion?"

"Of course," I said, and Berta nodded.

We worked out all the details. Sophronia would pay for our stay at Willow Acres, and we would endeavor to pry the diary from Grace Whiddle's clutches posthaste. Once we delivered the diary to Sophronia at her Long Island estate, Clyde's Bluff, we would collect our fee of five hundred clams.

The Discreet Retrieval Agency was back on its feet.

2

The next morning, Berta and I made a bright and early start of it and motored the forty-odd miles to Willow Acres in my cinnamon-and-cream-colored Duesenberg Model A. With its white-wall tires and dazzling chrome, the Duesy is a relic of my former prosperity. *Sigh*.

Cedric snoozed on the backseat. I couldn't afford a dog-minder, and Cedric isn't welcome at my parents' Park Avenue apartment, because he gives my sister, Lillian, hives. The only wrinkle was that I hadn't mentioned I'd be bringing Cedric when I telephoned Chisholm yesterday.

Green farms and forests gave way to the quaint villages, misty sea cliffs, and mansions of the Gold Coast. It was a smidge past eight o'clock when I braked at iron gates next to a gatekeeper's lodge. A brass plaque said WILLOW ACRES. Laurel hedges obscured the property.

"Here goes nothing," I said to Berta. "I have a qualmy feeling about this."

"The job is cut-and-dried."

"If you say so." I gave the gatekeeper our names and he let us through. I glanced in the rearview mirror just in time to see the gates shut. We rolled to a stop in the drive before a faux-Gothic mansion complete with arched windows and a couple of turrets. Flat lawns, pruned shrubs, squeaky-clean windows. "Looks like a loony bin," I said. "The kind they lock you up in and then flush the key down the lav."

"It is not particularly homey-looking," Berta said.

"We really should've stopped for a nice, greasy breakfast at a roadside hash house." I switched off the engine. Berta and I had left the city after only a cup of coffee and three pancakes each. "I'm already hungry, and I'll bet orderlies will try to slip stewed prunes down our gullets."

"Here comes the insect," Berta said. "He is ever so stiff. I suppose it is a result of the health bread. It is so difficult to digest."

Dr. Chisholm Woodby came toward us like a tall, dark, and handsome revivified corpse. Chisholm—aka the Prig—was my former brother-in-law by virtue of being the sibling of my deceased spouse, Alfie, and, alas, my *future* brother-in-law by virtue of being engaged to my sister, Lillian.

He stopped at my open window. "Hello, Lola. I trust you had a pleasant journey?"

"Peachy," I said.

"Good. I am not a man given to sentiment, as you are doubtless aware, but I must confess that I was moved by your telephone call yesterday. So many people are unable to come to grips with their problems, believing that they are simply moral failings. Morality does, naturally, play its part in problems such as yours, but—"

"Wait," I said. "Which problems are we speaking of?"

"This is a health farm, Lola. Hence, I speak of your health problems."

"Um." I glanced down at my middle, almost—but not quite!—touching the steering wheel. The truth is, I don't have a flapper's lollipop figure. It's at times difficult to spot my ankles, and I rely upon scientifically engineered girdles to simulate a waist. But I've got style, and the fellows seem to like me. "My health problems," I said. "Right." On the telephone yesterday, I'd told Chisholm that Berta and I wished to book into Willow Acres for a few days' respite from the hot city. Not to slim.

"The same goes for Mrs. Lundgren, of course," Chisholm said, stooping to give a terse nod to Berta in the passenger seat.

Berta maintained a stony silence. She had recently quit her post as cook in Chisholm's household on the grounds that she could not work for a man who banned butter, cream, sugar, flour, and everything else that tastes good.

Cedric barked in the backseat.

Chisholm's eye twitched. "I did not realize you were bringing your canine, Lola."

I'd already concocted my argument. "Isn't your clientele mostly ladies in the hoity-toity set?"

"Well—"

"The Carnegies are awfully fond of their dogs, and so are the Astors. You don't wish to give people the wrong idea about Willow Acres by banning dogs, do you?"

"Are you threatening me, Lola?"

I beamed. "Of course not. I'm *helping*."

"Very well," Chisholm snapped. "But do clean up after the dog. Nurse Astrid will see you to your room. Good morning."

Nurse Astrid was a bony young woman with brown curls, a white pinafore, a white cap, and glasses. She directed one male orderly to park the Duesy in some hidden lot, and another to collect our luggage.

"No, no, I prefer to carry my own suitcase," Berta said.

Nurse Astrid said, "But—"

"I insist." Berta wriggled her suitcase from the backseat.

I picked up Cedric, and we followed Nurse Astrid inside. In the lobby, twin staircases spilled to a sweep of marble floor. Plushy furniture, potted banana trees, gilt-framed landscapes, an antiseptic hush.

"'Room,' in the singular?" I said, huffing and puffing to keep up with Nurse Astrid.

"Yes, I am afraid we are quite booked up, so you and Mrs. Lundgren must share a room. You will not spend much time there, anyway. We keep the patients busy here at Willow Acres." Nurse Astrid led us up the stairs and along empty corridors.

"Where is everyone?" I asked. "Still asleep?"

"Willow Acres guests rise at six o'clock sharp," Nurse Astrid said.

"Then they're at breakfast?" I asked in a hopeful voice.

"Oh, no. Everyone supped upon bone broth and herbal tea at six fifteen, and they are now stimulating their muscles at the morning vigorology session. You must change quickly, and then you will be able to participate in the second half of the session." We stopped at a thick oak door. Nurse Astrid unlocked it with a key from her apron pocket. "You will be staying just through here."

"Why is the door locked?" I asked.

"Merely a precaution. We prefer to keep patients out of their quarters during the day to encourage full participation in the treatment program, and at night we will lock you *in* so you aren't tempted to undo all your hard work by sneaking away to the fish and chips stand down the road." Nurse Astrid ushered us down a corridor to the small room that Berta and I were to share. "Your vigorology costumes are in the wardrobe. Please change quickly. There is a small bathroom inside your room. I shall be waiting outside in the East Ward lounge at the end of the corridor in order to escort you outside." She left.

I shut the door and let Cedric loose to sniff around. Berta slung her small suitcase on one of the narrow beds and flipped the clasps.

"Did you hear her?" I whispered. "She said 'ward.' I think we have been roped into one of Chisholm's loony bins!" Did I mention that Chisholm is also the chief nerve specialist at Babbling Brook Hospital? His zeal for bettering other people knows no bounds.

"Nonsense," Berta said. "They think of this place as a hospital, and in a hospital, floors are called wards. Do stop panicking. It makes that vein stand out on your forehead like a—"

"Chocolate!" I cried. Berta's suitcase was neatly packed with about a dozen Hershey's chocolate bars and several yellow tins of Rold Gold butter pretzels.

"Shhh," Berta said. "The nurse will hear."

"But you've brought *chocolate* in your suitcase." I might've swooned.

Berta shut her suitcase. "I brought those items for professional reasons, Mrs. Woodby. The guests of this establishment are being deprived of every pleasure in life, so I conclude that they will be more than willing to pay top dollar for respite."

"Black-market chocolate and pretzels?"

"You need not make it sound so unclean. The items could also be used for bribes, if necessary. For the diary job, I mean to say."

"Could I have some chocolate? Please?"

Berta sighed. "Oh, very well." She opened her suitcase, selected a Hershey's bar, and handed it over. "But that is the last one."

"Sure, okay," I said, ripping through paper and foil.

Berta went to the wardrobe, opened it, and made an alarmed whinny.

"Is everything all right?" Nurse Astrid called through the door.

"Is she spying on us?" I whispered. I joined Berta by the wardrobe. "Oh. Zowie."

"These must be the vigorology costumes," Berta said.

"They certainly aren't cocktail dresses." Even though it was likely that Nurse Astrid was spying on us through the keyhole, I broke off a couple squares of chocolate and crammed them in my mouth. For courage. I hid the rest of the chocolate bar between the radiator and the wall.

A few minutes later, Nurse Astrid escorted Berta and me outside. Cedric followed, panting. The sun was already set to Broil. Four groups of patients populated the huge rear lawn, each being led through calisthenic rituals by an instructor.

"You will perform your vigorology sessions with the other occupants of your ward," Nurse Astrid said. "You will take all your meals with them, too."

Like a chain gang, I supposed. "Do you know if Grace Whiddle is staying in our ward?" I asked.

"Why, yes, she is. Are you her—?" Nurse Astrid gave me an assessing glance. "Are you her mother's friend?"

"Yes," I said through gritted teeth.

Berta was peering hard at the group to which Nurse Astrid was leading us. "But this group includes gentlemen. Do you mean to say that we will be sleeping in a ward occupied by gentlemen?"

"Think of it as a hotel, Mrs. Lundgren," Nurse Astrid said in a soothing voice.

Berta clucked her tongue.

Nurse Astrid left us.

I ushered Cedric to a bench in the shade, and Berta and I took our places behind six patients writhing on the lawn. Everyone was facedown and everyone wore—like Berta and me—black knee-length pantaloons, short-sleeved white cotton shirts, and canvas tennis shoes. Not a look from the pages of *Vogue*.

"One, two, three, four!" chanted our vigorology instructor, whom Nurse Astrid had referred to as Mr. Ulf. Ulf was clothed in nothing but a petite pair of white shorts, the kind circus strongmen wear. Although his face was that of an elderly man, his torso and limbs were muscled and spry. He had a thick German accent. "One, two, three, four!"

The six patients thrashed and moaned.

"We really need not do this," I whispered to Berta.

"Indeed we must, Mrs. Woodby," Berta whispered back.

"We could hide out in the dining room until lunch."

"That would be unprofessional."

"Who's going to notice if we—?"

"Ladies!" Ulf boomed, stone-faced. "Take your places." He pointed to the grass at our feet.

Berta placed her big black handbag on the grass. She rarely went anywhere without her handbag. We knelt, and Berta's knees creaked and popped. Wait. Were those *my* knees?

"One more round of wheelbarrows!" Ulf yelled. "One, two, three, four!"

On and on it went. The sun slid higher in a vivid blue sky. Perspiration dripped from my hair and trickled down my back. Cedric looked smug on his shady bench.

I guessed it was Grace Whiddle up in the front row. Grace was by far the youngest, tall, fair, blond, and only slightly plump. Her glasses slipped down her nose with every corkscrew and gyration. Next to her was a short, wiry young man with muscular arms. He looked familiar.

Two more men made up the second row: one tall, lanky, and handsome; the other squat and redheaded. Two ladies made up the third row, both of whom I knew by sight. The first was the authoress

Violet Wilbur, America's unrivaled doyenne of tasteful home décor. Her photograph always accompanied her weekly magazine column. Violet was thin and droopy, with frizzled graying hair and a sour mouth. The second woman was Muffy Morris, the thickset, yellow-coifed wife of Senator Winfield Morris. She wore diamond earrings and pearls with her regulation getup. What a show-box. She probably wore those jewels in the bathtub.

Muffy seemed to have her eyes stuck on Grace, and then it hit me: Muffy Morris was Grace Whiddle's future mother-in-law. Just imagine visiting a fat farm with your future mother-in-law. Shudder.

At last, Mr. Ulf instructed everyone to rise for the final exercise. He called them "sunbursts," but the sad truth is, we looked like a bunch of overweight toddlers leaping for the cookie jar.

"I'm going . . . for . . . the diary," I panted to Berta as the class disbanded. "Would you . . . look after . . . Cedric?"

Berta, borscht-red and shiny with sweat, could only nod.

I crossed the lawn, went inside the mansion, and found my way to the door of the East Ward. I twisted the doorknob. Locked.

"Could I assist you with something, Mrs. Woodby?" Nurse Astrid asked, appearing beside me.

"I'm, um, simply dying to change out of this vigorology costume," I said.

"Oh, that isn't only your vigorology costume, dear. You will wear that during all your waking hours, unless, of course, you are in your bathing suit."

That confirmed it: I was trapped in my own worst nightmare. Style or no, I won't be caught dead in a bathing suit. Exposing my tender white flesh to the glare of sunlight and scrutiny? No, thanks awfully.

"Come along," Nurse Astrid said crisply. "I'll escort you to the exercise-apparatus room. I believe Dr. Woodby has prescribed for you and Mrs. Lundgren extensive time on the hip-slimming machines."

3

The exercise-apparatus room must once have been the mansion's ballroom, with its expanse of parquet floor, vaulted ceiling, and tall windows. But now, with all those steel contraptions and grimacing people, it could've been an up-to-date torture chamber. Three ladies pedaled stationary bicycles. A man trudged to nowhere on a grinding treadmill. Another man hoisted strongman weights, snorting, and two ladies wrestled huge rubber bands on the floor. Fun, fun, fun.

I caught sight of Berta in a chair, leafing through a magazine. Cedric sat at her feet. I went over.

"Did you retrieve the diary?" Berta asked me.

"No. The ward is kept locked, and I was intercepted by Nurse Astrid. Why aren't you on a hip-slimming machine? I happen to know Chisholm prescribed those for both of us."

"I informed the nurse that vibration of any sort riles up my heart-burn."

"Why didn't I think of that?"

"As soon as I see Grace Whiddle, I will attempt to insinuate myself into her confidences."

"Good plan."

"This room smells quite overwhelmingly of underarm, does it not?"

"That, and despair."

A nurse appeared and strapped me to a hip-slimming machine. "Simply stand still for thirty minutes," she said to me, "and the strap's vibration will melt your fat away." She flipped a switch and left me. My hips joggled and buzzed.

Exercise? A cakewalk.

My teeth were still vibrating when I went to luncheon, but my hips didn't feel a bit more svelte.

The dining room was elegant, with wainscoting and stained glass windows. Pristine linens, bone china, silver, and fresh roses decorated the East Ward's table. Berta and Grace Whiddle were in the midst of a hushed heart-to-heart. Muffy Morris and the squat redheaded man spooned up broth side by side.

I sat, settled Cedric on my lap, and introduced myself to everyone.

"How do you do, Mrs. Woodby?" Grace said in a sweet voice. "I believe our mothers are the best of friends." She went back to her heart-to-heart with Berta. Berta gave me a surreptitious nod: she was making progress.

The squat redheaded man turned out to be Hermie Inchbald, Muffy Morris's brother. "How nice of you two to come to Willow Acres together," I said.

"Hermie is an angel," Muffy said. Her eyes and skin were dull, but her diamond earrings sparkled.

"My sister is my best friend," Hermie said. "No one else understands me. Except Bitsy, of course."

"Your wife?" I asked.

"His poodle," Berta whispered.

The handsome, lanky man sat down next to me and stuck out a large hand. "Raymond Hathorne," he said easily.

"Lola Woodby."

"Well, I'll be." Raymond grinned. "I know you."

"Do you?"

"Your mother, Mrs. DuFey, sings your praises every time she corners me. Saw her just two days ago at a polo match at the country club. She had on the most astounding hat." Raymond's Rs were ever so slightly throaty.

Raymond Hathorne. Of course. Mother had been attempting to throw me together with Raymond Hathorne for more than a month, ever since she met him aboard a Cunard ocean liner. I'd pictured him as one more bloated patriarch, but he was actually a bit of a sheik with his dark hair and eyes, sculpture-museum bone structure, and elegant strut. Honestly, Raymond was the only person in the entire dining room who didn't look like Bobo the Clown in the regulation bloomers and tennis shoes. "That's right," I said. "Mr. Hathorne. You're in—what was it?—soda pop?"

"That's the ticket. Hathorne's the name and soda pop's my game. Fizz-Whiz—heard of it?"

"No."

"Only available in Canada. Came down to make a go of the American market." That explained Raymond's throaty Rs; he must've been French Canadian. "Still in the research phase, though. Something tells me maple-flavored soda pop wouldn't be much of a hot seller here."

Maple-flavored soda pop sounded tasty to me.

The short, wiry man with the muscular arms sat down and introduced himself as Pete Schlump.

Berta peeped with excitement.

"Pleased to meet you, Mr. Schlump," I said. "Of course. You're the Yankees pitcher." I'm no sports nut, but Pete had made the news a few weeks back when his pitching took a sudden nosedive. Schlump's Slump, the newspapers called it. His rotten pitching had dragged the Yankees down a few notches in their standing.

"That's me," Pete said, looking a little sheepish.

Violet Wilbur perched on my other side, and I introduced myself.

"Hello," Violet said, offering me her tiny, limp hand.

"I often read your column in *Tête-à-Tête* magazine," I said. "Wasn't it you who declared that rose damask upholstery by any other name is just as sweet?"

"Mm," Violet said with a prickly smile. "Do you know, I'm just now up to my elbows in redecorating your former house for your sister, Lillian."

"Oh? How lovely." What a sucker punch. After my husband died, Chisholm inherited what had been my house, and since Lillian was to marry Chisholm . . . well, you get the picture.

"You've just published another instructional book, too, I understand," Muffy said to Violet.

"Yes," Violet said. "*The Tasteful Abode.*"

"Perhaps I ought to give dear Grace a copy as a wedding gift," Muffy said with a spiteful glint in her eye. "She will need all the assistance she can find in attempting to make a proper wife for my Gil."

The table fell silent.

"Now, see here," Pete Schlump said.

"Petey," Grace whispered in a warning tone. Maybe it was because Grace wasn't wearing her glasses, but when she looked at Pete, her eyes had a dreamy, Vaseline-on-the-camera-lens glow.

Good thing I need not break *that* news to Sophronia Whiddle.

"Golly, what I wouldn't give for a highball and some smoked salmon sandwiches," I said in a chummy undertone to cut the tension. "I'd even settle for some rum punch in this positively tropical heat."

"Oh, I do agree, Mrs. Woodby," Muffy said, leaning forward eagerly. "Although, of course, not rum. I never touch that vile stuff. But a highball, yes, a highball would be refreshing—"

Hermie touched Muffy's arm; Muffy clammed up.

Well, well. Looked like Muffy was in the clink for tippling.

A waiter appeared with a dish of sautéed steak for Cedric. I cut up the steak and set the dish and Cedric on the floor. I'm ashamed to say my mouth watered.

"That's a Pomeranian you have there, isn't it, Mrs. Woodby?" Hermie asked me. "I breed poodles myself."

"Oh?"

"It's a balm for the soul. I first encountered the breed in France during the war. They're trained to sniff about for truffles in the forests, you know. Awfully clever beasts."

"I didn't know you were in France, Inchbald," Raymond said.

"Yes." Hermie poked his gold-framed glasses back up his nose. "I don't like to talk about it, but I have a Silver Citation Star and all that."

"Indeed!" Berta said. "Those are awarded for 'Gallantry in Action,' are they not? You are a war hero."

"Were poodles and truffles the defining characteristics of France for you, Inchbald?" Raymond asked.

"I suppose so, yes. That and the pâté. Oh—and the fighting, of course."

For the briefest moment, something like rage rippled over Raymond's features.

"France is just great," Pete Schlump said. "No one cares about baseball over there. I go to take a break. The French are too busy with their wine and cigarettes to care about much else, is my theory."

"I disagree," Violet Wilbur said in an acid tone. "My column is translated in a French magazine, and it is extremely popular."

Waiters whisked away our bowls of broth and replaced them with celery salads. After that I suppose we were all too depressed to talk much.

Berta and I made a second attempt to retrieve Grace's diary later that afternoon, when Nurse Astrid let us all into the locked ward to change into bathing suits.

"Grace has taken me into her confidence," Berta whispered to me as soon as we shut ourselves in our room. "It seems she looks upon me as a grandmotherly figure."

"Is the diary in her room?"

"I believe so. She mentioned it in passing. What is more, she wishes to purchase some of my chocolate and pretzels. She claims those revolting vitaminizing drinks make her ravenous."

"Oh? Mine made me gag."

Berta dug a tin of Rold Golds and a Hershey's bar from her suitcase. "Come along, Mrs. Woodby. I shall create a distraction while you purloin the diary."

We poked our heads out the door, looking for Nurse Astrid. The coast was clear.

Grace's room was right next door to ours. Her smile faded when she saw that I'd tagged along. "Why's she here?" she asked Berta.

"Don't worry," I said. "I wouldn't dream of tattling to your mother about the pretzels and chocolate."

"All right, come in," Grace said, "but let's make it snappy. Nurse Astrid is always popping up when you least expect it."

While Berta and Grace haggled over the price of the Rold Golds, I scanned the room. *Aha.* That must be it: that green leather book on the bedside table. I strolled over, as though to look out the window.

Grace cut me off, snatched up the diary, and hugged it to her chest. "Fine, one dollar," she said to Berta. "I'll just find my coin purse."

Berta sent me a frown.

Sorry, I mouthed.

"Are you certain you do not wish to pop into a bathing suit?" Berta said as we made our way to the outdoor swimming pool. "It will feel so lovely plunging into the cool water."

"Not as lovely as retaining my last shreds of pride," I said. I did not speak with total conviction, because I still wore the regulation bloomers, blouse, and tennis shoes. "Anyway, I had my share of cold water during my mineral bath therapy after luncheon. My toes turned blue for a minute."

Berta went to the swimming pool. I found a shady spot on a wicker chaise, plopped Cedric by my feet, and slathered on a thick coat of Pond's Vanishing Cream to protect my skin from the sun. Then I settled back with the copy of *Thrilling Romance* I'd brought from my suitcase.

I began to read "The Captivating First Installment" of a story titled "Hello, Darling." Beautiful, petulant farm girl Maude, staying in the lavish Chicago apartment of her aunt Clarinda, meets the smoldering Bill Hampton at a party. Bill has a penchant for beautiful, petulant farm girls. Maude has a penchant for secretive baddies with broad shoulders. What could go wrong?

Maybe I was too old to be reading that sort of thing, but the fact of the matter was, I was a rookie when it came to men. Every day I saw flappers playing fellows like forty-seven-string pedal harps while I was stuck on the bongo drum.

I was a rookie when it came to love, too. I'd never loved Alfie, and during our marriage he'd kept himself busy giving *other* ladies experience. And Ralph Oliver? No flowers and bows and cupids there, and certainly no *I love yous*. Before he left for Cuba, we'd been too busy dancing, flirting, kissing, and drinking like it was going out of style. Sure, I had a soft spot for Ralph. I might've even been falling in love. But when it came to talk of feelings, well, both of us had kept as quiet as a queen's burp.

I continued reading. Insects droned. A gardener was trimming a nearby hedge, and his clippers went *zing zing zing*. People splashed and murmured in the swimming pool. I closed my eyes and sank into sleep.

"Is this your dog?" a man said sometime later.

I opened my eyes and struggled upright. "What? Oh. Hello, Mr. Hathorne. Yes, he's my dog."

"Found him wandering across the lawn." Raymond placed Cedric on my lap, sat down on the chaise next to mine, and studied my tennis shoes. "Say, Mrs. Woodby, you look like a million bucks in those ground-grippers."

A million bucks? Hah. I had no beau, zero highballs, and I was wearing flat shoes. I didn't feel like a million bucks. I felt like a buck-fifty.

"You know, despite everything your mother told me about you, I'd love to take you for a drink," Raymond said.

"What did my mother tell you?"

"That you're an angel."

"She lied."

"Trouble is, there isn't anything but seltzer water for miles around. I shake a mean cocktail, by the way."

"Do you?"

"Not that I admitted *that* to your mother. I caught a whiff of temperance about her."

"Good nose."

"Lucky I'm one swell actor."

"Oh yes?"

"In an amateur sense, of course, when I'm not minding the soda pop business. Shakespeare's always been a favorite."

"Shakespeare? How hoity-toity. You must be an excellent actor—and you must have a wonderful memory, too."

"Oh, I do."

"You could be acting right now," I said.

"I could be, couldn't I? Say, stop by my place anytime for that cocktail. I purchased the Pitridge estate outside of Hare's Hollow—do you know it?"

"Can't say that I do."

"Beautiful old place. Desperately needs repairs, of course. Plenty of time for that." Raymond stood and strolled away. He looked a bit like a pirate in those bloomers. *Ahoy.*

"What's the matter with me?" I muttered to Cedric. "Making googly eyes at Mr. Handsome the soda pop sultan?"

Cedric twisted himself to lick his tummy.

"You're right. Ralph is out of the picture. And soda pop sounds delicious in this heat."

4

Berta and I made our third attempt to retrieve Grace Whiddle's diary after lights out that night. I had fallen asleep promptly, my nerves threadbare as the result of another round on the hip-slimming machine, an evening vigorology session, and rye bran biscuits for dessert. Berta had stayed up late, delivering her black-market wares. She had taken pretzel and chocolate orders from everyone in the East Ward except Muffy.

Berta shook me awake.

"All right, all right," I mumbled, groping for my dressing gown. "Hold your horses."

First, I tiptoed out into the corridor and twisted Grace's door-knob. Locked.

"Locked?" Berta whispered when I returned to our room.

"Yes. On to plan B."

Plan B was infiltrating Grace's room by crawling along the ledge that ran outside our second-story windows. Thick ivy grew on the stones, and before dinner, Berta and I had tugged the ivy to test its strength. We'd managed to rip off only a few vines.

Berta toddled to our open window and removed the screen. "Go on, then."

"I still don't know why *I'm* doing this." I straddled the window-sill, and my bare toes dangled in the warm night air. The lawn was a long way down.

"The fact that you are half my age springs to mind," Berta whispered back.

"I think you're scared of heights."

"Being twice your age seems reason enough, does it not?"

I found a toehold, grabbed on to ivy, and brought my other leg out so I was standing tippy-toe on the stone ledge, fists full of crunchy vines. I inched over, ivy leaves tickling my face. Then there was the death-drop below me. I wouldn't consider that part.

I made it the few yards to Grace's open window. I peeked in.

Grace lay in bed, faintly illuminated by the driveway lamps outside. Her head tossed from side to side and she muttered inco-herently. She was dreaming.

I slung my leg over the windowsill. Grace started thrashing in bed and muttering more loudly.

Uh-oh.

I pulled my leg back out, inched along the ledge, and clambered back over my own windowsill. I thumped to the floor.

"Well?" Berta whispered.

"She's asleep, but just barely." I picked an ivy leaf from my hair. "It's a no-go."

Berta sighed.

"The funny thing was, Grace was wearing makeup," I said.

"Makeup? She was not wearing any during the day."

"I know, but she is now. Mascara, lipstick, the works. And she'd done something with her hair."

"How peculiar."

"I know."

In the morning, Berta and I trudged to our vigorology session on the rear lawn. I put Cedric on the grass and he romped to the shade. Wise pup. Violet Wilbur, the home décor authoress, was already marching in place on knobby legs. Red-haired rich boy Hermie Inchbald looked puffy and bad-tempered. Pete Schlump, the disgraced Yankee pitcher, stretched his brawny arms overhead. Grace Whiddle and her bejeweled future mother-in-law, Muffy Morris, weren't there yet. The Canadian soda pop sultan Raymond Hathorne grinned as I drew near.

"Good morning, angel," he said to me. "I see you got your beauty sleep. Nice stilts, by the way."

"Who, me?" I said. I had thought my legs resembled blocks of cheese in those bloomers.

"Now begin stretches!" the vigorology instructor, Ulf, yelled as he strode toward us. He was once again in nothing but small white shorts. His chest muscles jumped under leathery skin.

We all tried to touch our toes. Some of us failed.

I was just squinting at the blazing sun overhead, trying to calculate the time, when a woman's scream pealed out from the mansion.

Everyone froze mid-bend. A bird twittered.

More screams.

Ulf took off at a jog across the lawn. Violet hugged herself, and Raymond, Pete, and Hermie hurried toward the mansion.

"Come on," I whispered to Berta. I grabbed Cedric from his shady spot and started toward the mansion, too.

Berta caught up with me. "What are you doing, Mrs. Woodby?"

"You heard the screams."

"I am not in the habit of running *toward* screaming."

"But it's a perfect distraction. Grace's diary is in her room. Un-guarded."

"The ward is locked."

"I don't think I'll last another day here without starting to hal-lucinate talking strips of bacon, Berta, so if there's even a possible opportunity to collect that diary and skate, well, I'm taking it."

Inside the lobby, people clustered around a sobbing blonde in a nurse's uniform.

"Calm yourself, Nurse Beaulah," Chisholm said to her. "It simply will not do for you to become hysterical."

Nurse Beaulah sobbed still more loudly. Her tall, curvaceous body looked like it might pop her white pinafore.

"Now, what do you mean, Mrs. Morris is dead?" Chisholm asked her.

Muffy Morris *dead*? I looked around for Hermie and spotted him a few paces away, his face as white as skimmed milk.

"She's in her—her—her room!" Nurse Beaulah wailed.

"Did you leave the ward unlocked?"

"Yeah." Beaulah smeared liquefied kohl under her eyes.

"Everyone stay here while I step into my office to telephone the police," Chisholm said. "No one should go upstairs."

This could be our chance to nab Grace's diary, because if Nurse Beaulah had left the East Ward unlocked, Berta and I would have the place to ourselves.

Consulting each other was not necessary; Berta and I slipped past the clump of people and up the stairs. No one stopped us. Chisholm had already gone, and Nurse Beaulah's theatrical sobs and heaving bosom held everyone else rapt for the moment.

....

"Just think," I whispered to Berta as we slipped into the—unlocked!—East Ward. "We'll be eating a celebratory lunch at the Foghorn. I'm going to have the chicken-fried steak."

"How can you think of eating when there is a corpse on the premises?" Berta asked.

"I don't know."

We tiptoed down the corridor.

"Muffy's room is third on the right, I believe," Berta said. "That is the only room I did not enter last night to deliver the goods."

"Your aptitude for criminal lingo is astonishing, Berta."

"Thank you."

Sirens wailed in the distance, tinny but coming closer. The police station must've been just down the road. "I'd like to see her for myself," I whispered. I peeked through Muffy's door, which had been left open. I recoiled.

Berta gasped.

Muffy Morris was sprawled facedown on the floor in a pink dressing gown. Her blond head was cocked at a terrible angle and her slippered feet were skewed. Her outstretched hand clutched an empty booze bottle by its neck. Diamond rings glittered on her fingers. She looked stiff.

"Rigor mortis." Berta touched the locket she always wore. "Oh, is there anything more appalling?"

Cedric whined and fidgeted in my arms. I placed him on the floor.

"Looks like Muffy kicked the bucket in the middle of a bender," I said. The desk chair was on its side and the potted fern on the windowsill had been knocked over, scattering black dirt.

"Staggering drunk," Berta said. "We should go." The sirens were growing louder.

"That looks like a rum bottle she's holding, doesn't it?" I went over and peered at the bottle. A little brown liquid remained inside. Palm trees and the words RHUM CARIBE decorated the label.

"We really should go to Grace's room, now, Mrs. Woodby."

"Funny—that's a full bottle of gin over there on the desk."

"Do not dare nick that."

"No! I mean, why would Muffy get woozled on rum, which she said was vile, when she could've been drinking gin? I want to check the bathroom." I stepped into the small pink-tiled bathroom. It reeked of alcohol, and a faint garlicky smell arose from the urine in the unflushed lavatory. I gagged, covered my mouth, and darted out.

Sirens wailed just outside.

"Mrs. Woodby, we really must attempt to locate Grace's diary before it is too late. It sounds as though the police have arrived."

Just outside, the sirens blipped off.

"You're right." I scooped up Cedric. No sooner had we entered the hallway than we heard men's voices outside the ward's main door.

"Quickly," Berta whispered. "There is a second stairway at the other end of the corridor. I dodged into it briefly last night to hide from a nurse when I was making my deliveries."

We turned tail and ran. Along the way, we passed Grace's room. The door was open. I glanced in. Neat as a pin. "We'll search it later," I said.

"I do not believe there is any point."

"What do you mean?"

"I shall tell you when we are no longer in peril."

We pushed through a door and shut ourselves into what looked like a service stair.

"Muffy Morris was murdered," I whispered.

"Do not dramatize. You should have outgrown that when you formed your first wrinkle."

"What wrinkle?" My hand flew to my forehead. I thought I was the only one who'd noticed that. "Listen. Muffy hated rum. So why would she drink herself to death with a bottle of rum?"

"Perhaps her tastes changed." Berta hurried down the steps.

I followed. "Not since yesterday. Something is fishy."

"Be that as it may, it is none of our affair."

"Should I tell the police my suspicions?"

"And thus reveal to them that you were snooping at the crime scene? No. At any rate, the more pressing problem is, Grace Whiddle has flown the coop."

I stopped on the stairs. "What do you mean?"

"You did not see? Her room was empty."

"I simply thought it was clean."

"No. I suspect she's gone. You see, she hinted that she might flee during our chat yesterday. She does not wish to marry young Gilbert Morris. It is not a love match."

"Why didn't you tell me all this?"

"Because I believed we would collect the diary before any of it became relevant."

We reached the bottom of the stairs, swung through a door, and found ourselves blinking in sunlight at the side of the mansion.

"Grace scarpers the very same morning her future mother-in-law dies under suspicious circumstances?" I said. "Berta, I don't like this one little bit."

5

O odles of policemen arrived, and Willow Acres was plunged into pandemonium. Since Berta and I had decided to keep mum about having inspected the scene of the crime, we wouldn't be edisoned by the police. We decided to hang about until the police were done in the East Ward, and then we'd grab our suitcases and leave. If Grace and her diary weren't at Willow Acres, the Discreet Retrieval Agency needn't be there, either.

I saw Chisholm speaking with one of the other doctors in the lobby. I sidled up to him and coughed.

Chisholm didn't notice me and kept talking in low tones. ". . . and she had indeed taken the full dose of her cure last night. Nurse Beaulah removed the empty vial from her room."

I jabbed Chisholm with my elbow.

He turned. "A simple 'excuse me' would be sufficient, Lola."

"I hate to be the bearer of bad news," I said, "but I think Grace Whiddle is gone."

Chisholm turned putty-colored. "What do you mean, 'gone'?"

"She never turned up for the morning vigorology session, and I—um, there is talk that her room has been cleared out."

"Oh dear heaven. First Mrs. Morris drinks herself into an early grave, and now—" Chisholm pressed his lips tight.

"Is that the verdict, then?" I asked. "Death by tippling?"

"Lola, would it be too terribly much to ask for you not to meddle?" Chisholm and the other doctor hurried away.

In under ten minutes, it was confirmed that Grace Whiddle had packed her bags and fled. Another ten minutes led to an admission by the swimming pool cleaner that he'd seen her burrowing, suitcase in hand, through a hedge at the crack of dawn. Several minutes after that, the milkman reported that he'd seen Grace Whiddle step into the backseat of a blue Cole Aero-Eight motorcar on the road outside Willow Acres, after which the Aero-Eight had headed west.

"She planned it," I said to Berta.

"Indeed. With at least one accomplice."

Chisholm pleaded with the patients to go ahead with their usual daily regimes, but no one listened. I heard someone say the local press was already clamoring at the gates.

"We should telephone Mrs. Whiddle," Berta said.

"Probably."

We left the chaos of the lobby and went in search of a telephone.

"Mrs. Whiddle won't be pleased with this new development," I said.

"She can hardly blame us if her daughter is a flibbertigibbet," Berta said. "Poor girl. She was probably driven to madness by the rations. Perhaps she has returned to her mother."

"Her mother is the one who corralled her here in the first place. If I hadn't seen Pete Schlump loitering in the lobby just now, I would have guessed Grace had eloped with him. Look. Here's a telephone." We were in some sort of office adjacent to the kitchen, filled with grocer's lists, stacks of clean napkins, boxes of rye bran biscuits, and crates of celery. I dialed the operator and had her put me through to Clyde's Bluff.

"Well?" came Sophronia's shrill voice down the line. "Did you retrieve it?"

Nuts. She hadn't heard. "There have been . . . developments."

"Developments?"

I explained how Willow Acres was in an uproar because of Muffy Morris's death—I didn't mention my suspicions of murder—and that Grace had taken the opportunity to tootle off to parts unknown in an Aero-Eight. By the time I was finished, I was somehow holding a box of rye bran biscuits and munching away.

"My daughter is missing? Muffy Morris is dead? This simply cannot be. Do you understand what a feat it was for me to secure Grace's engagement to Gil Morris? Now the entire wedding could be called off! This is a disaster. How could you allow this to happen? I hold you entirely responsible, Lola Woodby."

"Mrs. Whiddle, you employed my agency to retrieve Grace's diary, not to baby-mind her."

"Do not make excuses."

I rolled my eyes at Berta—who could hear every word since her head was squashed against mine next to the telephone earpiece.

"What would you like us to do next, Mrs. Whiddle?" I asked. "Track Grace's movements?"

"Certainly not. You're fired."

Fifteen minutes later, Berta and I were back in our own dresses and hats, suitcases in hand, marching across Willow Acres' front drive to the motorcar parking lot. Cedric trotted along behind us, wagging his plume of a tail. If I'd had a tail, it would've been between my legs. We had failed. Dismally.

Berta was the first to speak. "I did not mention it before,

Mrs. Woodby, but I have been offered a cook's position at an estate in Gloucester, Massachusetts. At this stage, I suspect it might be prudent for me to consider the job."

"Maybe we should go and see Mrs. Whiddle," I said. "Maybe she'll reconsider. Someone has to find Grace, right?"

"I have always thought it beneath me to beg."

"You're right. Dignity is the name of the game." Oh, what would become of me? I'd never cut it as a waitress.

I stuffed my suitcase in the Duesy, placed Cedric on the backseat, and shoved a package of rye bran biscuits into the glove box. The biscuits had tasted like a mattress when I first had them last night, but they were growing on me. Maybe my appetite was becoming, by some miracle, healthful.

I was about to climb behind the wheel when I noticed the limousine in the next spot. A Packard, brand-spanking-new, its black paint slick in the sunlight. A chauffeur stared out the windshield. Someone else was in the back.

Odd, but none of my beeswax. I got behind the Duesy's wheel.

The rear door of the limousine swung open and a man stood up. "Mrs. Woodby?" He was heavy-jawed and hairy, like a gorilla in a snappy suit and a fedora.

"Yes?" I said.

"Senator Morris—Winfield Morris."

Of course. I'd seen him not only in the newspapers, but also from afar at social functions. "How do you do?"

"I know that my wife is dead," Winfield said. "That's what you're wondering, isn't it? Dr. Woodby telephoned and I came right away."

"I am terribly sorry for your loss, Senator Morris," I said. "Muffy was a . . . a . . ."

"Don't pull a muscle trying to make nice," Winfield said. "Muffy was a harpy. As a matter of fact, Mrs. Woodby, I was waiting for you."

"Me?"

"Dr. Woodby told me you drive a brown-and-white Duesenberg. She's a beauty, all right. Look at the curve of that front wheel well. Wowza."

Purring about motorcars when his wife had only just kicked off? What a fink. "Well, I was just leaving," I said, "but it was nice to meet you, Senator—"

"We ought to talk." Winfield tipped his head toward the limousine's dim interior. "Come on in."

"May I ask why?"

"I hear you're a detective. I want to hire you."

Part of me felt like leaping into my motorcar and zooming away. Senator Morris gave me the creeps. But another part of me felt like doing the cancan across the parking lot. Hallelujah! The Discreet Retrieval Agency was saved!

Berta tossed her suitcase in the Duesy, slammed the door, and bustled around to my side. "I am Mrs. Lundgren, Mrs. Woodby's detecting partner," she said to Winfield. "Did you say you would like to do business in your motorcar?"

Winfield's face stretched in an oily smile. "Yes. Yes, I would."

I lowered my driver's-side window so Cedric would have some fresh air. Then Berta, Winfield, and I scooted into the backseat of the limousine. I was in the middle. Winfield reeked of spicy aftershave lotion and sweat. His stubby thighs strained his trousers.

"How did you hear of our agency?" Berta asked. "Was it the one-and-a-half-inch-square advertisement in *The New York Evening Observer*?"

"Sure," Winfield said. "Yep."

"But how did you know we'd be here at Willow Acres?" I asked.

"Do you always grill your clients like this? Seems like *I* should be grilling *you*, not the other way around."

"We are a discreet agency," Berta said. "We take only the most select jobs."

"That's right," I said.

"Well, how's this for a select job?" Winfield said. "My wife was murdered, and I want you to figure out who did it."

I swallowed. "Why do you believe she was murdered? I was told she, ah—"

"Drank herself to death? That's what Dr. Woodby said. But he also told me a couple of other things. He said she was holding an empty bottle of rum. Muffy hated rum. He said there was a full bottle of gin in the room. If Muffy could've lived in a fish tank full of gin, she would've."

I gave Berta an *I told you so* look.

Winfield continued, "Fact is, that's why Muffy was booked into Willow Acres in the first place—to dry out. Seems like the murderer tried to make it look like Muffy drank herself to death in order to damage me. Politically, I mean."

"You believe that political sabotage was the murderer's motive?" I asked.

"Of course. What else could it be? Muffy didn't have any enemies. She was a lump. Never did much but drift around the house in her dressing gown and drink herself silly—when she wasn't going to expensive health farms to try and dry out. With the dough I spent last year on her health farms, I could've bought a Rolls-Royce. But I was only too happy to keep her out of sight. At a dinner at the British embassy last month, she passed out facedown in a bowl of soup."

"Oh my," Berta said.

"Why don't you go to the police about this?" I asked.

"I can't have all this go public. Shamuses never keep their traps shut."

"Will you give us a list of your political enemies?"

Winfield hacked out a laugh. "Course not! What, you think I want you two dames trying to blackmail me? No. It's your job to figure out who killed my wife, and keep the whole thing hush-hush."

Winfield removed his fedora and smoothed back his thinning hair with a palm. He replaced the fedora. "So. Are you taking the case or not?"

Berta and I exchanged a glance.

"Yes," I said. "We'll take the case."

6

....

Senator Morris is a cheapskate," Berta said. We rumbled out of Willow Acres' gates, passing a few shabby reporters. All the Duesy's windows were down; the day was heating up. "No payment at *all* until the murder is solved?"

"What can I say?" I said. "He's a politician."

"I must make him reconsider. How will we ever get by?"

"We'll find Muffy's killer before we run out of savings."

"What have you in the way of savings, Mrs. Woodby?"

"Oh, something in the ballpark of sixty-three dollars. You?"

"One hundred. But the rent—"

I stomped on the gas pedal.

I hoped we weren't out of our league. Sure, we had one cracked murder case under our belts, but we'd bumbled around a great deal. What if our success had only been beginner's luck? Winfield had told us to check in with him at his country house at ten o'clock tomorrow, and he'd made it clear that he expected results.

"The Foghorn?" I called over the wind.

Berta was clutching her battered felt hat. "Yes. And do step on it. I am faint with hunger."

"Have a rye bran biscuit. They're in the glove box."

"I would rather eat nails."

We didn't speak again until we'd resuscitated ourselves with chicken-fried steak, potatoes, buttery green beans, and coffee at the Foghorn Inn's restaurant in Hare's Hollow. Hare's Hollow is a shingled seaside town six miles from Willow Acres and only a few miles from the mansion I used to call home. The rambling Foghorn is a popular spot for economical holidaymakers, and the scent of fryer grease permeates every leatherette booth in the restaurant.

The waitress stopped by our table again, and Berta and I both ordered a slice of lemon meringue pie. It was going to take a lot of pie to erase the memory of those celery salads.

"We'll be systematic this time," I said. I dug a pen out of my handbag and smoothed out a scrap of paper. "Professional. No bumbling. Let's list the possible murder suspects."

"To narrow things down," Berta said, "Muffy's corpse had entered full rigor mortis. That means she had been dead for at least four hours."

"Where did you learn that?"

"*Mexico City Mayhem.*"

"If Muffy had been dead for at least four hours when we saw her," I said, "then she was killed while the East Ward was locked up for the night."

"Yes."

"Well, that limits the suspects to those *inside* the ward, doesn't it? Besides you, me, and Muffy, there was only Violet Wilbur, Hermie Inchbald, Grace Whiddle, Raymond Hathorne, and Pete Schlump. Five suspects. This'll be as easy as ABC." On the floor, Cedric made sticky gobbling noises. I ducked my head under the oilcloth. "No!" He'd found a french-fried potato; I caught a glimpse of it before it disappeared between his chops. I sat up. "Cedric shouldn't be eating starchy foods. They'll go straight to his tummy, and then he'll be out of a job."

Berta sipped her coffee. "If I may be so bold—do you realize how absurd you sound?"

I tapped my pen on the table. "I wish we knew how Muffy was killed, since it wasn't the tiddly."

"Poison, I presume."

"Okay, but what *kind?*"

"I cannot think how we could come by such information without directing unwanted attention to ourselves. We would have to ask Dr. Woodby, or the police. It simply would not do."

"We could poke around Muffy's room at Willow Acres a little more."

"That would be most imprudent, Mrs. Woodby."

"Probably." I studied the list of five suspects. "Who seems the most like a stony-hearted killer to you?"

"Grace Whiddle."

"Really?"

"Her upcoming marriage was not a love match. What better way to stall or even prevent the wedding than to kill her future mother-in-law?"

"I can think of several better ways, but all right." I scribbled on the scrap of paper: *#1 Grace Whiddle.* "It doesn't make her look cherubically innocent that she ran off right after the murder. When you were speaking with her privately, did you get the impression she could kill someone?"

"No. She seemed mild and rather dim. However, I once knew a young boy in Sweden who was believed to be a half-wit, yet he won a scholarship to study engineering at university. You never can tell."

"Next, Hermie Inchbald, Muffy's brother," I said. "He ought to be at the top of the list, if only because as a family member, he could have scads of motives."

"Are there Inchbald millions?"

"Naturally. Haven't you heard of Inchbald and Sons, Fine Clothiers? The company has been around since before the Civil War."

"Could the Inchbald millions be at stake?"

"We should find out." I wrote, *#2 Hermie Inchbald.*

"Then there are Raymond Hathorne and Violet Wilbur," Berta said. "Oh yes, and Pete Schlump."

"Raymond is a newcomer to New York. He comes from someplace in Canada—Quebec, judging by his accent. Pete runs in a completely different social set than the rest. And Violet Wilbur? Would the doyenne of tasteful décor indulge in murder?"

"I can envision it quite perfectly. It is not as though *her* floor was soiled by Muffy's death."

The waitress brought our pie. My first heavenly bite was ruined by a terrible thought. "Wait," I said. "Senator Morris suggested that the murderer was one of his political enemies."

"Well," Berta said, "could not one of those suspects be his political enemy?"

"Difficult to picture. Raymond Hathorne, maybe."

"That reminds me—just between you and me, Mrs. Woodby, Raymond Hathorne seems rather too forward."

"The year is 1923, Berta. Guys and girls flirt these days. Besides, I'm a widow, not some naïve young prune who requires a chaperone."

"I cannot disagree with that. However, his sweet talk seemed most familiar."

I stuffed my mouth with meringue. Truth was, Raymond Hathorne's flattery could get him everywhere with me, if only because I was desperate for a distraction from Ralph Oliver's absence. "Let's stick to business," I said. "Could Violet Wilbur be Senator Morris's political enemy? Could Grace be? That sounds absurd, doesn't it?

"It occurs to me that, although Senator Morris believes his wife's murder was motivated by politics, he could be mistaken. Politicians are paranoid. Narcissistic."

"Well, okay, Dr. Freud. Let's keep all possibilities open, then." I ate more pie. "What about Pete Schlump?"

Berta's fork hovered midair. "Oh, no. No, no, no. Pete is a national treasure. He has more important things to do than dabble in crime."

"I'm not so sure. He is taking a hiatus smack in the middle of baseball season."

"I did not like to mention it, since he confided to me in the strictest confidence," Berta said, "but his nerves are, as he termed it, shot."

"Is that the reason for Schlump's Slump? Nerves?"

"'Schlump's Slump' is such an unkind phrase, but yes. He said that he checked in to Willow Acres in the hopes of saving his nerves and, hence, his pitching career. No. Pete could not have killed Muffy. He has no motive."

Privately, I thought Berta was starstruck. Last year she listened to the entire World Series broadcast—New York Giants versus Yankees—on the radio set in the butler's pantry.

"Then it's settled," I said. "Grace Whiddle and Hermie Inchbald are our top suspects, so the first order of business is gathering more information about them. Foremost, where Grace might've run off to, and also whether or not Hermie stood to gain anything in the way of family money with his sister dead. We should try to convince Sophronia Whiddle to speak to us, and attempt to telephone Hermie Inchbald, too, wherever he lives. Oh—and if we have a chance to quiz anyone about Muffy Morris, we should take it."

Berta nodded.

The waitress brought the bill, and Berta and I split it fifty–fifty, leaving more pennies and dimes on the table than was entirely swish.

"I do not believe we have enough money for a hotel tonight," Berta said to me as I climbed into the telephone box under the stairs in the Foghorn's lobby. "But it seems that our plans may keep us on Long Island for at least a day more."

"I know." I settled Cedric on my lap and unhitched the telephone earpiece from its cradle. "I'll think of something."

I asked the operator to connect me to the Inchbald residence.

"Inchbald Hall in Oyster Bay?" she asked.

"Sure. Yes, that's the place." It had to be.

A butler answered. He told me that young Mr. Inchbald was still away on a holiday. I said thank you and disconnected.

"I think Hermie is still at Willow Acres," I said to Berta.

"That is odd. One would have thought he would wish to leave the place where his sister had died."

"I agree. Makes him look a tad suspicious, doesn't it?"

Next, I telephoned Sophronia Whiddle's house, Clyde's Bluff, but her butler told me that she was unable to accept my call. Butlers.

I hung up. "Does that mean Sophronia doesn't wish to speak with me, or that she's in hysterics about her runaway daughter?"

"Probably both," Berta said.

"This leaves us no choice but to call upon her in person."

I gave the fellow at the lobby desk a dime for the two calls and we headed for the Duesy.

Twenty minutes later, we rolled to a stop in the side porte cochere at Clyde's Bluff.

"Looks like Sleeping Beauty's castle," I said, switching off the engine. "Imagine building a French château on Long Island." I checked my makeup in the rearview mirror. My precious Guerlain lipstick was faded from lunch, but I hated to reapply it. The tube was down to its last creamy, vamp-red dregs. I would have to bite the bullet and buy a—gulp—*drugstore* lipstick.

"The French château style does suggest a certain misplaced sense of grandeur," Berta said. "Although, Mrs. Whiddle does not appear to have enough funds to pay a gardener."

Where the lawns must've once been, a field hummed with insects. A dry, crumbling fountain sprouted weeds. "Mr. Whiddle worked on Wall Street, but he died several years ago," I said. "If Sophronia is low on lettuce, that would explain her eagerness to hitch Grace to Gil Morris, love or no. She wants Grace to marry money."

The door under the porte cochere swung open and Sophronia Whiddle appeared. Her face went white and then pink. She charged at Berta's open window. "I fired you two," she whispered hotly. "Leave."

"We've been hired on another case," I said, "and we'd like to ask you some questions about Grace."

"Do you truly think you can go and bungle the simplest of jobs and then turn around—after I *fired* you, mind—and *interrogate* me?"

Another motorcar's engine chugged behind us.

"Oh, for pity's sake," Sophronia said, glancing down the drive. "It's your mother."

"My mother?"

"She and your sister, Lillian, are staying with me for the week."

My windpipe went all wonky and I coughed. "Oh. We'll just be going then, so—"

"No," Sophronia said. "Come inside—quickly!—or she'll see you."

"There is no reason for subterfuge," Berta said.

"Oh yes, there is," I said. I grabbed Cedric and bounded out of the car.

7

Sophronia herded Berta and me through the side door and into
a cramped powder room. Berta wedged herself between a wall
and the sink. I ended up sort of hovering over the lavatory, holding
Cedric with one arm and using the other to brace myself against
the wall. My face was about two inches away from a garish oil painting in a gilt frame. I longed to sit down on the lavatory lid, but
that would not have been dignified.

Sophronia shut the door behind her. "Well, then. What is this
about being hired on another case?"

I said, "We cannot say who hired us—"

"That would be indiscreet, you see," Berta said.

Sophronia scoffed.

"—but we are investigating Mrs. Morris's death."

"Investigating?" Sophronia said. "Everyone knew Muffy had
one foot in the grave for years—her drinking problem, you know."

"Of course," I said quickly, "but there are a few loose ends our
client would like to sort out."

"Is your client Senator Morris?"

"No," Berta and I said in unison.

"It is. Your mother told me what a terrible liar you are, Mrs. Woodby. And I see that little wrinkle on your forehead twitching. How disappointed Senator Morris will be when he discovers you two are more suited to be court jesters than detectives."

"You haven't heard from Grace since we spoke on the telephone this morning?" I asked.

"No. You know how girls of that age are. They all loathe their mothers."

"Grace wasn't keen on going down the middle aisle with Gil Morris, was she?" I said.

"I made Grace see reason. It was—it is—a brilliant match. I've hired another detective to find her. Come along. Your mother must have gone in through the front door by now, so I'll just let you out." Sophronia twisted the doorknob.

"You do realize," I said, "that Grace sneaking away so soon after Mrs. Morris's demise causes a certain—"

Berta cut in, "Your daughter may be difficult to locate, Mrs. Whiddle, because she is quite possibly a murderer."

Sophronia let loose a scream that made the pipes under the sink twang. "How dare you, you horrid little woman!"

Berta drew herself up. "I will not be spoken to in that manner."

"Mrs. Whiddle," I said, "you said yourself that Grace wasn't keen on the marriage. Did she have any other suitors besides Gil?"

"Of course not. Her first social season was this year—she only finished at Miss Cotton's Academy for Young Ladies in May—and she did not precisely cause a sensation. You've met her. Pudgy. Poor posture. Those glasses of hers—they're so thick, she could see into next week."

"Does she have any close girlfriends to whom she might've confided her plans?" I asked. "Some relative who would harbor her?"

"My family is all in Philadelphia, and the only remaining member of her father's family, Great-Aunt Dottie, is at the moment on a tour of Panama. But friends . . . yes, she has one close friend, Josie Van Hoogenband."

A lead! I hid my smile of victory. "We'll just be going, then. By the way, cute painting." I nodded toward the garish picture in the gilt frame. "Did Grace make it when she was little?" I was fairly sure it was supposed to depict a farm: sheep like blobs of cotton, pigs like wads of chewing gum, grimacing cows.

"No," Sophronia said coldly. "That was painted by Gil Morris."

"When he was a little boy, you mean."

"No, he painted it this spring and gave it to Grace as a token of his affection."

Berta and I gawked at the painting.

"Modern art," Berta whispered.

That must've been it.

Berta and I took turns smushing past Sophronia and out the door.

"I do think the powder room is the best place for that painting, Mrs. Whiddle," Berta said over her shoulder.

"Oh, one last question," I said to Sophronia, stopping. "Do you know if Hermie Inchbald stands to come by any additional family funds as the result of his sister's demise?"

"Get. Out."

Berta and I had almost made it outside when my mother said behind us, "I heard a scream, Sophronia."

I froze, sighing inwardly. I turned. "Hello, Mother."

"*Lola?*" Mother, several paces down the hallway, squinted. "Lola, what are you—?"

Sophronia said, "Lola was just stopping by to—"

"I stopped by to use the powder room," I said. "I was motoring past and I was dying to go, so—"

Mother blinked her large blue eyes. "How vulgar." She was still pretty, with dark waves threaded with gray, and a figure that amply filled out her chic dress.

"No, no, it's quite all right," Sophronia said, yanking open the side door. "They were just leaving."

"Just leaving? Why, I haven't seen my own daughter for a month. Still lugging that silly little dog about? Men don't like little dogs, Lola. I had no notion you were even here in the country. I thought you had decided to stay in the city all summer, although goodness knows how you could bear it, even if you are staying at the Ritz— you are still staying at the Ritz?"

"Where else?" I said with a tight smile. Mother somehow could not comprehend how utterly broke Alfie had left me, and I'd decided to keep her in the dark. It gave me more freedom.

"And I see that Berta is still your . . . cook?" Mother looked askance at Berta.

Berta sent back a steely glare.

"She's not my cook," I said. "How silly! I don't need a cook at the Ritz. I have all my meals sent up from the restaurant. No, Berta is my, um, she's my maid now."

Mother's eyes flicked to my last-season's cloche hat, down my wrinkled dress, and landed on my battered T-straps. "Perhaps you should hire someone else, dear," she stage-whispered.

"Mother, did you know Muffy Morris?" I asked. "She's dead."

"You are so very lurid, Lola. I blame those dime novels you've been devouring since the age of fifteen. Yes, I knew Muffy a bit, but I refuse to gratify your morbid curiosity."

On to the next question, then. "I've met Raymond Hathorne at last."

"Oh!" Mother's face softened. "Such a gentleman, isn't he? Such exquisite clothes! I hear that Fizz-Whiz is going to make a mint. Did he—did you enjoy each other's company?"

"He's the berries. Say—where did you meet him again? On a steamship?"

"Yes, on our return voyage from Europe in May. We shared a table in the dining room."

"What was he doing in Europe?"

"I gathered that he'd been in Scotland, golfing at someone's castle."

"Have you met any of his family?"

"Well!" Mother was positively radiant now. "You *did* hit it off! Why, yes, I know his mother."

"From Canada?"

"Yes. She was at Delphina Madison's place on Lake George last summer. A very good family. French Canadians, you know. Practically European aristocrats. They have some sort of château up in Quebec with timber as far as the eye can see. You aren't too old to bear children, you know, Lola—"

"Well, I really must be going," I said, inching toward the door.

"But you've been neglecting your family," Mother said. "Lillian is to be married soon, and she would so enjoy the assistance of a seasoned older sister to—"

"Mrs. Woodby is in mourning, Mrs. DuFey," Berta said, "and she cannot be expected to engage in frivolity from dawn till dusk."

Mother tucked her chin back, affronted. "Oh. I see. Then I will not remind her of the yacht club luncheon—"

"Toodles, Mother," I said.

"Where are you staying here in the country?"

"Well, I've just had the most refreshing visit to Chisholm's health farm—"

"Oh? You do not appear at all slimmer."

"—and now I'm off to the Ocean Princess Hotel." These days, I couldn't afford a bar of soap at the Ocean Princess Hotel. Back in the city, I slept on the sofa behind a folding screen.

"But—"

Berta and I were already swinging out the door.

"Now do you understand the reason for subterfuge?" I asked Berta as we jostled down Clyde's Bluff's potholed drive in the Duesy.

"I have known your mother for years, Mrs. Woodby, and her behavior comes as no surprise. What *is* surprising to me is your reluctance to stand up to her. If you simply told her that you have gone into business as a lady detective, you would avoid much strife."

"I'll come clean soon," I lied. If I told Mother I had become a lady detective, I might not have eardrums left once she'd finished screeching. And as I said, I wasn't about to demolish the reputations and prospects of my family members. They could do that for themselves. "Where next?"

"Josie Van Hoogenband, Grace's friend, seems like a promising lead. Girls do talk to their friends, you know, so Josie may be the one person to whom Grace confided her plans."

"You mean her plans for clipping off her future mother-in-law?"

"And running away. Even if Grace did not tell Josie her plans, Josie will still be able to provide valuable insight into Grace's motivations and personality."

"All right. Let's telephone Josie. I know where she lives. Her father, Eugene, is a bigwig in my old social set. Alfie was forever kowtowing to him because he's one of the founding members of the Titan Club."

"That stuffy gentleman's club on Forty-fourth Street?"

"That's the one. Alfie was a member, too. I got the impression it was all about drinking and cards and cigars—and giving each other preferential treatment in their business deals, naturally."

"Have you made Eugene Van Hoogenband's acquaintance?"

"Only in passing. I can't picture him inviting me in for tea, if that is what you're hinting at."

We motored over a bridge, beside which a new bridge was being built. ANOTHER QUALITY PROJECT BY V. H. STEELWORKS, a sign said. Construction workers toiled in dungarees, and a crane lifted steel beams.

"It seems as though new bridges are being built everywhere this summer," I said.

"Indeed. And nothing seems the matter with the old ones."

We motored back to the Foghorn and went once more to the call box in the lobby. We waited for a man whining into the receiver about how some girl had jilted him and taken off for Niagara Falls with another fellow. Finally, he hung up.

"Cheer up," I said to him as he passed. "It happens to everyone." Except Ralph Oliver hadn't had the decency to properly jilt me. He'd gone straight to the taking off bit.

A woman identifying herself as Mrs. Jasper the housekeeper answered the telephone at Breakerhead, the Van Hoogenband house.

"Could I please speak with Miss Josie Van Hoogenband?" I asked.

"May I ask who is calling?"

If I gave my real name, word could get back to Mother. "I am Miss Cotton, the headmistress from Miss Cotton's Academy for Young Ladies. I must speak with Miss Van Hoogenband about an examination she took last month."

"You do not sound like the Miss Cotton who attended Miss Van Hoogenband's piano recital at the house last week."

I forced a little laugh. "These telephones, you know—"

"Do not ring again, whoever you are," the housekeeper said, and hung up.

I sighed. "We're having the rottenest luck getting through to people on the telephone today," I said to Berta as I climbed out of the call box.

"Indeed, and now we must pay the front desk clerk five more cents. We cannot afford this."

"Speaking of being on the nut, I nearly forgot—Mother reminded me where we could stay for the night. Alfie's yacht."

"He had a yacht?"

"He had three, but the repo men left one they didn't think was worth taking."

"Oh dear."

"I'm sure it was only because it was too small or something. I've been meaning to try to sell it off, but I believe the deed of sale is at my . . . at *Chisholm's* house, and I haven't had the heart to ask him for it. It's moored in the Hare's Hollow Marina." I glanced around the lobby and lowered my voice. "Having a place to stay here frees us up nicely for *nocturnal detective work.*"

"You don't mean—?"

"Yes. Let's sneak into Breakerhead tonight and get Josie Van Hoogenband to talk to us. Who knows, Grace might even be hiding there."

"This seems rather extreme, Mrs. Woodby."

"Then what do you propose?"

"We could motor to Breakerhead now, in the pleasant sunshine, and endeavor to gain admittance."

That did sound less extreme. I checked my wristwatch. "It's almost three o'clock now. We could stop there on the way to Willow Acres."

"Willow Acres?"

"Hermie Inchbald's butler said he was still there, remember? Hermie will be going to the swimming pool soon, and we wished to learn if he has come into big money as the result of his sister's death."

"What has the swimming pool to do with any of that?"

"If Grace Whiddle's escape this morning taught us anything, Berta, it's that it is possible to burrow through the hedges next to the swimming pool."

Berta sighed.

8

....

L ush old trees and thick hedges hid everything but a few of Breakerhead's chimney tops from view. A high iron fence stretched as
far as the eye could see. Golden eagles and spikes topped the glossy
black gates. A gatekeeper hurried out from the lodge when we slowed.

"How might I help you ladies?" he asked. "You tourists?"

"No," I said, "we're, um, lost. Where is Hare's Hollow?"

"Straight down this road." He pointed. "And I'd stay away from
this house if I were you. The master don't like snoops."

"Right." I toed the gas pedal.

"Evidently, Josie Van Hoogenband is penned in like a veal calf," I
said over the roar of the engine. This was no surprise. Ten minutes in
the public eye for any reason—short of publishing a volume of poems
about flowers—could permanently cloud a debutante's marital forecast.

"Then there is no choice in the matter," Berta said. "We must
partake in nocturnal detective work, after all. We might throw pebbles at Miss Van Hoogenband's window and convince her to speak
with us."

"We'll frighten her. She'll raise the alarm."

"You and I are many things, Mrs. Woodby, but I would not say that we are especially frightening."

Good point. Maybe we could tell Josie we were a couple of tooth fairies.

I motored to the country road behind Willow Acres and parked on the grassy verge. Tall laurel hedges hemmed in the property on all sides, but there wasn't a fence—only a shut gate at the rear service entrance.

"Ready?" I asked Berta.

She made a grim nod. She disliked burrowing through hedges.

I gathered Cedric into my arms and we walked along the verge until we came to the place in the hedge where the swimming pool had to be.

"Thank goodness it's a laurel hedge instead of boxwood or something." I hugged Cedric close, hunched forward, squeezed my eyes shut, and plowed through the hedge. Twigs scratched my cheeks, and a branch almost ripped my hat off. I tripped on a root and stumbled through. Cedric leapt from my arms just before I sprawled, palms-first, on the lawn.

"*Oof,*" Berta said, landing next to me.

We'd landed in the shady spot with the wicker chaises set back from the pool. Several patients in bathing suits lolled on the chaises, all staring at Berta and me from over the tops of books and magazines. No Hermie. I didn't recognize any of them, actually.

I wobbled to my feet and dusted myself off. "Ah, it's Willow Acres," I said loudly, helping Berta up.

The patients kept staring.

"Could any of you tell me where I might find Mr. Inchbald?" I called to them.

Silence. Then a lady in round sunglasses said, "Mr. Inchbald checked out this morning. A terrible tragedy in the family."

"Are you certain he's gone?"

"Quite."

The butler at Inchbald Hall must've been behind the game, or lying. Rats.

"You know," the sunglasses lady said, "this is private property. I'm afraid I must ask you to leave. Are you reporters of some sort?"

"Where's Cedric?" I whispered to Berta.

"Over there." Berta pointed. Cedric was a mere orange puff bouncing across the lawn toward the mansion.

I whistled; Cedric ignored me. I took off after Cedric as fast as a lady can in two-and-a-half-inch heels on a recently watered lawn.

"Stop!" the sunglasses lady shrieked behind me.

"Kindly mind your own potatoes," I heard Berta say.

I caught Cedric as he was padding through an open door into the mansion. "Naughty," I said into his fuzz.

He panted, wearing his usual oblivious sock-monkey expression.

Berta arrived breathlessly beside me. "What in heaven is your dog doing?"

"Looking for sautéed steak, I'll bet. Unlike you and me, Cedric ate like royalty here."

"Well, we really should go. Mr. Inchbald is not here." Berta threw a worried glance across the lawn. The sunglasses lady was on her feet, talking to one of the male orderlies and pointing at us.

"But now that we're here, we may as well try to take another look at Muffy's room."

"Are you mad?"

"If anyone asks, we could say we forgot something in our room. Besides"—the orderly was striding toward us, waving a hand—"I think it would be best if we took a detour."

Berta and I darted inside the lobby. Empty, thank goodness, since we stood out like sore thumbs in our everyday dresses and hats. We hurried up the stairs and made our way to the East Ward.

The East Ward's door was slowly falling shut when I saw it. I held Cedric close and ran. I grabbed the knob just before the door hit home, and peeked through. A maid pushed a big wheeled laundry hamper down the hall.

"What luck!" I whispered to Berta.

We waited until the maid disappeared into a room. Then we slid through the door and tiptoed past—the maid was humming as she worked—and made it to Muffy's room. We shut ourselves in and looked around.

Neat as a pin. No trace of Muffy's messy death remained. The bedsheets looked like they'd been steam-pressed, and a new potted fern sat on the windowsill. The bathroom sparkled.

My heart sank. What had I expected? That the police—that *Chisholm,* of all people—would leave the place a disaster?

"Well, that's that," I said. My glance fell on the radiator by the window. My first thought was, *Darn it, didn't I leave a half-eaten Hershey's bar behind the radiator in my room?* My second thought was, *I ought to look behind Muffy's radiator.*

I went over and stuck my hand in the crack between the radiator and the wall. I felt something small and hard. I gently wiggled it free.

"What is that?" Berta asked.

I held it up. Brownish liquid trembled inside a small glass vial with a metal screw top. A typed label said M. MORRIS 7-15-1923 P.M. "I think I know how the murderer poisoned Muffy," I said.

Footsteps clacked out in the hallway.

"Good gravy," I muttered. I stuffed the vial into my brassiere, tightened my grip on Cedric, and made for the door.

The door swung open. Nurse Astrid blocked our path, two brawny male orderlies just behind her. "Good afternoon, ladies," she snapped. "May I ask what you are—?"

I pushed past her and ran down the hallway. Berta's boots tapped behind me.

"Don't let them get away!" Nurse Astrid screamed.

Then there were two more sets of footsteps pounding behind me.

I shoved through the ward door, ran down the hallway, and jogged down the swooping stairs into the lobby. I'd meant to run out the front doors, but I saw another nurse standing there, speaking with a patient. I skidded to a stop and turned a right angle. Berta huffed and puffed at my heels.

"Excuse me!" the nurse called.

"They've been poking about in the East Ward!" Nurse Astrid shrilled. I caught a glimpse of her and the two orderlies pounding down the stairs, and then Berta and I were racing along a hallway.

"The . . . kitchen," Berta gasped. "Door . . . out."

"Swell notion," I said all in one go, to pretend I wasn't as breathless as she was.

We shoved through a swinging door at the end of the hallway and found ourselves in a service passage. We raced down the passage and burst into a steel-and-white kitchen. Deserted. We went out the kitchen door and squinted, wheezing in the sunlight.

A delivery truck rolled out of nowhere. Berta and I stopped. Pink letters on the truck read YELLOW DUCK ICE CREAM.

My mouth watered. But wait. Why the heck would an ice cream truck make deliveries at a health farm? Was this a mirage?

A man in a white cap and a yellow bow tie leaned an elbow out the driver's window. "You two look like you need a ride," he said, and winked.

This *was* a mirage. Surely. Because . . . how could this be? Ralph

Oliver, delivering ice cream to Willow Acres? Impossible on a number of fronts, foremost being that Ralph Oliver was in Cuba.

"They went through here!" I heard Nurse Astrid scream behind us.

Berta was already climbing aboard the ice cream truck. "Do get a move on, Mrs. Woodby," she cried.

The kitchen door crashed behind me.

I bundled Cedric and myself into the ice cream truck, and Berta scooted over to the middle of the seat. I hadn't even shut the door when Ralph hit the gas. We zoomed toward the front drive, gravel spraying. I stuck my head out the window just in time to see Nurse Astrid and the orderlies staring after us. Then we rounded the corner of the mansion.

Cedric squiggled in my lap, whimpering and barking. He always went gaga over Ralph.

I glanced at Ralph. He was concentrating on driving at racetrack speed down the front drive. His thick ginger hair was just visible beneath his cap, and so was the white shrapnel scar on his forehead, a souvenir of his service in the Great War. Gray eyes shone in a craggy, lightly freckled face. How the heck did he make an ice cream uniform look manly? If Berta weren't between us, I might've thought about sliding my hand under his suspenders. . . .

Nix that. Undignified. Besides which, Ralph was a rotter. If he was back from Cuba, why hadn't he telephoned?

He caught me looking. "How's business, kid?"

"Nifty." How I wished I'd reapplied my Guerlain lipstick.

"Looks that way."

Berta said, "We have been hired to investigate the death of Mrs. Morris. It is very big business."

Ralph braked at the health farm gates and honked. The gatekeeper scurried out and opened up. "I heard about that," Ralph said. "Senator's wife. Murder?"

"Maybe," I said.

"How'd you get that gig?"

"From Senator Morris himself."

"Cripes," Ralph said, pulling through the gates. "That *is* big business. All right—where are you two headed next?"

"I parked around the back," I said.

Ralph turned onto the road.

I stole another glance at him. Then I had to look away because of the way things started sizzling and popping inside me. "Nice bow tie," I said.

"Thanks. Bought it special."

"What were you doing at Willow Acres disguised as an ice cream man, Mr. Oliver?" Berta asked.

"Yes," I said. "I'd love to know the answer, because last time I heard, you were in Havana on a case. Remember? You let me know with a one-line note written on the back of your card that you stuffed through my mail slot in the middle of the night?"

"I was in a hurry. Say, aren't you happy to see me?"

Yes. "No!"

Ralph's jaw tightened.

"You simply vanished!" I said. "I didn't expect daily telephone calls, but it's been weeks. I thought I'd at least get a postcard."

"Let's just say things got a little sticky, and getting to the post office in Cuba wasn't really feasible."

"Why is it such a contortionist's feat to get a straight answer out of you?"

"Wouldn't want to bore you with details." Ralph's hands were relaxed on the steering wheel, but his sidelong glance was searching and almost . . . wary. Could he be as uncertain as I was about where we stood? No. Ralph worked ladies like a sailor works knots.

I glanced behind the seat. Metal refrigerator compartments lined the back of the truck. "Is there any ice cream back there?"

"Nope," Ralph said. "Only frozen peas."

Sigh. "Are you working on the Muffy Morris case, too?"

"Nope—"

Phew.

"—I'm searching for young Grace Whiddle. That's what I was doing in disguise back there at the health farm: talking with the staff. I was wrapping things up with a gardener when I happened to see you two running through the lobby. Went to my truck here. Figured you'd need a lift."

"Well, thank you," I said. "Who hired you?"

"Grace Whiddle's mother, just this morning."

"That was *our* job."

"Mrs. Whiddle told me she had a couple of lady detectives trying to get her daughter's diary, and I figured it was you two. Said she fired you, though."

"Well, yes, but—"

"Don't mention it to anyone," Ralph said. "Mrs. Whiddle doesn't want to involve the police yet. Thinks it'll cause a scandal and ruin Grace's chances of marrying Mr. Moneybags. If it were my daughter, I'd have every flatfoot on it, and the Feds, too. This is your motorcar, isn't it?" He braked beside the parked Duesy. "Are you two headed back to the city?"

"Certainly not," Berta said. "We have several hot leads."

Several was a stretch, but I nodded.

"I'm staying at the Foghorn," Ralph said. "I've got a few more things to take care of right now, but maybe I'll see you two there around, say, six o'clock for dinner?"

"Maybe," I said.

"Of course," Berta said.

Ralph grinned and tipped his cap. "All right, then. See you soon, Mrs. Lundgren, Mrs. Woodby. Cedric."

Berta and I climbed down from the ice cream truck and boarded the Duesy. I settled Cedric in the backseat and fired up the engine. We watched as Ralph made a U-turn and rumbled away.

"Oh dear," Berta said, straightening her hat. She was still flushed and out of breath. "What excitement. If we are to break into the Van Hoogenband house tonight, I must have a lie-down."

"A lie-down? What about this?" I pulled the glass vial I'd found behind Muffy's radiator from my brassiere.

"We can wait a bit to discuss that. You must remember that I am over sixty years of age, and before we launched our agency, I seldom took more exercise than kneading bread dough. Although, mind you, kneading bread dough is quite strenuous."

"How about taking a gander at Alfie's yacht, then?"

"If there is a neat little berth on which to rest, I shall be as happy as a clam."

"Neat little berth? If I knew Alfie, it'll be gold-leaf staterooms." I put the vial in my handbag for safekeeping.

We motored off in the direction of Hare's Hollow, and I told myself not to think about Ralph. Things were still popping and sizzling inside me, but I'll come clean: My heart ached. He had called me Mrs. *Woodby*, not Lola. For some mysterious reason, Ralph and I had returned to GO on the Monopoly board.

9

I parked the Duesy in front of the Foghorn. Berta and I collected our suitcases and handbags and walked along Main Street. Cedric followed slowly, sniffing for the perfect spot to go. We waited while he went.

"Look, a new bakery," I said, pointing across the street. An arched shop window read LITTLE VIENNA BAKERY in gilt. Tiered stands displayed treats too far away to identify. Still, I sighed with longing. Cookies can, at least temporarily, fill a man-shaped hole in a lady's heart.

"Come along," Berta said with a sniff.

"Are you jealous?" I asked. "Someone else's baked goods turned my head?"

"Do not be ridiculous."

Behind Hansen's Bait Shop, a wooden stair led down to the harbor path. Four docks stretched into a gently bobbing inlet. Dozens of yachts gleamed with white and gold and polished wood. Beyond, Long Island Sound sparkled.

"Do you know where you are going, Mrs. Woodby?" Berta asked.

"Sure." We tromped down a dock, footsteps hollow, lugging our suitcases. Cedric trailed a few steps behind, sniffing the boards. Everything smelled of sun-heated tar and lapping brine. "Alfie's lawyer sent me a letter about this yacht and told me it was all mine. Said it was moored in number thirteen. How could I forget *that?*"

We arrived at number 13. We stood side by side and stared at Alfie's one remaining yacht. Faded letters on the side said SEA NYMPH.

"It appears to be listing to the left," Berta said.

My daydreams of maritime splendor came crashing down. While all the other yachts in the marina looked fit for displaying the sunning bodies of motion picture stars, Alfie's yacht looked as though it had just returned from an around-the-world cruise while manned by ogres. Barnacles studded the hull. White paint curled, and the teak wasn't that orangey gold it was supposed to be, but gray. A sail flapped limply in the breeze, revealing badly stitched patches.

"Sorry, Berta," I said.

Berta stepped aboard. "Beggars cannot be choosers."

I wobbled aboard, too.

Down inside the yacht, mildew itched my nose and the climate was decidedly dank. A hundred things creaked with every roll of the water beneath us. But there were two small cabins, each equipped with a bunk bed, and a tiny galley that had a kerosene stove and a coffeepot. That was all we needed, right?

Berta and I shut ourselves into our respective cabins. I tossed aside my suitcase, kicked off my shoes, lay down on the bunk with Cedric, and fell promptly asleep.

Ralph was alone in a corner booth at the Foghorn restaurant when Berta and I entered a little after six o'clock. My heart went pit-a-pat. I balked. How could I do this? Be a cheerful lalapazaza when I hadn't the foggiest why the bonfire we'd gotten going before he left for Cuba had poofed out?

"Oh, for goodness' sake, Mrs. Woodby," Berta said without stopping. Even Cedric kept going to the booth without me. He knew where his bread was buttered.

Berta positioned herself and Cedric in the booth in such a way that I had no choice but to sit beside Ralph. My knees sagged like saltwater taffy. Granted, that was possibly the result of having walked from the yacht in my highest heels. I had no intention of looking ankle-less in front of Ralph Oliver.

"Good evening, Mrs. Lundgren, Mrs. Woodby. Don't the two of you look as pretty as pictures."

Berta touched her freshly plaited silver hairdo. "Thank you."

Yes, I'd spent lots of time making my bob shiny and I'd used a hairpin to dig out the last bit of Guerlain lipstick from the tube. But if Ralph was going to play his cards close to his chest, I was going to play mine even closer. "Let's get down to business," I said briskly.

Ralph lifted his eyebrows. "Well, okay."

"You're working on the Grace Whiddle disappearance," I said, "and we're working on the Muffy Morris murder. My partner and I see no reason why we cannot, for mutual professional benefit, trade information with you, our colleague." Berta and I had talked this over on the walk from the yacht.

"I'm your *colleague*, huh?" Ralph studied his menu.

Berta was rummaging in her handbag. "I was going to give you one of our business cards, Mr. Oliver, but I seem to have forgotten them all in the city. Have you any, Mrs. Woodby?"

"Of course," I said. I checked in my handbag. The only business card in there had been floating free amid coins, makeup, hairpins, biscuit crumbs, and the vial of brown liquid I'd found behind Muffy's radiator. "Here you go, Mr. Oliver. Colleague to colleague." I slid the card over.

"What's this?" Ralph poked the inky-black blotch in the middle of the card.

"Oh. Mascara, I suppose." My cheeks went hot. The hinged lid of the cake mascara compact I kept in my handbag had broken, and I couldn't afford to replace it.

"Mrs. Woodby," Berta whispered, "how unprofessional." She looked at Ralph. "I am sorry, but I must keep this card if it is the only one." It disappeared into her handbag.

Ralph shrugged, mouth serious, eyes twinkling. "Never mind. Let's share. What have you got?"

I placed the medicine vial on the table. "This, according to the label, was Muffy's evening dose of whatever medicine she was being treated with. See? It says 'M. Morris 7-15-1923 P.M.' But Muffy never took it. The funny thing is, this morning I overheard an exchange between Chisholm and another doctor to the effect that Muffy *had* taken her medicine. Chisholm even said that Nurse Beaulah collected an empty vial from Muffy's room this morning."

Berta said to Ralph, "Muffy appeared to have died as a result of drinking an entire bottle of rum. We inferred that she did not, after all, drink the rum since she loathed the stuff and there was an untouched bottle of gin in the room." Berta tapped the vial. "But what to make of this?"

"Here's my theory," I said. "The murderer planted the booze bottles in order to make Muffy's death *appear* to be the result of excessive tippling, to cover up how he or she really did it, which was poisoning Muffy with a vial that looked just like her medicine vial. I think the murderer dumped most of the rum down the sink— Muffy's bathroom reeked of alcohol. Muffy took the poison— which was in the vial Nurse Beaulah later removed from the room—and the murderer hid this vial of her *real* medicine behind the radiator."

"Adds up nicely," Ralph said.

I unglued my gaze from Ralph's rugged profile. Never mind about playing my cards close. Why didn't he just kiss me, darn it? We'd been doing an awful lot of kissing before he skedaddled to Cuba, and I wouldn't have said no to starting up where we'd left off.

"I wish I knew what kind of poison was used," I said.

"Were Muffy's pupils dilated?" Ralph asked.

"Her eyes were shut."

Berta said, "She appeared to have suffered a certain amount of delirium. Her room was in disarray."

"Maybe there was a struggle," Ralph said.

I hadn't thought of that. "Wait a minute," I said. "In Muffy's lavatory, well, she hadn't—" I cleared my throat. "—she hadn't flushed it, and it smelled of, strange to say, garlic."

Ralph's eyebrows shot up. "Garlic? Garlic in the urine or on the breath, that's arsenic. Rat poison."

Berta chirruped. "How clever you are, Mr. Oliver!"

"Only problem with that is," Ralph said, "any Tom, Dick, or Harry can get their hands on rat poison at any garden or feed store."

"Still, you are brilliant," Berta said.

"Should we order?" I grumbled. "I'm famished."

After we ordered, Berta said, "I have just remembered something. When I was delivering my goods last night—"

"Goods?" Ralph said.

"Black-market chocolate and pretzels," I said.

"Course." Ralph grinned.

"—when I was delivering them, a nurse came into the East Ward and I hid myself in the second stairway until she was gone."

"What time?"

"A little after eleven—I began my delivery rounds at eleven."

"Did you see who it was?"

"No. I caught the briefest glimpse of her white pinafore before I hid myself."

"Then the thing to do is discover who was on duty last night," I said. "That nurse might know something crucial about the killer."

"Yes," Berta said. "Or she could *be* the killer."

We mulled that over. I hated to think that our list of suspects was longer than the five East Ward patients.

"I'm not too keen on sneaking back into Willow Acres again," I said. Actually, I suspected I'd pulled my hamstring while fleeing Nurse Astrid and the orderlies, but I'd say *hamstring* in front of my colleague Ralph Oliver when pigs flew. One doesn't say *hamstring* while playing it close.

"I am certain you will think of something, Mrs. Woodby," Berta said. "You always do."

After we all polished off our desserts and split the bill, Berta and I excused ourselves. I tried to be nonchalant about it, but Berta was acting mysterious.

"We have *somewhere to be*," she said in a meaningful voice.

"Got it," Ralph said with a smile. "Nocturnal detective work. Do it all the time myself."

After dinner, I telephoned Inchbald Hall again in the hopes of getting hold of Hermie. This time, the butler said he was at home.

Success! Except . . . how could I learn if he'd come into the family millions as the result of his sister Muffy's death? Asking him in person would be best. Then I could see if his face twitched.

"Mr. Inchbald," I said when I had him on the line, "this is Lola Woodby—we met at Willow Acres."

"Yes?" Hermie said dully.

"I'm awfully sorry to bother you after, well, what happened to your poor sister, but I simply can't stop thinking about what you said about poodle breeding—how it's a balm for the soul and all that."

Hermie's voice perked up. "Oh, yes?"

"I was thinking of putting my dear tiny Cedric up to stud, and I was hoping you might be able to offer me a few tips. Could I pop by for a visit, say, tomorrow?"

"Tomorrow?"

I crossed my fingers.

"What about the next day," Hermie said, "at, say, half past twelve?"

"That'd be the duck's quack, Mr. Inchbald." I said good-bye and rang off.

10

....

Berta and I killed the time till eight thirty tidying up the yacht by lantern light. I discovered several big cans of drinking water and an unopened crate of caviar. If only I could also find a case of champagne; teetotaling didn't agree with me.

After tidying up, Berta and I changed into black clothing.

"Is that what you are wearing, Mrs. Woodby?" Berta asked when I arrived on deck. An orange sherbet sunset streaked the sky.

"What's wrong with it?" I glanced down at my black silk dress that showed some leg, and my spiky Pinet pumps. "It's all black." Mentioning the foil-wrapped Hershey's bar I'd wedged in my bodice was not necessary.

"There is such an expanse of calf, you are in danger of glowing in the moonlight."

"I have stockings on!" Sheer stockings, yes, but geewhillikins, my calves weren't exactly in danger of being mistaken for signal buoys, were they? "You're going to be sweltering in that getup." Berta wore a long-sleeved black wool dress, thick black stockings, and her painful-looking Edwardian boots.

"I do not wish to be eaten alive by mosquitoes."

We motored through the balmy night to a sprawl of farmland behind the Van Hoogenband estate. I parked in a rutted tractor turnout and switched off the engine. The headlamps faded out and darkness expanded around us. Crickets chirped.

"We neglected to discuss one pertinent point," Berta said. "You do not intend to bring the dog, do you?"

I glanced into the shadowy backseat, where Cedric sat, pert and panting gently. "I hadn't thought about it."

"He is like a goiter on your neck, if you do not mind me saying so."

"The cutest goiter *I've* ever seen." I addressed Cedric. "Sorry, peanut. Mommy will be back in jig time. Promise." I was a terrible dog mother.

Berta and I set off.

"We really ought to invest in a flashlight," I said after I twisted my ankle for the second time on the dirt road.

"Mm. Or perhaps you ought to invest in proper shoes."

"These are more than proper. They're Pinets."

"You are lucky you are not in a full body cast."

How could I admit that I didn't want to go traipsing around in flat oxfords because of the 1 percent chance I'd run into a ginger-headed rotter?

We traced the iron-fenced perimeter of Breakerhead until we found a side gate. I gave it a shake. Locked, of course.

"We'll have to scale it," I whispered.

"You first."

After some trial and error, I managed to get a toehold on an iron crossbar. Getting over was a bit tricky in a dress and I lost a shoe on the B-side, but I made it.

I coached a huffing and puffing Berta over, too. She landed at my feet, and I gave her a hand.

"I hope fleeing in a hurry won't be necessary," I said, stuffing my foot back in my shoe.

"We shall move about utterly unseen, two stealthy shadows of the night."

I wished.

Breakerhead's windows blazed. Keeping to the shadows, we crossed the lawn and came to the side of the house. I stood on tiptoe and peeked through a lit-up window. Rich furnishings filled a large unoccupied room. We crept to the next window. Another unoccupied room, this one a library.

We circled around and at last found where the household was congregating: the dining room. A Camelot-sized table glimmered with white linens, silver, crystal, and an urn of luscious-looking fruits. Jewel-hued tapestries covered the walls. Several servants scurried about—maids in black and white, a fellow with a towel over his forearm and a wine bottle at the ready—but only four people sat at the table.

"That's Eugene Van Hoogenband at the head of the table," I whispered to Berta. He was fifty or so, with thick brown waves; a large, handsome face; and intelligent eyes.

"He appears sneaky and arrogant," Berta said.

"Well, you don't get to be one of the richest men in New York by being a dear old thing."

"He looks like a banker."

"Steel baron. Mills upstate. He's a widower, from what I recall. That must be Josie at the foot of the table." Josie was brown-haired and slim, with the prettiness of a girl in a soap advertisement. She stared at her plate.

"Who is the elderly gentleman?" Berta whispered.

"Not sure." A gaunt old white-haired gent in a wheelchair sat on

Van Hoogenband's left. He gestured angrily with his fork. "Looks like he's on a rant."

Someone else sat on Van Hoogenband's right, but we couldn't see around the high-backed chair. After a moment, the person leaned over to speak to Josie.

"Golly," I breathed. "It's Senator Morris."

"Dining with friends while his wife is laid out on a slab somewhere?"

"I suppose he couldn't bear to be alone at such a tragic time."

Winfield tipped back his head and brayed with laughter.

"Or maybe he's in shock," I said.

"Disgusting."

A servant darted close to the window and Berta and I squatted out of sight. Our knees crackled like campfires. The servant pushed open the window, I guess to let in some fresh air, and then he was gone.

"We must simply wait until dinner is over," I whispered to Berta, "and then we can try to speak with Josie alone—the men will probably send her away so they can have their brandy and cigarettes."

"Brandy? Is not Senator Morris one of the foremost proponents of the Hearthside Movement?"

"Well, sure. But Chisholm is the only politician in the entire state who actually lives by the Hearthside creed of temperance and family wholesomeness. The rest of them are the usual sort of politician."

We made ourselves as comfy as we could underneath the window. When Berta wasn't looking, I took the Hershey's bar from my bodice and broke off a few squares. The gents' talking went on and on, but I couldn't distinguish their words. Josie never spoke, which wasn't surprising. She was destined to be a wealthy wife, and her training had doubtless begun in the cradle. From time to time, I stole a peek through the window. Servants whisked a parade of lavish courses on and off the table. Wine flowed.

It was between dessert and the cheese and fruit course that I saw the figure in the garden. I sucked in a breath.

"What is it?" Berta whispered.

"Look." I pointed. A human-shaped black figure, barely visible against the inkpot saturation of the gardens, crept along. It disappeared around the corner of the house. "Do you think the Van Hoogenbands have some sort of night guard?"

"They very well may. Surely their silver alone is worth a king's ransom."

"We've got to be careful, then."

"I was already being careful, Mrs. Woodby. Did you steal one of my Hershey's bars?"

I swallowed chocolate. "Borrowed it."

We waited some more. No second sighting of the figure. I took a peek through the window just in time to see Josie get up and pass into the next room.

"She's on the move," I said softly.

There was no time to stash the chocolate away. Berta and I hunched below window level and crept to the next portion of the house. We peeked through. Josie was in a sitting room with a mounted tiger's head and scarlet wallpaper. She shut the doors and went to a sideboard, where she poured herself a large portion of what looked like whiskey from a crystal decanter. She knocked it back.

"Goodness," Berta whispered, "she does that with as much practice as a merchant seaman."

"What do you know about merchant seamen, Berta?"

"Enough."

Josie dried the whiskey glass with a cloth and left it on the sideboard. She crossed to yet another set of doors.

Once again, Berta and I scrambled along the side of the house and came up for air outside the music room. The music room had those floor-level French windows, and they were wide open to the warm night. We lurked in the shadows. Josie sat at the grand piano. She began to play. Well, sort of.

Berta winced. "Do you suppose her musical abilities have been weakened by the large portion of liquor she consumed?"

"The piano sounds like broken factory machinery. How is she *doing* that?"

"I cannot bear it any longer. Besides, the gentlemen will not stay in the dining room forever." Berta stepped through the windows.

Since Berta was correct and we didn't have forever, I followed her inside.

11

....

Josie screamed when she saw Berta and me coming through the French windows. Her piano exercise tinkled to a stop. She half rose from the piano bench. "Who are you?"

"Miss Van Hoogenband, I beg that you keep your voice low," Berta said.

Berta's homey voice had a calming effect on Josie, who repeated more softly, "Who are you?" She eyed our black clothes and the twigs and leaves stuck to them. "Have you been spying on me?" Her gaze fell on the chocolate in my hand. "And eating candy? Like you're at the *pictures*?"

"No, no," I said. I stuffed the chocolate down my bodice. "I mean, we have been watching you, but only to look for an opportunity to speak to you alone. We are private detectives and we've been hired to look into the disappearance of your friend Grace Whiddle."

Josie's eyes went hard. "Who hired you?"

"We're not at liberty to say," I said, borrowing a line from Ralph Oliver's book.

"You don't look like detectives," Josie said. "In the pictures, they're always fellows, and they've got fedoras." She pointed at Berta's huge handbag. "What's in there?"

"Cookies," Berta snapped. "Oh yes—and this." She pulled the mascara-blotched business card from her handbag and passed it to Josie.

Josie looked at the card with a smirk and set it on the piano.

"Miss Van Hoogenband," I said, "have you seen Grace Whiddle since she disappeared from Willow Acres Health Farm this morning?"

"No."

"Do you have any idea where she is?"

A pause. "No."

"Any contact with her? Telephone calls, a note?"

"No."

"Did she have any beaux other than Mr. Morris?"

Josie chewed her lip.

"Miss Van Hoogenband," I said, "Grace could be in danger."

"Why's that?"

I decided not to tell her that Muffy's death hadn't been an accident. No need to alarm her. "Because she's a young, innocent, naïve girl out in the world alone."

Josie burst out laughing so hard, she had to brace herself against the piano.

Berta and I exchanged a glance.

"Are we meant to understand that Grace Whiddle is *not* innocent and naïve?" Berta asked.

"She has everyone fooled." Josie wiped a tear of mirth from her eye. "Her mother. Mrs. Morris. Gil, especially."

"Her fiancé, Gil Morris?" I asked.

"That's right. Poor sap is always writing her treacly poems and giving her wilted bouquets and his absolutely hideous paintings, that sort of thing. Completely goofy about her—and he never even saw Grace without her glasses on."

"What does that mean?"

"You'll figure it out. You're detectives, aren't you? Now, if you don't mind, I must return to my piano practice or Father will scold me."

"It is a wonder your father does not pay you to keep away from that thing," Berta muttered.

"I beg your pardon?" Josie said.

I said, "Tell me about Grace's diary, Miss Van Hoogenband."

"How do you know about that?"

"We suspect that her diary is related to her disappearance. Was there anything written in it that might've provoked someone to, say, kidnap her?" I didn't think that Grace had been kidnapped, but I'd decided to put the fear of God in Josie. Little snot.

Josie sat on the piano bench. "She's crackers about that diary. She writes in it every day, sometimes more than once, and she carries it with her everywhere."

"But what does she write?"

"She won't tell me. I always thought it was histrionics about her mother—she's always pipped about her mother, who's just about the biggest flat tire in the state—and maybe her feelings about getting married to Gil."

"She isn't in love with Gil?" I asked, playing dumb.

"Gosh, no. Have you met him?"

"No," I said. But I had seen his oil painting of the farm animals in Sophronia's powder room. That painting would stop love dead in its tracks. "What about her feelings for Muffy Morris? Did she describe those in her diary?"

"I *told* you," Josie said, "I've never read Grace's diary. But I know who has. Miss Cotton."

"Of Miss Cotton's Academy for Young Ladies?"

"Do you know it?"

"Vaguely." I had, in fact, attended Miss Cotton's Academy, a stuffy Manhattan finishing school, during my eighteenth year. "How did Miss Cotton come to read the diary?"

"Well, Grace was writing in her diary during Personality Development class one day, and the teacher, Miss Ames, caught her at it, confiscated the diary, and handed it over to Miss Cotton. Grace was in an absolute panic, but we got it back. We sneaked into Miss Cotton's office one evening."

"Wowie," I said. "That couldn't have been easy."

"We bribed the janitor with absolute bushels of ciggies."

Note to self: Speak with Miss Cotton.

"Do you suppose Grace was capable of, say, killing a person?" I asked.

"Killing?" Josie giggled, but then her face went serious. "Well, maybe her mother."

"What about her mother-in-law?"

"You don't mean that Mrs. Morris was *murdered*? Senator Morris told me it was her heart."

"No, no," I said quickly. "I'm only attempting to understand what sort of girl Grace is."

"A dumb Dora. Her head is in the clouds—she talks about running away to be a burlesque dancer or a motion picture actress, but she's as glamorous as a steamed mussel."

"I thought you were friends."

"We are. But I'm the head friend, and it's handy having Grace around. Father says you never get anywhere in life by being a patsy."

The double doors swung open, and a huge man in evening clothes lurched into the room. His mug was fringed with spiky hair and, along the hairline, a long scar. It looked as though someone had sawed off the top of his head like a boiled egg, rummaged around inside, and then stitched it back on in a hurry.

Berta and I shrank back. *A brain surgery scar?* was my only coherent thought.

"Hands up, ladies," the man said in a voice like a broken outboard motor. He waved a hefty pistol.

Berta and I raised our hands. As I did so, the chocolate bar remnant came unwedged from my décolleté and fell on the carpet.

"Miss Van Hoogenband," Mr. Egghead said, "your father wants you ta go ta your room."

"Go to my room?" Josie crossed her arms.

Mr. Egghead made a gurgling sound.

Josie took the gurgle as her cue to scurry away. Just before she shut the double doors and disappeared, she gave me a silent raspberry.

Brat.

"Siddown on the piana bench," Mr. Egghead said, waving the gun at Berta and me. His movements were a bit slip-sloppy. Not a comforting feature in a fellow who's holding a five-pound gun.

Berta and I scurried over to the piano bench and plopped down in tandem. There was barely enough room for so much in the way of hips on the bench. Mr. Egghead stuffed his pistol in a pocket, pulled out a ball of twine, and trussed Berta and me together at the shoulders like a couple of chicken drumsticks. "Mr. Van Hoogenband's real upset 'bout this," Mr. Egghead said. "He don't like people bugging his daughter, see. He's gonna deal with you later, when he's done with his guests."

"Ah," I said.

"How are we going to explain ourselves?" Berta whispered.

"Shuddup!" Mr. Egghead finished tying us. "Now, you stay right there," he said, and left.

Berta and I waited two beats. Then we both stood up—because Mr. Egghead had tied only our shoulders together—and waddled toward the windows.

I tripped on the carpet and took Berta down with me. We were struggling around like kittens in a sack when a pair of battered wing tips appeared in my line of vision.

"Looks like I missed the three-legged race," Ralph Oliver said.

"So *you're* who I saw skulking around in the garden earlier," I said. "I should've known."

Ralph disentangled us from the twine and helped us to our feet. The three of us stole outside.

We ran across the dark lawn, under the trees, and to the gate Berta and I had climbed over earlier. We stopped there, and I doubled over, trying to catch my breath. "What are you doing here?" I asked Ralph.

He stood with his hands in his baggy trousers pockets. He wasn't even out of breath. Maddening. "Same thing as you."

"But I'm sure I never mentioned Josie Van Hoogenband at dinner."

Ralph shrugged. "I've got my own sources. Is this the thanks I get for busting you out of there?"

"He has a point, Mrs. Woodby," Berta said.

"Yes, well," I muttered. "Thanks." I still couldn't understand how Ralph had known to go to Breakerhead. He was hiding something. No surprise.

Ralph boosted Berta up so she could squeeze a boot onto the gate's crossbar.

"Avert your eyes," she said to Ralph.

Ralph turned around.

Berta went up and over, and thumped to the ground on the other side.

My turn.

Ralph's white grin flashed through the darkness. "Need a hand?"

"I'm able to do it myself."

"Well, sure, but everything's more fun when there's two involved."

I started up the gate. It was not the most graceful of ascents or dismounts, but I did it all by myself. I didn't even lose a shoe. By the time I'd dusted myself off, Ralph had hopped down next to me.

"Sorry we beat you to Josie," I said. Ralph was so close, I could smell him, that fresh-air scent with the faintest touch of caveman somewhere in the mix. My body started writing an enthusiastic RSVP to the party.

Ralph grinned in a way that made me suspect he'd somehow gotten the RSVP. "Not to worry, kid. It turns out, it worked out pretty nice for me. I heard everything Poor Little Rich Girl said through the window."

"You *pill*."

"Call it teamwork."

"We're not a team."

"Suit yourself."

I would say something. I must. "You and I should have a private talk sometime, Mr. Oliver."

"Oh yeah? About what?"

He was going to pretend he hadn't well-nigh jilted me? That we were mere colleagues? That last month our kisses hadn't generated enough electricity to light up the Atlantic Mutual Building?

"Berta, we're leaving," I said through clenched teeth.

"It is I who is waiting for you, Mrs. Woodby," Berta said.

"Hold it," Ralph said.

Awash with luscious thoughts of apologies and kisses and giant rose bouquets, I gave him my most disdainful look. "Yes?"

"I think this is yours." Ralph pushed the foil-wrapped nub of Hershey's bar into my hand. "Maybe I'll see you two at breakfast. Mrs. Lundgren. Mrs. Woodby." He merged with the shadows and was gone.

12

....

I'm not one to get gussied up for brekky. In my former days as a Society Matron, I often took my morning coffee and cinnamon rolls on a tray in bed. More recently, I'd been taking my coffee and cinnamon rolls in pajamas at the kitchen table. However, as any reader of *Thrilling Romance* well knows, a lady must be well turned out if she wishes her former fellow to be consumed with remorse.

To that end, I managed to wash my bob with a bowl of hot water heated on the galley's kerosene stove, air out a leaf green cotton dress by hanging it over the yacht boom, and put on my munitions with only a powder compact for a mirror. I was out of lipstick, so I did my best with a dab of cheek rouge on my lips. After that, I was so exhausted, I thought about lying down, but my finger waves weren't dry yet.

Berta knocked on my cabin door. "Mrs. Woodby? Are you quite ready to go to breakfast? It sounds as though you are wrestling bears in there."

I swung open the door.

"Goodness," Berta said. She was impossibly neat in a chintz dress and a smooth bun, even though I thought she'd only just woken up. "Look at you. So very groomed."

"I merely wish to appear presentable for our visit to Senator Morris's house this morning—you haven't forgotten, have you?"

"No, I have not. I lay awake last night wondering how I might demand an advance fee from him when we have not made any progress on the case."

We disembarked the yacht, Cedric in tow, and walked along the dock. The morning air was salty-fresh and cool. Mist hovered like silk scarves over the water. I almost tripped in my high, bone-colored Perugia T-straps.

Berta clucked her tongue.

"What?" I said crossly.

"If you do not mind me saying so—"

"I probably will."

"—you, like all prideful women, wish to be adored even when you're behaving badly. But is that not, perhaps, unfair?"

"Behaving badly? Me?"

"Poor Mr. Oliver looked quite stricken when you told him you were not happy to see him yesterday."

"He wasn't stricken! He was as sphinxlike as ever. *Stricken.* Hah." Stricken? Truly?

When we stepped into the Foghorn's lobby, Ralph was leaning an elbow on the front desk, fedora tipped, chatting with the cute, titian-haired front desk clerkette. The clerkette was all giggles and fluttering eyelashes.

Girls and Ralph? Like flies to honey.

Ralph stopped mid-sentence when he saw me. He murmured something to the clerkette and came over. "I was hoping I'd see you this morning," he said. His smile was guarded. "Nice dress."

"Nice hat."

"Nice shoes."

"These old things?"

Berta sighed noisily.

Ralph crouched to scratch Cedric, who was skittering around his ankles like a tiny tap dancer. "Actually, I was hanging around to let you know I'm headed to the city. Let's go outside. More private."

We went out onto the creaky wraparound porch overlooking Main Street.

"I'm following a tip about Grace's whereabouts," Ralph said softly. "I'll probably be back in the neighborhood at some point to collect my payment from Sophronia Whiddle. I'll see if you're still around then."

"You sound very confident, Mr. Oliver," Berta said. "It must be a very hot tip indeed."

"Hope so. You two may have a hot one, too, with what Josie Van H told you last night about that schoolmistress. The schoolmistress might've read all about Grace's big plans to poison you-know-who in that diary. Could be the key to your case."

"I know, I know," I said, "but I'm not sure how to find Miss Cotton. School isn't in session during the summer."

"Telephone the school. Maybe there's someone there, working the office."

Good idea. "Just a minute," I said. I dashed inside and went to the lobby call box. I had the telephone exchange girl plug me into Miss Cotton's Academy on the Upper East Side. The telephone rang ten times and I was just about to disconnect when a fluting woman's voice said, "Hello?"

"Is this Miss Cotton's Academy for Young Ladies?" I asked.

"Yes."

"I am Lola Woodby—née DuFey—an alumna of the school. I must speak with Miss Cotton regarding an urgent matter."

"Miss Cotton is in the country for the summer."

"Where?"

"Goodness. I cannot disclose her private address."

"The matter is pressing."

"Then telephone the police." The woman hung up.

I gave the front desk clerkette a nickel. She tossed the nickel in the till and looked me up and down. Why must ladies size each other up as though they were inspecting beef brisket on special at the butcher?

I returned to Ralph and Berta on the porch. "No luck. Miss Cotton has gone to the country for the summer, and the woman on the telephone—a secretary, I suppose—said she can't disclose her private address."

"Then I'll stop by the school first thing when I get to the city and see if talking to her in person is more effective," Ralph said, "as a special favor to the prettiest detectives on the Eastern seaboard." He gave me a lingering look that made me shiver like a whippet. I couldn't help it. I'd tried the cold tap, but now here *he* was running hot. We had some serious plumbing problems.

"Where's the school?" Ralph asked.

"East Ninety-first Street, a block and a half from Central Park," I said. "You can't miss it. It's a cross between a French château and a penitentiary."

"Okay, then." Ralph was already going down the steps. "I'll telephone you here in the lobby call box at, say, one o'clock with the address. That should give me enough time."

"He is very sure of himself," Berta whispered to me. We watched Ralph climb into his junky Chalmers touring motorcar with its saggy fold-down top.

"I know." I couldn't decide if Ralph's self-assurance was exciting, aggravating, or both.

Ralph reversed out of his spot, braked, and called over the *whappety-whappety* of the engine, "Say, I almost forgot—you might want to take a look at the newspapers." The Chalmers rumbled away down the street.

Several minutes later, Berta and I were settled in a corner booth with piping cups of coffee and all the latest newspapers our waiter could scrounge up. We ordered breakfast and started leafing through.

"See anything?" I asked Berta.

"No. You?"

"No . . . oh. Yes. Gee." I'd picked up yesterday's edition of *The New York Evening Observer*.

MUFFY MORRIS TEETOTALED! the headline said, followed by, SENATOR'S WIFE IN FOR TIPPLING CURE, OUT ON A STRETCHER.

"By Ida Shanks, no less," I said.

"Oh my." Berta poured cream in her coffee. "Miss Shanks is making her way in the world, is she not?"

"Really pulling herself up by the bootstraps."

Some people have a nemesis; I have Miss Ida Shanks. One part boiled fowl, one part witch, and one part writer for New York's most muckraking newspaper. Ida and I grew up together in dusty Scragg Springs, Indiana, but while my father made his fortune on Wall Street and I'd married money, Ida had attended a ladies' college in Illinois and gotten a job as a writer. Strictly on the qt, I admire her gumption. But I loathe her, too, because when she was the *Observer*'s society columnist, I was her favorite target.

"Chisholm is probably spouting steam," I said. "This could ruin his business." I considered. "Wait. No one was supposed to know about that empty rum bottle except Chisholm and the police."

"And Nurse Beaulah. Recall that she discovered the body."

"You know, I'll bet the *murderer* leaked the news of the rum bottle to the press, to spread the story around that Muffy's death was due to drink. As a cover, you know. I'll ring Chisholm up after we eat and ask if he'll allow me to speak to Nurse Beaulah—I'll think of some fib. And I suppose I'll try to ring up Ida Shanks, too." You may think I would've already sprinted for the nearest telephone to ring up Ida Shanks, but the truth is, I knew in my heart that she would never reveal her leak to me. She's not exactly a Good Samaritan.

The waiter brought my scrambled eggs, bacon, and toast, and I dug in.

Berta ate a few bites of sausage and then said, "I cannot help wondering if it was a mistake to give Miss Van Hoogenband our card."

My jaws froze mid-chew. "Why?"

"Well, surely she will alert her father to the existence of the card. He will know our address in the city. Perhaps he has even told Senator Morris that we entered his house last night."

"Senator Morris can't complain if we were there last night," I said. "We were only doing our job."

But . . . had the Discreet Retrieval Agency bitten off more than it could chew? After all, when we started the agency, we'd sworn not to investigate murders. We'd meant only to be a couple of bounding Labrador retrievers fetching things for people. Murder was different. Murder was sticky.

Berta and I paid our bill and returned once more to the lobby call box. "This call box is beginning to feel like my summer cottage," I said to Berta as I slid inside. "And is the front desk clerkette giving me the stink eye?"

"Of course she is giving you the stink eye. Mr. Oliver abandoned her company for yours."

He had, hadn't he?

"I shall just take Cedric out for a walk," Berta said. "He seems agitated."

"Probably indigestion from all that sausage you slipped him at breakfast."

Berta and Cedric toddled off.

First I rang up *The New York Evening Observer*'s offices in the city, but Ida Shanks wasn't in yet.

Phooey.

Then I telephoned Willow Acres and asked for Chisholm.

"Hello, Lola," Chisholm said. "I understand that you and Mrs. Lundgren trespassed upon Willow Acres by way of the hedge yesterday afternoon and fled Nurse Astrid and two orderlies?"

"Oh, that? All a misunderstanding."

"Why are you telephoning? I am very busy."

"You sound a little hot and bothered, Chisholm. I take it you saw the newspapers?"

"Of course I saw the newspapers. I suppose it was you who leaked that information to the press?"

"Me?"

"You overheard my conversation in the lobby the day before yesterday, in which I mentioned Mrs. Morris's cure—"

"The leak wasn't me, Chisholm. We might not be the best of pals, but I'd never leak your secrets to the press. You're family."

"This is a scandal, you do realize. If Senator Morris chooses to believe that my staff and I were anything but perfectly tactful about his wife's health problems—"

"I telephoned to ask a favor," I said.

Silence. "A favor."

"The night I stayed at Willow Acres, I thought I lost an earring between the floorboards of my room. I searched for it everywhere, and the night nurse helped me, too. I wished to tell her not to worry, because I found the earring in my shoe." I cleared my throat. "What was that darling night nurse's name, again?"

"Meddling again, Lola?"

"What?"

"You are lying. There are no cracks between the floorboards in *my* establishment. I do realize that you recently found it gratifying to meddle in a murder investigation, but wishing to do it again makes me fear for your already fragile mental state. There are curative measures you could take for your barren condition, you realize. There have been some recent advances in electroshock—"

"I'm not barren," I said through gritted teeth. At least, I didn't *think* I was barren. By the time Alfie croaked, we hadn't canoodled for eons. Thank goodness.

"Why don't you call upon your sister?" Chisholm said. "Lillian will be a bracing influence upon you. She is redecorating Amberley in preparation for our conjugal life there, with the help of Miss Wilbur—you do know Miss Wilbur?"

"Violet Wilbur? Scourge of tacky wallpaper and regrettable rugs? Sure." I gripped the telephone cord so tightly, my knuckles went white. I already knew about Lillian redecorating what once had been my house, but it still made me feel icky-boo. "Toodles."

"Good-bye, Lola. And do cut down on your chocolate consumption, mm?"

13

After my chin-wag with Chisholm, I needed a little pick-me-up, so I convinced Berta that we had time to stop in at the Hare's Hollow five-and-dime before motoring to Senator Morris's house. After some deliberation I purchased a crimson Delica Kissproof lipstick for ten cents. As soon as we were back in the Duesy, I applied a coat using the rearview mirror.

"Tastes waxy," I said, popping the cap back on. "I suppose that's how it's kiss-proof?"

"That is a very optimistic lipstick, Mrs. Woodby."

We set off for Senator Morris's house, stopping at a gas station along the way. With gas at a quarter per gallon and all the driving we were doing, Berta and I needed to crack this case, pronto.

"Another palace," Berta said as we drove up the Morris house's front drive.

"You'd never guess that Senator Morris's family made their bucks in bathroom fixtures, would you?" The place was a brick Georgian colonial: thick ivy, tall windows, white pillars, lots of marble figures in their birthday suits. I parked in the shade since I figured it would be unprofessional to take Cedric inside. I left the Duesy's windows open, and Berta and I went to the front door. I rang the doorbell. No answer.

"Maybe everyone is outside somewhere," I said. "Let's go around to the back." We circled the house. "By the way, do we or do we not admit to Senator Morris that we broke into Breakerhead last night?"

"I would rather not discuss the matter with him," Berta said.

"So we lie."

At the back of the house, we found ourselves on a terrace with a long stone balustrade. Stairs led down to a lawn edged with pyramidal topiaries, and the lawn terminated in a cliff. Beyond, the sea sparkled indigo. Boats dotted the horizon.

"There is someone," Berta said, pointing down at the lawn.

"That must be Gil." A thin young man stood slump-shouldered at an easel, facing the sea and painting. "Let's go ask him about his mother. Could be our only chance."

Berta glanced back at the house. "But Senator Morris—?"

"He can hardly fault us for being friendly."

We went down the steps and approached Gil.

Gil wore a seersucker suit and a straw boater hat. No mourning togs, then. He didn't seem to notice us, I suppose because he was concentrating so fiercely on his painting. His tongue stuck out between his front teeth.

"Lovely painting," I said. Then I looked at the painting. It wasn't lovely.

"Oh. I didn't hear you coming. When I paint, I am deaf to the world." Gil lowered his brush. Blue eyes bulged in a long, weak-chinned face. "Who are you?"

"Mrs. Woodby, and this is Mrs. Lundgren. We're here to meet your father, but I'm afraid no one answered our ring at the front door."

"Oh, the servants are all off today—mourning Mummy—but

Dad is home. He's in his study, I suppose. The study is soundproofed, so he probably didn't hear the bell." Gil spoke in a wispy tenor.

Berta said, "I beg your pardon—did you say 'soundproofed'?"

"You don't know Dad very well, do you? He's—how shall I put it?" Gil waved his paintbrush. "He's paranoid and self-absorbed. Thinks everyone is out to get him. I suppose he told you that Mummy died because of something to do with him?"

Berta said, "He did mention that your poor dear mother—"

"*Dear?*" Gil tipped back his head and laughed so hard, the ribbon on his boater hat quivered. "Mummy was an alcoholic old hag. I'm pleased she's gone. One parent dead, one to go. Once Dad pops off, I'll live in comfort without having to jump through hoops for anyone."

Sweet Jujyfruits. No love lost in *this* family.

Gil went on, "Mummy never did understand my art. As soon as I finished at Harvard two years ago, she never stopped hinting I should be cut off unless I joined the family business. Uncle Preston runs it now. Morris Water-Closets. He wishes to start me off in the mail room. That would simply crush my soul. At least Dad foots the bill, although with an endless litany of complaints and insults."

"How does your father foot the bill, exactly?" I asked. Berta and I looked at Gil's work in progress. A lumpy boat perched atop rows of pantomime waves. Two bloated seagulls dangled beside a lemon-shaped sun.

"For my trips to Europe, where I study painting."

"I see," I said.

"Do you study . . . modern art?" Berta asked.

"God, no." Gil tucked his chin in disgust. "Loathe it. I'm a classicist, quite obviously."

"And your mother thought you ought to be more, um, conventionally employed?" I asked.

"Yes. The only way I could get her off my back was to agree to marry Grace and endeavor to produce a few brats to carry on the Morris name. Mummy said Grace had the most tip-top birthing hips—although, of course, I adore Grace with every fiber of my being."

"Mr. Morris," I said, "have you any idea where Grace might be?"

"No! And oh gosh, I am so desperately worried about her! If something were to happen to her, if the wedding weren't to go off . . . well, I'll positively die."

"The wedding is supposed to be in five days' time," I said, "so in all likelihood, it will be . . . delayed."

"No. *No.*" Tears glistened in Gil's eyes. "Grace will come back. She wouldn't leave me at the altar. She is such a sweet little saint— except for that vile, wretched diary of hers." Gil's lips peeled back from his teeth. "She's cuckoo about that thing. You haven't seen it anywhere, have you?"

"No," I said.

"What was she always writing in there? Why wasn't it enough to talk to me? She'd tell me good night and slip away, and the next thing I knew, she'd be sitting on her bed and scribbling madly. Sometimes I thought she must be writing about me."

Wait. Had Gil spied on Grace in her *bedroom*?

Gil looked over my shoulder. "Here's one of Father's trained apes come to fetch you."

I turned. A man with slicked hair and a dark suit strode toward us, waving. "You the detective dames?" he called when he drew near.

"I suppose that could refer to us," I said to the man.

"Then come with me. Senator Morris is waiting."

Senator Winfield Morris's study was done up in the usual green leather, mahogany, and those gold-embossed books you buy as a set. More eyebrow-raising were the gun cabinets flanking the fireplace. They were crammed full with what I was sure were tommy guns.

"Just like women," Winfield called from his seat at a massive desk. "Late." He grinned. "Buster," he said to the man who'd fetched us, "stay."

Buster shut the door and stood in front of it with a wide stance.

"Good morning, Senator," I said. Berta and I stopped in front of Winfield's desk.

Winfield looked us up and down, his beady eyes coming to rest on my bosom. "Glad to see you cleaned yourself up, Mrs. Woodby. I hate to see a pretty lady let herself go. When I saw you at Willow Acres yesterday—*whew*."

I ached to whack Winfield with my handbag. But one doesn't whack one's sole client with handbags.

"Have a seat," Winfield said.

Berta and I sat in the two chairs facing the desk.

Winfield steepled his hairy fingers. "Have you found the murderer?"

Was he kidding? "You must understand, Senator, that these things take time," I said. "But we have a lead." So far, Winfield had given no indication that he knew we'd been at Breakerhead last night. Maybe Van Hoogenband hadn't told him. Better yet, maybe Van Hoogenband had never found our business card on the piano.

"A lead?" Winfield hunched forward over his desk.

"We discovered how the murderer managed to kill your wife." I launched into a description of the vial of medicine we'd found behind the radiator in Muffy's room, and how we figured that the murderer had swapped it out for a vial containing arsenic.

Winfield interrupted me. "I don't care *how* they did it. Come on, girls. I'm not paying you to dig up all the cute little details. I want to know who, and I want to know now."

Berta said, "Strictly speaking, Senator, you have not paid us a red cent."

"*Berta*," I whispered.

"That's right," Winfield said. "I haven't. How about we keep it that way and I find someone else to collar Muffy's killer?"

"That won't be necessary," I said quickly.

Berta cut me an annoyed look. "Senator Morris, we require an advance fee if we are to continue this investigation. We have expenses, and it is agency policy. Furthermore, I do not believe it is necessary to remind you that our agency provides a cushion of discretion and an understanding of New York society that other agencies simply cannot."

I held my breath.

Winfield looked at Berta and me in turn with his unreadable eyes. At last he said, "Fine," opened a desk drawer, and pulled out a stack of greenbacks as thick as my wrist. He counted some out while Berta and I watched, mesmerized. He slid the bills over. "One thousand okay?"

Holy moly.

"For now," Berta said briskly. Her handbag absorbed the cash.

"Now that that's settled," Winfield said, "any other leads— anything useful?"

"Well, we suspect that whoever leaked the story about the rum bottle in Muffy's room to the *Observer* could be the murderer himself—or herself," I said.

"How do you figure?"

"No one else besides the murderer, Mrs. Lundgren and me, one of the nurses, and Dr. Woodby were supposed to have seen Muffy's room. Oh—and the police."

"Well, that's more like it," Winfield said. "*That* sounds like a political saboteur. Slandering me to the papers, damn it! *Get them.* Now, listen, I can't talk tomorrow. This is a busy time of year for me. Giving a speech at a beauty pageant tomorrow. For once, I'll be with a bunch of gorgeous girls instead of smelly old men. Come by again the day after tomorrow, same time. I'll be expecting progress. If not—" Winfield shrugged. "—well, I just might have to terminate. Got it?"

Terminate? My eyes flicked to the tommy guns. "I believe we do. But before we go, I have two questions. First, could I ask you again who you believe killed your wife?"

"I told you, that's your job."

"Your hunch could be helpful."

"Fine. You want to know who did it? I'll tell you. It was the anarchists."

"The . . . anarchists?"

"Scummy Europeans invading the States with their red propaganda. They hate everything I stand for, everything all Hearthside politicians stand for. Mark my words, when you find out which one of those creeps at the health farm killed my wife, you'll find a sleeper anarchist."

Gil had been correct: Winfield was paranoid. "And another thing," I said. "Could we look through Muffy's things? We might unearth a clue."

"I can't see how you'd unearth a clue about a goddam anarchist in my dead wife's things, but sure, fine, go right ahead. Buster will show you to her room." Winfield twiddled his fingers, and Buster opened the study door.

Berta and I practically tripped over each other getting out of there.

14

....

Buster led Berta and me along corridors and up a back stair, and left us at Muffy's bedroom door.

"See yourselves out," he said.

Berta and I shut ourselves into the room. "Just how I pictured it," I said. Blue chinoiserie wallpaper and dainty white furniture, head-achy floral perfume emanating from the squashy carpet.

"It is very clean," Berta said. "Muffy seemed such a disaster, I would have expected a bit more of a mess." She began rifling through a dresser.

"I'm sure they have battalions of maids."

"True."

I went into the bathroom. Gold taps, veined marble, and a large perfume collection on mirrored trays. All spick-and-span. Another of Gil's putrid paintings hung over the lavatory. It depicted either a castle at sunset or a gelatin salad.

I went back out into the bedroom and inspected the built-in bookshelves on either side of the fireplace. One side held a collection of romantic novels. I'd read a few of them myself, so I knew they were tales starring medieval knights, masked highwaymen, and passionate sheikhs. They weren't highbrow, but they were just the ticket to see a neglected wife through a lonely evening. Sympathy for Muffy fluttered through me. I knew what being married to a bastard was like, and while it hadn't driven me to a jugging problem, I certainly had eaten an unreasonable amount of buttercream icing over the years.

The bookcase on the other side of the fireplace held a few photograph albums, the *New York Social Register*, a Hare's Hollow Country Club directory, and a few other volumes of that ilk. I paged through a photograph album. Babies, weddings, petulant children, dewy-eyed debutantes—including one of the young Muffy herself. A series of travel photos of European landmarks, ocean liner dining rooms, and palm-treed beaches in which Muffy posed with her brother, Hermie. I shut the album and replaced it on the shelf.

"Find anything interesting?" I asked Berta.

"Nothing. Shall we go?"

We motored away from the Morris house after I'd let Cedric loose for a surreptitious visit to the shrubbery.

"What did you make of Winfield's notion that it's the anarchists out to destroy him?" I asked Berta.

"Implausible. Any anarchist worth his or her salt would kill the senator himself, not his wife, and they would take credit for it, too. I tend to believe the senator is, as his son said, paranoid and self-absorbed."

"Have you ever known any European anarchists, Berta?"

"Well, no, but I have read of them extensively in Elmo Bentley's *Secret Empire* penny serial."

"This anarchist business has gotten me thinking. Our murder

suspects do have links to Europe. Hermie seems to have traveled all over the Continent with Muffy."

"As a tourist, surely."

"Could've been a cover."

Berta snorted.

"Then there's Raymond Hathorne," I said. "Even though he's Canadian, Mother and Lillian first met him on an ocean liner returning from Europe last month."

"Your mother said he had been golfing in Scotland."

"And Pete Schlump said how fond he is of France—remember?"

"Pete Schlump could not be an anarchist! The very idea."

"Violet Wilbur said something about her magazine column being madly popular in France, too. Maybe it's only a coincidence. But maybe Europe—anarchists or no—is mixed up in this somehow."

When we reached Hare's Hollow, we lunched at a fish and chips shanty, after which Berta carefully logged the cost in her expense book.

"It isn't necessary to be so scrupulous," I said. "It's only lunch."

"I wish to be professional. And I do wish you would keep track, too."

I shrugged.

"Oh, by the by," Berta said. She took the stack of money that Senator Morris had given us and counted out half for me. "Do not spend it all at once."

We headed back to the Foghorn to await Ralph's call. To my relief, the cute clerkette had been replaced by a fellow in a waistcoat.

At one o'clock on the dot, the call box telephone jangled. I picked it up.

"Lola Woodby."

"Hi there, kid," came Ralph's voice, distant and crackly. "I have Miss Cotton's address for you."

"How did you manage it? That school secretary was as tough as shoe leather."

"Oh, I figured out how to soften her up."

I rolled my eyes. "What is the address?"

"Number eleven Rosebud Lane, Stony Brook."

"Peachy." Stony Brook was about thirty miles from Hare's Hollow. "I owe you one, Mr. Oliver."

"I'll remember you said that, Mrs. Woodby."

We disconnected at the same time.

I didn't notice the black Chevrolet Touring Car tailing us until we were about five miles out of Hare's Hollow. And really, for the number of twists and turns in the road, it wasn't safe for a motorcar to follow me so closely.

"You should keep your eyes on the road, Mrs. Woodby," Berta said, "rather than incessantly checking your makeup in the rearview mirror. Yes, your lipstick is bleeding, but you might fix it once we stop."

"What?" My hand flew to my lips and I rubbed. "No—it's, well, I think we're being followed—no, don't turn around!"

Berta turned around and glared out the rear window. "It is true." She swiveled forward. "Do not be alarmed, but it is that lumbering fellow with the forehead scar from the Van Hoogenband house last night."

"Mr. Egghead?" I yelled. My foot jabbed harder on the gas of its own volition.

"Surely that is not his name." Berta clutched the dashboard as we sailed around a bend.

"Didn't you see the scar straight across his head? He's either had his head popped open like a ring box by a brain surgeon, or—"

"Calm yourself."

"I'm *calm*," I said through clenched teeth.

"Good. Because there is a second person with him."

I shot a glance in the rearview mirror. "Are you sure that's another person? It could be a dog."

"It is a small person. Perhaps a child. I saw a hat. Oh dear. When you grimace in that fashion—"

"I'm trying to concentrate!"

"—I am able to see that some lipstick has found its way to your teeth."

I wouldn't look in the rearview mirror at my teeth. I wouldn't.

I looked in the mirror. My mouth was a vampirish crimson mess. "It melted!"

"Mrs. Woodby, watch out for that guardrail!" Berta cried.

My eyes flew to the road just in time to see a guardrail hurtling toward us. I slammed on the brakes. We skidded.

SMASH!

My torso slammed against the steering wheel. Berta screamed. Mr. Egghead's motorcar had rear-ended us, and it pushed us along like a snowplow for several yards before coming to a stop.

Berta was hanging on to the passenger door, and her hat had fallen over her eyes. "Go! Keep going!" she cried.

I hit the gas and we zigzagged before straightening out on the road. We rumbled around a bend.

"Is Cedric all right?" I half sobbed.

Berta twisted. "Yes."

"Do you see them? Are they coming?"

"I do not know. Drive a bit more, and then find a secluded place to turn off."

I zipped along, my nerves fizzing like dynamite fuses, and when I saw a hedge-lined turnout, I turned. The Duesy bumped on the narrow lane. Something rattled, Berta peeped, and branches screeched along my door. I braked hard and switched off the engine.

No noise but the sound of two ladies and one Pomeranian panting. Then, a motorcar engine.

In the rearview mirror, I watched Mr. Egghead's Chevrolet sail past. I caught the briefest glimpse of a small woman in a cloche hat sitting in the passenger seat.

"It worked," I said. "I can't believe it. They didn't see us." I turned. "I'm so sorry, Berta. I don't know what came over me."

"I know what came over you. Your lipstick melted and you panicked."

I felt like bursting into tears, from fright and relief and embarrassment. Instead, I took the Delica Kissproof lipstick and a hankie from my purse and, hands shaking, repaired my lips.

We arrived in Stony Brook without seeing Mr. Egghead's motorcar again. When we parked in front of 11 Rosebud Lane, I had to peel my thighs off the hot leather seat. The first thing I did when I got out was inspect the damage to the Duesy's rear.

"Oh dear," Berta said. "The spare tire looks as though it has been chewed up and spit out."

I told myself to buck up, that it was frivolous to have a lump in one's throat about a spare tire. But I couldn't afford to fix it, you see.

I collected Cedric, and the three of us approached Miss Cotton's house. It was a neat shingled cottage with white trim surrounded by a picket fence and climbing pink roses. Bees droned and birds twittered.

"What a charming little house," Berta said, opening the gate. "I could not think poorly of a lady who keeps a house such as this."

"You'll be singing a different tune once you meet her," I whispered. "Miss Cotton has a frozen giblet for a heart."

"But just look at her petunias."

15

....

I hit Miss Cotton's door knocker.

"I am in the back!" a woman called.

Berta and I circled the cottage, following a moss-edged stone path.

Miss Cotton sat at a table, wearing sunglasses and smoking a cigarette. A floral scarf held back graying hair.

I stopped. "Miss . . . Cotton?" The Miss Cotton I had known wore tailored tweed and crisp blouses. Not . . . embroidered gypsy dresses. Yet I recognized her rigid posture, her scarecrow limbs, her prominent nose.

Miss Cotton took a pull from her cigarette in its long holder and blew smoke. She set aside a book. "If you're peddling those cheap cleaning supplies—"

"Miss Cotton," I said, "I am Lola Woodby, née DuFey. I was a pupil at your academy several years ago."

Miss Cotton looked over the tops of her sunglasses. "Lola. It *is* you. What a surprise. The years have treated you well."

"Thank you," I said.

"I always thought you would come to no good, but now, well, look at you." Miss Cotton swept her cigarette down and up. "All grown up. Healthy, hearty, and hale, just like your sister, Lillian."

In my arms, Cedric warbled a growl. I shushed him.

"And who is this?" Miss Cotton turned to Berta.

"Mrs. Lundgren," Berta said. "Private detective."

I opened my mouth and shut it again. I hadn't thought to discuss it with Berta, but I wasn't too keen on revealing my new trade to the ruthless tormentor of my eighteenth year.

"Did you say 'private detective'?" Miss Cotton asked.

"Go on," Berta whispered to me.

I swallowed. "Yes. Both of us are private detectives."

Miss Cotton laughed.

Berta said, "We are the Discreet Retrieval Agency."

"Oh my. Lola Woodby, lady gumshoe in last year's hat. Mm. Now I recall hearing something to the effect that your husband left you penniless. I commend you, Lola. Most women in your position would simply remarry."

"We would like to ask you some questions about Grace Whiddle," I said.

"I do not speak of my students. What is more, during the summer holiday, I make it a point not to think of my students. How did you find my house, anyway?"

"Gumshoes have methods," Berta said.

I said, "Miss Cotton, did you know that Grace Whiddle fled Willow Acres Health Farm yesterday just before Muffy Morris's corpse was found? No one knows where she's gone."

"What are you suggesting?" Miss Cotton tapped ash. "That Grace murdered her future mother-in-law? Shouldn't the police be handling this? Who hired you?"

"I am not at liberty to say," I said. Golly, but that was a liberating phrase.

"Oh, very well," Miss Cotton said. "Why don't you sit? Would you like a highball? I seem to remember that's what you were drinking when I found you and your horrid little friend Daisy getting lathered on the roof during ballroom dancing class."

My mouth watered as Berta and I sat. It had been ages—okay, three days—since I'd had a highball. "Why, yes, I—"

"We do not partake of spirits on the job," Berta said in a stony voice.

I squelched a sigh.

"I thought that only applied to the police," Miss Cotton said.

"You will find that we are more serious about our work than the police are," Berta said.

"What I would like to know first, Miss Cotton," I said, "is what sort of girl Grace Whiddle is."

"What sort of girl? Why, the same as the rest of them. Spoiled, sullen, rich little princess. She was one of the wallflower set. I must admit I was surprised to hear of her engagement to Gilbert Morris, because I had her pegged for one of those three-season debutantes who eventually marry a businessman from Kansas or else one of those elderly European aristos who are on their third wife and always seem so very sinister."

"Grace is not a good matrimonial prospect?" I asked.

"Well, no, she isn't. Rather dull and plain, hideous posture, plump, prone to spots on the chin, that sort of thing. And she scarcely ever speaks."

"But she is an avid diarist," I said.

"Oh? I had no idea."

"Cut the cauliflower," I said. "We know for a fact that you confiscated Grace's diary at school only a few weeks ago, and that you read it."

"Of course I didn't read it."

"What was in Grace's diary?"

"I shall say it again: I did not read it."

I was convinced Miss Cotton was fibbing. Her sunglasses hid her eyes, but she had that sneezy look people get when they're bottling up a secret.

"The contents of the diary could be the key to Mrs. Morris's death," I said.

"But I read in the newspapers that she drank herself to death."

Oops. "Of course she did. But *why* did she drink herself to death?"

Miss Cotton blew smoke. "Oh, very well. You two are persistent, aren't you? Like fruit flies. I did dip into the diary—briefly—but I assure you it contained nothing but girlish nonsense about her mother and her fiancé and the servants' gossip and what she ate for dinner. She simply recorded all the mind-numbing minutiae of her useless existence. No cloak-and-dagger stuff, I'm sorry to say."

Berta said, "Did anyone besides you see the diary before the girls stole it back, Miss Cotton?"

"Yes. Eugene Van Hoogenband saw it."

"Van Hoogenband?" I said. "But why?"

"Why?" Miss Cotton toyed with her silver cigarette lighter. "Because he is Josie's father, of course. Josie had been passing notes in Personality Development class—to Grace, you see—at the same time that Grace was writing in her diary. It was, as it were, a two-girl crime."

Josie hadn't mentioned that bit.

Miss Cotton continued. "I called in the parents of both girls for a disciplinary meeting. Mrs. Whiddle canceled at the last minute, but Mr. Van Hoogenband came—although he is, as you must know, tremendously busy with his steel company. I allowed him to peruse the diary while I went to take a telephone call in the front office. Mr. Van Hoogenband wished to keep the diary, but I could not allow that. It did not belong to his daughter. In any event, you two are barking up the wrong tree with this diary nonsense. If it's murder—"

I said, "I didn't—"

"—then Miss Wilbur is your woman."

"Violet Wilbur?"

"Mm. You see, when I read the newspaper report about Muffy Morris's death, I was surprised to learn that Violet Wilbur was also checked into Willow Acres at the time, and that in a brief interview she indicated that she was not acquainted with Muffy."

"Neither Muffy nor Violet gave any hint of a prior acquaintance," Berta said.

"Well, that is peculiar," Miss Cotton said, "because Violet and Muffy knew each other for years. Decades, actually. They attended finishing school in Switzerland, near Lake Geneva, at the same time. Institut Alpenrose."

"How do you know that?" I asked.

"Because I attended Institut Alpenrose as well. I was one year behind them, but I remember them well. Both of them were rebellious troublemakers. Sneaking out to drink beer with local boys, smoking behind the carriage house, that sort of thing." Miss Cotton turned her sunglasses in my direction. "Rather like you, Lola."

"Why would they have pretended not to know each other?" I asked.

"You know how it is. Schoolgirls do silly things, things they sometimes regret for the rest of their lives. I don't know. Now, I really must ask you to leave. Be a couple of old dears and see yourselves out through the garden. Oh, and Lola—I don't like to point out such things, but I think you ought to know that you have lipstick on your teeth."

"Mrs. Woodby," Berta said when we were motoring away down Rosebud Lane, "do not look in the rearview mirror."

"Huh?" I jolted up in my seat to look in the rearview mirror. Holy gamoly. Mr. Egghead and his tiny pal in the cloche hat were back. Their front fender was mangled, and I got a better look at the pal this time. A blond-bobbed puppet with a red Cupid's bow. I re-wrapped my sweaty palms around the steering wheel. "What should we do?"

"Please focus on the road, Mrs. Woodby."

"But what does Van Hoogenband want from us?"

"He must be attempting to make certain that we leave his daughter alone. Recall how sheltered she is."

"I wasn't banking on thugs when we took on this case, Berta. I really can't contend with thugs."

"Of course you can."

I sneaked another glance in the mirror. Mr. Egghead wasn't try-ing to gain on us. It was more like he and his pal were keeping tabs on us. That was tolerable—for the moment. "I've got it," I said. "Violet Wilbur is redecorating Amberley. We could stop there to ask her about that schoolgirl scandal Miss Cotton mentioned—I can always say I wish to visit my sister. Even if Violet isn't there just now, those two thugs back there won't be able to get past Amberley's gatekeeper."

Mr. Egghead and his sidekick motored behind us all the way back to Hare's Hollow, through fields lit with golden sunbeams, past tree groves, train stations, villages, strawberry stands, and mansions.

Chisholm's gatekeeper let us through Amberley's gates without question. After all, he had very recently been *my* gatekeeper. Mr. Egg-head didn't try to get past the gates; he parked across the road. He'd be waiting.

I drove up the long, leafy drive and parked in front of Amberley, with its brown-and-white half-timbering and ivied chimneys.

Mullioned windows sparkled in the late afternoon sunlight. It still looked like home to me.

But it wasn't.

I felt like laying my forehead on the steering wheel and screaming. I also felt a bit like being sick on Chisholm's drive. Instead, I lifted my chin high and climbed out of the motorcar.

Berta settled back in her seat and shut her eyes. "It is fine to leave Cedric here with me."

"You're not coming in?"

"For your sisterly chat? Oh no, no, no. I must have a bit of a nap."

"Oh, fine," I grumbled. "Would you let Cedric out for a stretch?"

"His legs are four inches long. I do not think they require stretching."

"Well, he's slimming."

"So you say."

Lillian answered the door. "Lola," she said, her blue eyes widening. "What a . . . nice surprise."

"Might I come in?"

"Oh. Yes, of course. Miss Wilbur's here, though, seeing to the decorating, so *please* don't act eccentric like you do and upset her. She has fragile nerves, you know. Chisholm's treating her." Lillian led me into the drawing room. White drop cloths shrouded the furniture, and one wall was being papered in puce-and-gold stripes by workmen. "I've started with the drawing room since Dr. Woodby and I will be entertaining ever so much. You didn't really entertain here, did you, Lola? Unless you count the tawdry drunken frolics you and Alfie had with people you barely knew."

"Is that how Chisholm described it to you?"

"Yes." Lillian said this without even a flicker of shame. She is nineteen years old and devoid of the capacity for shame or humor.

Which, since she resembles a marshmallowy pre-Raphaelite angel, is appropriate. I imagine angels never cringe or crack jokes.

"I'll have you know, Chisholm never once attended a party in my home," I said, "so he doesn't know what he's speaking of."

"Well, it's *my* home now," Lillian said with a vicious smile, "or it will be soon. Once I'm married and after I've managed to dispose of all the bottles of booze and trashy novels I keep finding in cupboards and closets, things are going to be different. Proper."

"Speaking of proper—" I glanced around. "—I'm surprised you're here without a chaperone."

"Mother is upstairs having a lie-down in the guest bedroom. Headache. The paint fumes brought it on."

There was a God, then.

"Oh, I nearly forgot," Lillian said. "Raymond Hathorne telephoned Mother at Clyde's Bluff, trying to find you. Said he met you and was utterly charmed. So nice to know that there is a little hope for you, Lola. Even if it's with a man in soda pop."

"Oh. Hello, Mrs. Woodby," Violet said from the doorway with a stack of fabric swatches in her arms.

"Hello, Miss Wilbur," I said. "Busted out of the health farm so soon?"

"My stay was but a short one."

Just long enough for her to be around when Muffy popped off, actually. "Mine, too," I said. "Those hip-slimming machines are marvelously efficient."

"Oh?" Violet eyed my hips.

Violet wore a chic dress, and her cheeks shone with rouge cream. Had her stay at Willow Acres brought about these changes in her grooming habits? Because even in her magazine column photograph, she appeared dowdy.

I needed to get rid of Lillian for a while so I could speak with Violet alone. "Lillian, dear, I'm absolutely parched," I said. "Could you ask the maid to bring some iced lime water? Not lemon." I smiled at Violet. "I find lemons to be so blasé."

Lillian opened her mouth as if to object, but she seemed to think better of it after a nervous glance at Violet. "Of course, sister dear," she said, and swanned away.

16

....

I eyed the puce-and-gold wallpaper the workmen were smoothing with brushes. "What scrummy wallpaper," I lied.

"It's hideous," Violet said in a flat voice. "Lillian insisted upon it, although I told her that gentlemen do not wish their living spaces to appear so very feminine." She touched a pearl earring. "When I marry, I shall let my husband make all the decisions. That is the road to matrimonial harmony."

Maybe, but it was also the roller-coaster ride to festering resentment and excessive éclair consumption.

"Are you to be married?" I asked.

"Well, perhaps. And believe you me, I am ready to defer to the man I love, even to walk the plank for him." Violet blushed under her rouge cream.

My, my. Violet Wilbur in love? Well, even cactuses bloom from time to time.

"Who's the lucky fellow?" I asked.

"I don't like to speak of my private life while working," Violet said.

Her dreamy expression slid off as she watched something over my shoulder.

I turned to see a delivery truck pass the side windows. They'd be heading to the rear service entrance. "Miss Wilbur," I said, "I must admit I'm surprised to see you back at work so soon after the death of Mrs. Morris."

"Why should it surprise you? I am a busy lady." As if to prove it, Violet barked orders at the workers to straighten a strip of wallpaper. "Boors," she said to me in an undertone. "And they leave buckets of wallpaper paste simply everywhere."

"I'm surprised to see you working because you and Muffy were friends," I said.

"We weren't friends. I barely knew her."

"But you went to school together. In Switzerland. Institut Alpenrose, wasn't it?"

Violet glanced at the workmen and lowered her voice. "That was decades ago. Who told you about that?"

Time for a whopper. "My aunt Penelope attended Institut Alpenrose, and I was just chatting with her on the telephone today and she thought it fishy that you told the newspapers that you didn't know Mrs. Morris when, in fact, you did."

Violet's nostrils pinched. "Well. You may tell your nosy aunt that I was not in the habit of acknowledging Mrs. Morris as an acquaintance because she was a degraded drunk and, what is more, I had not spoken to her since she humiliated herself with a schoolgirl scandal in Switzerland. She was a shockingly wayward and saucy young lady."

Muffy was wayward and saucy? Miss Cotton had said Violet and Muffy were both naughty as schoolgirls. "What did Muffy do?" I asked.

"I never repeat filth."

"The night that Muffy died—did you hear or see anything peculiar in the ward?"

"No. I sleep with wax stoppers in my ears. Now, I really must step away. A delivery has arrived that requires my supervision. So nice speaking with you, Mrs. Woodby." Violet clicked away on her high pumps. She was even wearing seamed stockings.

Whoever Violet's fellow was, she was certainly head over heels. A lady won't fiddle with keeping stocking seams straight for just anybody.

Lillian hadn't yet returned, so I decided to follow Violet. I wished to know why this delivery had her so jumpy. Maybe her secret sweetheart was driving the truck.

Naturally, I knew my way around the house, so I took a shortcut through the dining room wainscoting to a hidden servants' passage. This led to a hallway outside the kitchen. The delivery was sure to be made at the service entrance at the end of the hallway.

I peeked out of the servants' passage. Sure enough, Violet stood at the open service entrance, speaking to someone in low tones. I darted across the hallway to the broom closet, slipped inside, and shut the door most of the way. My foot plunked into something wet and gooey, and I stifled a cry. I'd stepped into a bucket of wallpaper paste. My favorite pair of Perugias, ruined.

On the positive side, I was close enough to eavesdrop on Violet. I left my foot in the bucket of paste and strained my ears.

". . . took your sweet time with these, didn't you?" Violet was saying in a harsh whisper. "Come along. Bring them inside."

Another voice—a low-pitched woman's or a higher-pitched man's—said something I couldn't make out.

Violet again: "Very well. Good Lord. You really make me do all the leg work."

Mumbles.

Violet: "You, artistic? Hah!" Footsteps.

Violet went outside. I guessed that whoever was driving the truck had refused to help Violet unload the delivery because, bird-frail as she was, she heaved a huge, flat, paper-wrapped parcel from the back of the truck and carried it inside. Then she went out and got another one. No sooner had she slammed the truck's rear doors than it accelerated away. Violet carried the second parcel inside.

Lillian pushed through the kitchen door. "There you are, Miss Wilbur. The maid is bringing the iced lime water to the drawing room. No cookies, however, for if I serve cookies, I'll never be rid of Lola."

I scowled in the darkness. The very thought! I wouldn't hang about here simply for cookies; I'd stuff the cookies into my handbag and go.

"Good news, Miss DuFey," Violet told her. "Your Heyligers have arrived from Amsterdam."

"Dr. Woodby will be so pleased," Lillian said. "May I see?"

Violet tore the brown paper diagonally, exposing a big triangle of painting. It was one of those gloomy Dutch still lifes, a lobster sprawled on a plate and surrounded by glassier-than-glass wine goblets and half-peeled lemons.

"Is that wine in those goblets?" Lillian asked. "Because Dr. Woodby is the president of the Booze Is Bilge Club—"

"Wine!" Violet laid a hand on her chest. "No, no, my dear. Grape juice, surely."

"Oh. What a relief."

Lillian's best subject in school was lunch.

They set off down the hallway. "Dr. Woodby has just arrived home," Lillian said. "I saw his motorcar through the kitchen window. I cannot say he'll be terribly pleased to see Lola, though. She always was the black sheep of the family."

"I understand perfectly," Violet said. "Oh—have you an aunt Penelope, Miss DuFey?"

"No," Lillian said. "Why do you ask?"

"No reason."

Lillian and Violet pushed through a door, and their voices were lost to me.

Violet knew I was snooping into Muffy's death. Rats. And Chisholm was home. Double rats.

I pried the bucket of wallpaper paste from my foot. Cold, chunky sludge oozed down my ankles and onto the closet floor. I opened the door and hopped on one foot to the service entrance and outside. Once I was on the gravel path, I hobbled around to the front of the house. Pebbles stuck to the wallpaper paste as I went, weighing me down more and more with each step.

"Why are you limping, Mrs. Woodby?" Berta called from the Duesy.

"Could you drive?" I asked, breathless. "I have a bit of a problem with my pedal foot presently."

"I suppose so."

"Hurry!"

Berta got out and I climbed into her place. I tossed her the keys and she got in the driver's seat and switched on the engine.

"Lola?" I heard Chisholm's voice call over the growl of the engine. "LOLA!"

I caught a glimpse of Chisholm standing on the front steps with his briefcase in one hand, shaking a fist. Berta laboriously turned the Duesy around and motored down the front drive toward the gates.

"Wait," I said. "What if Mr. Egghead and that blond puppet are still waiting for us?"

"It would be my preference to contend with two thugs rather than with Dr. Woodby."

"Mine, too. But *neither* would be better. Take the other gate—you know, the one behind the caretaker's cottage? It leads to a side road. Mr. Egghead will never see us."

"But that gate will surely be locked."

"I think I still have the key to that gate on my key ring. I never bothered taking it off. Cross your fingers that Chisholm hasn't changed the lock."

Chisholm hadn't changed the lock, and I still had the key. When we eased onto the main road, we craned our necks left and right. No black Chevrolet.

"To the yacht?" Berta asked.

"Dandy."

"What happened to your foot?"

"I don't want to discuss it."

On the yacht, Berta said, "I must have a rest, Mrs. Woodby. All of this excitement with Mr. Van Hoogenband's henchpersons has fatigued me. We might review our clues at dinner, if you are in agreement."

"Sure," I said. I was prying my foot from the paste-crusted shoe and stocking.

Berta disappeared belowdecks.

I chucked my ruined shoes and stockings onto the dock because the paste was so stinky. I'd find a rubbish bin later. I carried Cedric to the galley and gave him a bowl of water. He lapped thirstily, spraying water everywhere.

After that, Cedric and I retired to our cabin. I opened the porthole to let in some fresh air and finished Part One of "Hello, Darling," which ended on a real cliff-hanger: Maude broke off her engagement with Bill Hampton, and he stalked away in a he-man sort of huff with a storm brewing on the horizon.

I checked the publication date on the magazine's cover. The issue was eight days old, so the next issue would be on sale now. Berta wouldn't approve, but I had to buy it. Besides, Senator Morris had coughed up a thousand bucks that morning. I could afford a little pleasure, couldn't I?

I fell asleep, and woke up groggy after sundown. Berta was waiting for me on deck in a canvas chair. Stars dappled the blue-black dome of sky, and the town lights twinkled over the marina. A few lights glimmered in other moored yachts.

I hugged myself despite the balmy evening. "You don't suppose Mr. Egghead and his pal know we're here at the marina, do you?"

"I do not expect so, but they will surely have noticed your motorcar parked in town."

I'd parked a few blocks off Main Street on a residential street, but still, the Duesy would be difficult to miss with its smashed spare tire.

"We must eat, though," I said. "I'm starving."

"I am as well. We will simply take our chances."

I fed Cedric a few jars of the caviar I'd found on the yacht, watered him, gathered up my ruined shoes, and then the three of us set out. I dumped the shoes in a rubbish bin behind the bait shop. I confess I felt a pang.

The Main Street shops were still open because it was tourist season. Noisy families congregated around Betty's Ice Cream Parlor, and several people stood at the counter inside Little Vienna Bakery.

I caught Berta glaring at the bakery.

"Let's go in," I said.

"Certainly not." Berta straightened her spine. "I bake my own things as a rule."

"But we don't have an oven in the yacht."

Berta didn't answer.

We stopped by the five-and-dime, where Berta purchased a scouring pad and a can of Bon Ami cleaning powder. "That yacht is obscured beneath a layer of grime," she said.

I fruitlessly searched the magazine shelf for the latest issue of *Thrilling Romance*. I asked the salesclerk about it.

"*Thrilling Romance?*" he said. "Naw, that sold out yesterday. Can't keep it stocked—it's the girls at the telephone exchange office two doors down. Addicted. Try the drugstore in Oyster Bay."

To console myself, in addition to picking up the evening newspaper, I purchased two Cadbury Dairy Milk bars and a new Coty lipstick. The lipstick was a demure pink. No more crimson smeary messes for me.

17

Berta and I made it to a corner table at the Foghorn without seeing Mr. Egghead, his pal, or his Chevrolet. Not that I felt as snug as a bug; they could've been watching us from the shadows.

The restaurant seemed to be short on staff, and we waited and waited for our meals. I tided myself over with a rye bran biscuit from my purse, slathered with butter. If only I'd known eating healthfully was such a cinch.

Once we were eating dinner, I told Berta how I'd hidden myself in Amberley's broom closet and seen Violet accept a delivery of paintings.

"That is where you had your tussle with the bucket of wallpaper paste?"

I waved my fork airily. "That's old news. Listen: the paintings were Heyligers. He's an old master. Those are valuable paintings, and what's more, Violet said they'd just arrived from Amsterdam."

Berta sawed at her beef. "I see that you are lifting your eyebrows in a meaningful fashion, Mrs. Woodby, but I cannot think what I am supposed to make of Amsterdam." She took a bite.

"Europe."

"Ah. You are thinking of Senator Morris's European anarchist suspicions."

"Exactly."

"Violet Wilbur was already connected to Europe by virtue of having been a student at Institut Alpenrose."

"True."

"Which reminds me: Did you gain any new knowledge regarding the schoolgirl scandal to which Miss Cotton alluded?"

"Sort of. Violet admitted there had been a scandal, but she said it was *Muffy's*."

"Indeed?" Berta's blue eyes gleamed. "How very interesting. What do we know of Violet, aside from her books and her magazine column?"

"Not much. She's very prim and boring. I do know that she grew up wealthy—her father founded the Gelleez factory—that boxed gelatin dessert."

"Disgusting stuff. And she never married."

"Not yet." I told Berta how Violet had alluded to an impending marriage. "We should look further into this finishing school scandal," I said. "Senator Morris might even approve of this lead, given that it could involve European anarchists. When would Muffy and Violet have been at school?"

Berta tipped her head. "In the '90s, I suppose, because Muffy and Violet both must be about fifty years of age."

"Why is it that fifty suddenly seems not very old anymore?" I said.

"Not very old? Mrs. Woodby, it is positively youthful."

I snapped my fingers. "I've got it. Remember that shelf of photograph albums and things in Muffy's bedroom? I'll bet there's an Institut

Alpenrose alumni directory of some kind mixed in—I saw a country club directory and the *New York Social Register*."

"But we are not expected at the Morris house until the day after tomorrow."

"Come on, Berta. We can't sit on our hands when there might be a hot clue just waiting for us."

Berta made a weary sigh. "I suppose not."

I unfolded *The New York Evening Observer* I'd purchased at the stationer's. "I thought I'd look this over, just in case Ida Shanks has another . . . Oh. She does."

A small headline on page three read, SECOND INCHBALD SCANDAL. The article conveyed that Inchbald & Sons, Fine Clothiers, the elegant company that had been around since the 1850s and which had made the family's colossal fortune, had a skeleton in its closet: The company had indulged in war profiteering during the Civil War.

"This is awful!" I said. "Listen to this: 'Inchbald and Sons manufactured uniforms for Union soldiers made of a material called "simulated wool," composed of sawdust and horsehair mixed with pulp from old cotton rags. When the uniforms were exposed to rain or snow, they dissolved, leaving Union soldiers wet and even freezing.'"

"That is monstrous!" Berta said.

"It gets worse, too. 'Untold illnesses and causalities among the noble Union troops resulted from this egregious slight of Inchbald and Sons. It is not known just how the company has kept this scandal hidden for well-nigh sixty years, nor is it yet known whether the American public will hear from the company head, Obadiah Inchbald, who, our source claims, was the primary decision-maker in the simulated wool scandal. Time will tell, and the Almighty will judge.'"

"It seems very much as though Miss Shanks's source is attempting to publicly humiliate the Inchbald family," Berta said.

"It also seems as though her source has something to do with

Muffy's death, don't you think? Otherwise, it would be too, well, too *coincidental*."

"I do agree. You must telephone Miss Shanks first thing in the morning and demand to know her source."

"I can demand, but you can bet your boots Ida won't sing." My words hung heavily.

At last Berta said, "Mrs. Woodby, I am afraid you have gotten gravy on your bodice."

We talked over our next steps. I had my appointment to call upon Hermie Inchbald in the morning—an appointment that had taken on a new urgency in light of the Inchbald & Sons scandal. For her part, Berta would endeavor to enter the Morris house tomorrow and search for an Institut Alpenrose alumni directory. After that, we would figure out a way to learn which nurse had been on duty the night Muffy died. That little question was still dangling out there like rained-on laundry. In the meantime, we would keep our heads low in case Van Hoogenband's goons were still searching for us, and attempt to get a good night's sleep.

We paid our tab and walked out onto the now mostly dark Main Street. Cinnamon-scented air wafted by. The source was Little Vienna Bakery, still lit and alive with customers.

"Come on, Berta, we've got to try it," I said.

Berta hesitated, and then the cinnamon air must've hit her, too, because she grumbled, "Oh, very well."

I picked up Cedric, and we went inside the bakery and got in line. A plump, aproned man with a large mustache stood behind the display counter, speaking to the customers with a Central European accent.

"—and the vanilla kipfels have a lighter, more, how do you say, *brisk* crunch. However, if it is chocolate that you desire, the Sacher torte . . ." His words died away. He didn't blink.

I turned. Yes. The whisk-broom baker was looking at Berta with a sort of amazed expression. But he remembered himself and continued on with his speech.

Berta smoothed her chintz sleeve, wearing a serene and, yes, smug expression.

"Of course you'd make an instantaneous conquest of a baker," I whispered to her.

"I cannot think what you mean, Mrs. Woodby."

I craned my neck to see into the display cases. Most of the trays held nothing but crumbs since it was the end of the day, but hand-lettered signs read APPLE STRUDEL, JAM TURNOVERS, CREAM SLICES, SPONGE ROULADE, CHESTNUT DUMPLINGS, and on and on. My mouth watered. Only a few of the kipfels—some sort of sugar-crusted crescent cookie—and a few slices of Sacher torte and something called, improbably, marmorgugelhupf remained.

At last it was our turn to order.

"Good evening, mesdames," the baker said, his brown eyes twinkling strictly for Berta's benefit.

Berta made a terse nod and said, "What a pity that your sponge roulade is sold out, for I believe the true merit of a baker is revealed in his or her sponge."

"Ah, you are a baker, madam?"

"Yes."

"But I should have known."

"What sort of butter do you use? Not salted, I hope?"

"Certainly not."

"And you always bring your egg whites to room temperature?"

"Do you take me for an apprentice boy?"

"The flour from the mills upstate is best. I never rely on the rubbish from New Jersey."

"Madam, please, wait here. I have one last sponge roulade that I set aside for Mrs. Parsons, but never mind her—it is for *you*." The baker disappeared through a swinging door.

"Good grief," I said. "I didn't know it was even possible to flirt about butter."

"I am not flirting," Berta said. "Oh. And do not turn around, but it seems that Van Hoogenband's thugs have caught up with us."

"*What?* Here. Take Cedric." My fingers shook as I unclasped my handbag and brought out my face powder compact. I dabbed my nose with the puff and looked into the mirror. Mr. Egghead and his pal loitered under a streetlamp. They were looking our way.

"Holy moly," I whispered. "Are they watching us or those chocolate cakes in the window?"

"Us."

18

....

I put away my compact and took Cedric from Berta's arms. "This is *awful*," I whispered. "If they follow us to the yacht—"

"We will evade them."

"How?"

"Return to the Foghorn, where it is busy, and attempt to shake them. Perhaps they will believe we are staying there. Ah. Here is my sponge roulade."

The baker returned, all smiles. "Taste this," he said, offering Berta a chunk of cake on a fork.

Berta set her paper bag on the counter, took the chunk of cake, and ate it. After she swallowed, she made an approving nod.

The baker beamed. "I have wrapped up the rest." He slid a white paper parcel over the counter. "On the house."

"Thank you," Berta said in a prim voice. She tucked the cake in her handbag.

I was pretty sure Mr. Egghead & Co.'s eyes were boring holes into my back. "Time to go," I said.

Berta and I ducked out of the bakery and made a beeline down Main Street.

"I am . . . so very . . . weary of . . . running," Berta panted.

I didn't answer. I was too busy being weary of running myself.

A block away, the Foghorn Inn glowed. I looked over my shoulder. Mr. Egghead and the blonde were striding toward us.

Clinking dishes, chatter, and a phonograph piano rag wafted from the Foghorn's windows. I was about to shove through the lobby doors when—yes!—I noticed two uniformed policemen sitting on the porch, eating pie.

I stopped. "Officers," I said, breathing hard. "Please. We're being . . . chased by . . . those two thugs!"

Mr. Egghead and the blonde were coming up the steps.

The plumper of the two policemen burst out laughing. "Haw! Thugs!" He nudged the other officer with his boot. "Van Hoogenband's valet a thug? Haw-haw-haw!"

Valet?

The other policeman chuckled and took another bite of pie.

"As useful as rainboots in the bathtub," Berta muttered.

We pushed into the lobby.

"Up the stairs," I whispered.

Berta and I climbed the stairs. As soon as we reached the landing, we peeked down. Mr. Egghead and the blonde stood inside the lobby doors, looking around.

"They didn't see us go up," I said softly. "Come on."

We mounted the rest of the steps, ran down the hallway, and pushed through a door leading to a back stair. Downstairs again, we fumbled around until we found a door out. We were at the side of the inn, where a strip of lawn met Walnut Street.

"Let's run for the yacht now, while they're still inside," I said.

"Run? I would prefer a brisk walking pace."

We made it to Hansen's Bait Shop and looked back. No one was following us, unless they were hidden in the shadows. There were plenty of shadows. We dodged to the back of the bait shop, down the wooden steps to the harbor path, and onto the dock.

Berta stopped. "Oh dear. I forgot my purchases on the bakery counter."

"What purchases?"

"The scouring pad and cleaning powder. I really must go back."

"Now? It'll still be there in the morning."

Berta shook her head. "I cannot abide living in squalor. Do not worry about me, Mrs. Woodby." She hitched her handbag up her forearm and started back up the steps.

"I should come with you."

"No. Certainly not."

Something told me Berta's desire to go back to the bakery—alone—was more about the mustached baker than a can of Bon Ami cleaning powder. Thugs or no, far be it from me to meddle in another lady's romantic machinations.

"Be careful," I whispered after Berta.

She waved a dismissive hand.

I walked down the dock, Cedric in my arms, and boarded the *Sea Nymph*.

"What a night," I muttered to Cedric, setting him down. "What I wouldn't give for a highball right about now."

"Well, that's a coincidence," someone said in the darkness, "because I brought a bottle of whiskey and some ginger ale special for you."

"Ralph!" I pressed a hand to my jolting heart. "I mean, Mr. Oliver." Cedric waggled away from me.

"Come on, now, Lola. Why the formality?" I made out Ralph

lolling in the canvas deck chair, legs stretched, hands clasped behind his head. Two bottles glimmered next to his feet.

"Why? Because you've been calling me *Mrs. Woodby* ever since you returned from your mysteriously long trip to Cuba, that's why."

"Must've been a mistake." Ralph bent to scratch Cedric's ears, and then got to his feet. "I'm sorry, Lola." Thin moonlight illuminated his forehead and cheekbones, but I couldn't quite make out his eyes. He came closer.

"Oh. Well. I accept your apology," I said. "Why are you here?"

"To let you know I tracked down Grace Whiddle—"

"Really?"

"—because I thought it might help you with your case."

"Where is she? Is she all right? Where did you find her?"

"I haven't seen her yet. I only traced a series of leads to Pete Schlump's apartment on the Upper East Side."

"Pete Schlump?" I thought of Grace's Vaseline-on-the-camera-lens glow when she'd looked at Pete, and how Pete had leapt to Grace's defense when Muffy Morris insulted her. "I knew it."

"I'm thinking she's in his apartment, but she's not coming out. I staked out the building till the doormen started getting antsy. Probably thought I was a Yankees fanatic out for blood over Schlump's pitching slump. I'll head back there tomorrow. Which reminds me. Foghorn's booked solid tonight. Mind if I sleep here? My neck can't take a night in my jalopy." Ralph stopped a half pace away.

"Here? Oh. I—"

"On deck should be fine. Nice and warm tonight."

He had *that* right.

Ralph brushed my hot cheek with his knuckle. "C'mon. You owe me one. You said so yourself."

True.

He went on, "I also came here tonight because I wanted to see you."

"Why is that?"

"To do this." Ralph's arms circled my waist and he pulled me up against his warm, hard, salt-scented chest. The core of me simply melted, like a fizzled-out lightbulb filament. "On the off chance you changed your mind. You know, about not being happy to see me back from Cuba."

"I might've changed my mind," I whispered against his lips.

"Yeah?"

"But fair is fair. You can't be the only one playing your cards close. Besides, don't you know that when a lady says she isn't happy to see you, there's still a twenty percent chance she *is*?"

Our lips touched.

The yacht bobbed. Someone had stepped aboard.

"Well, well, Ralphie," a girlish voice chirped. "I'm not surprised to see you petting another gal, don't get me wrong. But most fellers woulda taken a intermission or something."

Ralph and I pulled apart. We both turned.

Mr. Egghead's tiny blond sidekick stood with one arm akimbo and the other aiming a jumbo pistol at Ralph and me.

"Miss Mallone," Ralph said with a stiff nod.

"Everyone calls me Baby Doll, and last time I checked, you did, too, you big gorgeous sheik, you. When you weren't calling me other things, anyways."

"Do you two know each other?" I asked.

Ralph scratched his eyebrow. "Do *you* two know each other?"

"No," I said. "Well, yes. I mean to say, this Miss—Miss Mallone—"

"Call me Baby Doll," she said. "Everybody does."

"—has been pursuing me hither and thither all day. She's a hired thug."

"Gee, thanks, honey," Baby Doll said, and she didn't even sound sarcastic.

"Who are you working for this time, Miss Mallone?" Ralph asked.

"Van Hoogenband. Have been for months, which you woulda known if you paid attention when I talk." Baby Doll looked at me. "Now I see why you've been so cool, Ralphie. Got yourself a side dish. Say, cute dress, Mrs. Woodby. Ralphie likes smart dressers, don't you, Ralphie?"

I frowned up at Ralph. "What's going on here? Is this—this young lady your—?"

"Sweetie," Baby Doll said. "I'm his sweetie."

"Uh—" Ralph said.

"It's no skin off my teeth that you're here with this fancy dame," Baby Doll said to Ralph. "I'm not a jealous girl. Live and let live, that's my motto. I got my own coupla side dishes, and let me tell you, I like my beef with a side of beef."

"I'm not sure what that means," I said.

"Miss Mallone," Ralph said, "you are not my sweetie."

"No?" Baby Doll's dimpled smile was visible even in the weak light. "That's what you said when I was down in Cuba."

"You were in Cuba with *her*?" I asked Ralph.

He massaged his forehead. "It's—"

"Course he was," Baby Doll said. "Stayed in a fancy white hotel together and ate all *kinds* of fruits."

I sucked in a slow, shuddery breath.

"Say, honey," Baby Doll said to me, "Boss ain't too happy about the way you and your pudgy sidekick have been giving me and Eggie the slip."

"Eggie?" I said.

"Big fella? God-awful scar clear across his forehead like a soft-boiled egg?"

It was a vague comfort to know I wasn't the only one who occasionally thought people looked like breakfast foods.

"But now we figured out where you're staying." Baby Doll glanced around the yacht deck. "What a dump."

"What does Mr. Van Hoogenband want?" I asked.

"Don't know. Eggie and me's orders was to figure out where you and the pudgy dame are staying and report back. And now we know. Enjoy your spooning, you two. See you round." Baby Doll turned and minced down the gangway. Her hollow footfalls receded on the dock.

I spun on Ralph.

He said, "Lola, listen to me before you—"

"No! I loathe you and I never want to see you again." A *Thrilling Romance* heroine would have slapped Ralph's cheek at this juncture, but I felt like slapping myself for getting stuck on a ladies' man. I, of all people, should've known better. After all, I'd been married to a Casanova for a decade.

"Still jake if I sleep here on the deck?" Ralph asked.

"Argh!" I cried, throwing my arms up, "Come, Cedric."

Cedric didn't budge from his perch on the deck chair.

"Peanut," I said, patting my knees, "*come.*"

Cedric panted.

"Fine." I stomped down the ladder into the bowels of the yacht. Cedric could stick with Ralph. They could have a ginger-haired boys' evening. I certainly didn't care a snap of the fingers. Stumbling around in the near darkness, I ripped the wool blanket from the top bunk. I carried it back up to the deck and threw it beside Ralph's deck chair—he was lounging there with Cedric in his lap and looking inscrutable. "That's for Cedric," I said. "Not you."

"Got it," Ralph said.

I flounced toward the ladder.

Wait. I turned and went back.

"I knew you were a softie," Ralph said, starting to smile.

"I am *not* a softie." I snatched the bottles of whiskey and ginger ale and carried them down to my cabin. I slammed the door so hard, it bounced open again. I slammed it again, and it clicked shut.

I slumped on the edge of my bunk and unscrewed the cap of the whiskey bottle. I sighed. Highballs with Ralph would've been divine, but getting whiffled all alone on a mildewy bunk bed with gravy on my dress, my favorite shoes in a rubbish bin, no real progress on our murder investigation, and Van Hoogenband's thugs on my caboose? Simply depressing. I screwed the whiskey bottle cap back on and stashed it under the berth.

I rummaged in my handbag for a Cadbury Dairy Milk bar and tore into it. I waited for Ralph to come storming in and sweep me into his arms.

Ralph didn't show, and I fell asleep waiting.

19

I awoke to the *crick-creeek, crick-creeek* of the yacht as it rolled gently on the waves. Water slopped. Sunlight sliced through the open porthole. My mouth tasted of chocolate and my vision blurred with mascara and dried tears.

Ralph.

Baby Doll Mallone.

Fruit in Cuba.

Ugh.

I checked my wristwatch which, along with my clothes, shoes, and makeup, I still wore. *Phooey*—just after eleven o'clock, and I was due to call upon Hermie Inchbald at twelve thirty.

I tiptoed out of the cabin, praying that Ralph was gone. He was, and so were Berta and Cedric. Berta had left a note for me on the galley table: *Meet me and your dog at Little Vienna Bakery.*

I cold-creamed my face, fixed my hair, brushed my teeth, and got dressed. It was just as well that Ralph and I were out of business, because my undergarments weren't really up to entertaining a gentleman caller. Bathroom sink hand washings and fire escape dryings had taken their toll. The lacy silk frivolities I'd indulged in back when I was a Society Matron were as shrively gray as coal miners' hankies.

I buttoned myself into the last clean dress in my suitcase, a gauzy, drop-waist floral. I had no choice but to wear my black Pinet pumps, even though they looked all wrong with the dress. Topping it all off with a sun hat and a dab of my new Coty lipstick, I was on my way.

I found Berta sipping coffee at a table inside Little Vienna Bakery. The bakery was empty of customers, and warm. A ceiling fan whirred, and somewhere in the back, a phonograph piped out a symphony.

"Any sign of Van Hoogenband's goons?" I asked, sitting.

"No." Berta was blooming in a blue dress and a new style of plaited bun. "I am relieved to see you are in good health, Mrs. Woodby."

"Why wouldn't I be?" I bent to pet Cedric, who lay beneath the table. Pastry crumbs trembled on his whiskers. A bowl of water sat beside him.

"Mr. Oliver told me you disappeared into your cabin with a bottle of whiskey. I assumed you were on a toot."

"Didn't drink a drop. And Mr. Oliver is no longer welcome on the yacht."

"Lovers' spat?"

"No. Complete amputation."

"It won't last."

"Just you watch. Hold it—whose coffee cup is this?" A half-empty coffee cup sat at my place.

"Mr. Oliver's."

"Berta! Is he . . . here?" I looked around furtively.

"He has already gone to the city in order to continue his surveillance of Pete Schlump's apartment building."

"Did he tell you how Van Hoogenband's blond puppet—her name is Baby Doll!—found our yacht?"

"Yes—and he was kind enough to sleep on deck and stand guard for us all night."

"And did he tell you that he'd been in Cuba—*at the same hotel*—with Baby Doll?"

Berta's forehead creased. "That sounds most unlikely. That Baby Doll creature is built like a drinking straw, and Mr. Oliver has always been so very appreciative of your womanly figure—"

"Could we change the topic?" I wanted to kick something.

"Very well. Do you know, I am ever so disappointed in Pete Schlump. I had held him in the highest esteem, particularly after last year's World Series, but running off with a girl engaged to be married to another? It is so very low."

"Think Pete Schlump could be a murderer yet?"

"Certainly not. He is still a *Yankees pitcher*." Berta said *Yankees pitcher* the same way you'd say *canonized saint*.

"But what do we really know about him?"

"Everything. Have you been dwelling under a rock? His biography is known to the very masses." Berta took a deep breath. "Pete Schlump was born to a German saloonkeeper and his wife in Buffalo, New York, and grew up in a brick row house. He was a naughty little boy—chewing tobacco and throwing tomatoes at policemen while only seven years old—and so he was sent to a reformatory run by priests, where he learned to play baseball from the head disciplinarian, Father Marcus. Upon graduation at the reformatory, he signed to play with the minor-league Rochester Red Wings, but he was soon snapped up by the Yankees at the age of nineteen, when they noticed Pete's Hercules-like pitching arm."

"How old is Pete now?"

"Twenty-five. And he has lived his entire adult life fully in the public eye. He cannot have any secrets. He is recognized everywhere he goes."

The mustached baker emerged from the back of the shop in a white apron and wreathed in smiles. Berta introduced him as Mr. Wilhelm Demel, transplanted from Vienna by way of Queens.

"Pleased to meet you," I said.

Wilhelm gave me a limp smile and then turned up the watts for Berta. "Another strawberry turnover, Mrs. Lundgren?"

"No, thank you, but I am certain Mrs. Woodby requires coffee and pastry."

"Very good." Wilhelm bustled to the back of the shop.

"He is such a wholesome gentleman," Berta said, gazing after him. "Quite unlike the rakish characters I usually find myself mixed up with. There is something to be said for going against type, I do think."

"Jimmy the Ant is ancient history now?" I asked.

"A fossil, Mrs. Woodby."

After I gobbled up two strawberry turnovers and drank a cup of coffee, Berta and I reviewed our plan for the day: I'd go to Inchbald Hall, she'd finagle her way back into Muffy Morris's bedroom to look for an Institut Alpenrose directory, and then we'd devise a plan to, once and for all, find out who the nurse on duty had been the night Muffy died.

"And do not forget that we must ask Miss Shanks who her source for the Inchbald and Sons war-profiteering scandal was," Berta said.

"I'll do my best."

"Mr. Demel has a telephone at the back that I am certain he would allow you to use."

"Excellent. That'll save me five cents."

I poked my head into the kitchen—stuffed with racks of fragrant, cooling pastries and blindingly clean—and saw Wilhelm fussing with the oven. I asked if I could use his telephone, and he led me to a vestibule. The open door looked out onto the weedy alley.

"Thanks," I said, and waited till Wilhelm went back to the kitchen to dial. I asked the operator to put me through to the *Evening Observer* offices on Park Row, and at length got Ida Shanks on the line.

"Going begging again, Duffy?" Ida said after I'd asked her to disclose the identity of her informant. Ida calls me Duffy because in 1910, my family, the Duffys of 5 Polk Street, Scragg Springs, Indiana, became the DuFeys of Park Avenue. Ida would simply hate for me to forget my rags-to-riches biography.

"I'm not begging," I said. "I am suggesting that we trade information."

"Have you anything tasty for me?"

Perspiration sprang up on my forehead. I had to come up with something juicier than a medium-rare sirloin if Ida was going to reciprocate. *Aha:* Van Hoogenband. She'd love the sound of that. "Did you know that Eugene Van Hoogenband is mixed up in Muffy's death somehow?" I said. Strictly speaking, this was true, since *I* was mixed up in Muffy's death and Van Hoogenband had mixed his thugs up with me.

"That's good, Duffy. Van Hoogenband? Oh, his name will look gorgeous splashed across a headline—not as gorgeous as my byline below it, of course. Just how is he mixed up in it?"

"I'm not sure. Something to do with Grace Whiddle's diary, possibly." Wait. I shouldn't have mentioned the diary. Dumb, dumb, dumb.

"Diary?" Ida squawked. "What diary? No one has mentioned a diary to me."

"Oh. Not diary. I meant address book. Some brouhaha about who has been invited to Grace Whiddle's wedding—"

"You've always been a terrible liar, Duffy."

"Listen here, Miss Shanks—"

"That menacing voice isn't going to work with me. Goodness, no. After all, I've seen you flat on your back in an ice skating rink with the mayor of New York on top of you. Oh, wait—so has *the entire city of New York.*"

"That ice was slippery!" I drew a shaky breath. "I must know who your source is. Don't you see that this could be the key to getting to the bottom of her death?"

"My source is like a golden egg, Duffy, and I intend to sit on this as long as it takes to hatch. These stories are making my career. Those fat cats up in the boardroom, who never took me seriously before, now can't get enough of me. No, I'm in no hurry to wrap this story up. No hurry at all."

"Are you mad? More people could be killed!"

"Don't get ahead of yourself, Duffy. I happen to know that it makes those cords pop out on your neck in a most unsightly way."

In spite of myself, I touched my neck.

"On the other hand . . ." Ida said.

"What?"

"Well, if you gave me something *really* useful, perhaps I'd consider revealing a clue about my source."

"What do you want? Something on Dr. Woodby?"

"He's a big bore. No, I want you to give me an exclusive interview."

"Me? About what?"

"Why, about your absolutely sidesplitting former-Society-Matron-plus-cook detective agency, of course. The public will lap it up. Mind you, it would most likely be printed on the humor page—"

"Forget it," I snapped, and hung up.

Berta looked at me expectantly as I sat back down at the table.

"Nothing," I said.

"Nothing? Did you offer to trade information?"

I swallowed. I would not tell Berta about Ida's offer. Berta would expect me to give the interview for the sake of the agency. But why should I throw myself on the pyre just so Ida could get her jollies?

"Well, of course I offered to trade," I said. I checked my wristwatch. "Drat. I must leave for Inchbald Hall now." I squashed the last crumbs of turnover in the tines of my fork and ate them.

Berta stood. "Allow me to borrow an apron from Mr. Demel—"

"An apron?"

"For my disguise. And then I would be most obliged if you gave me a lift to the Morris house."

After dropping Berta off at the fence—not the front gate—of the Morris estate and promising to pick her up in the same spot in about an hour, I motored to Inchbald Hall. This turned out to be a mansion straight out of a ghost story. Everything was pointy: the windows, the gargoyles, those eerie spires on the roof. Not what you'd call a sunlit bower of domestic bliss. I parked, and Cedric and I went to the front door.

A couple minutes later, a Transylvanian butler had left me on the back terrace. Trees curved around close-clipped grass. A hedge maze and a rose garden lay to the sides. Hermie was jogging, red-faced, around a chalk circle on the lawn. A huge apricot-gold poodle pranced beside him on a leash.

Cedric warbled deep in his throat.

"Shush," I whispered to him. "You might learn something."

"Mrs. Woodby!" Hermie called, waving. He finished the lap and I joined him on the grass. He appeared moist and overheated in his black suit and hat. He was the first person, actually, whom I'd seen in mourning attire. "The Gold Coast Kennel Club Dog Show is next month," he said, out of breath. He gestured to the poodle. The poodle did not appear to be out of breath. "Bitsy won Best in Show last year. She is matchless, isn't she?"

Bitsy peered at me through her apricot bangs. Her eyes looked more like a little girl's than a dog's. Cedric growled some more; Bitsy didn't flinch.

Hermie went on, "Or, rather, I had thought Bitsy was matchless until the existence of a champion stud in Connecticut—he's called Honneker's Edmund Freeps—came to my attention. I am awfully eager to breed Bitsy to him. The litter would be perfection itself. Sheer perfection. Of course, Father refuses flat-out to pay the stud fee, and my allowance won't cover it."

Aha. Here we went with the money woes. "With your sister gone, perhaps your allowance will increase?" I asked. A rude question, but Hermie didn't seem to mind.

"No. Father said I won't see an extra penny until he's dead." Hermie patted Bitsy's head as though to soothe himself.

That ruled out a financial motive for Hermie, then. "You are able to . . . carry on despite your recent loss?" I asked.

"Muffy meant the world to me," Hermie said. "But life goes on, and I must keep Bitsy in top form. It is what Muffy would've wished. You could put your little fellow down, Mrs. Woodby. Bitsy won't harm him."

I placed Cedric on the lawn. He and Bitsy commenced their doggy circular-sniffing ritual.

"Fine flanks on him," Hermie said. "Buttocks well behind the set of the tail."

"Quite," I said. Obviously, I adore dogs. But not as science experiments. Nonetheless, I was here under the pretense of wishing to breed Cedric, so I asked Hermie a lot of questions about the whole business. Finally, I slipped in, "By the way, Mr. Inchbald, why were you at Willow Acres?"

"Muffy asked me to go with her," he said. "We'd always been close.

We spoke on the telephone most days—she was very lonely living with that ape Winfield, you know—and we took our holidays together. In the winter it was Bermuda, and in the late spring we took a long holiday in Deauville. Lovely hotel there, on the beach. Casino and golf and all that."

Europe again. Although, I couldn't quite picture Hermie or Muffy taking up with anarchists at a posh French seaside resort.

Hermie went on, "At any rate, Muffy was a bit nervous about her slimming course at Willow Acres—she'd done that sort of thing before, without success. I told her I'd go. Provide moral support and whatnot." His voice wobbled. "Never thought I'd b-be leaving the p-place alone."

"I'm not sure how to put this," I said, "but I got the impression Muffy wasn't in for slimming, but for—" I cleared my throat. "—for a drinking cure."

Hermie flushed so deeply, his freckles were obscured. "All right, yes, it's true—read that in the tabloids, did you?"

I made a noncommittal noise. "May I ask, did you hear or see anything peculiar the night Muffy died?"

"Yes, I did. But not from Muffy's room. From the other side. From Raymond Hathorne's room."

"What did you hear?"

"Talking. A woman's giggles."

"What time was this?"

"I'm not certain, but it was likely sometime after midnight. It woke me up, and I put a pillow over my head to muffle it."

"You, boy!" a gruff voice shouted.

We turned toward the house. A figure hunched in a wheelchair up on the terrace. White hair tufted above a dried-apple face. He was the same man who'd been dining with Van Hoogenband, Senator Morris, and Josie at Breakerhead two nights ago. Obadiah Inchbald,

I presumed. A nurse in white stood behind the wheelchair, holding the handles.

"Father." Hermie cringed.

Bitsy barked. Obadiah shook a fist.

"Father's b-been on the warpath ever s-s-since that libelous story was published in th-the newspaper yesterday," Hermie said, backing away from the terrace. "About his company. Inchbald and S-sons. Did you see it?"

"As a matter of fact, I did."

"F-Father thought he'd go th-through life without ever paying for his s-s-s-sins." Despite the stutter, despite the cowardly hitch of his shoulders, Hermie was smiling. "If he k-keeps up with this red-hot rage, he just m-m-might blow the last fuse and I'll be f-free of him. I won't have to s-snap to and walk on eggshells and wheel him around the T-titan Club like a sl-slave j-just because they won't let his n-nurse in th-there."

"Your father belongs to the Titan Club?" I asked.

"Y-yes. He's a f-f-founding member."

"Oh really?" I thought of Obadiah Inchbald and Senator Morris dining with Eugene Van Hoogenband at Breakerhead. "Tell me, is Senator Morris a founding member of the Titan Club as well?"

"Y-yes. It's the three of th-them, ruling the r-roost. Horrible men. L-lording over everyone else l-like k-k-kings."

Interesting. Very interesting.

"Boy!" Obadiah bellowed. "Who's that you have down there? Entertaining visitors when your sister's body hasn't even gone cold, eh? I'll bet you killed her, boy!" Obadiah snarled something at a lower volume to the nurse, and she turned the wheelchair and pushed it away down the terrace.

I squinted. "Is that Nurse Beaulah from Willow Acres?" I recognized the brassy glint of her hair under her nurse's cap.

"Th-that's right. Sh-she comes here t-t-to administer his rheuma-ma-matism c-cure." Hermie turned his back to the terrace, ignoring his father, and launched into an elaborate description of what happens to a lady dog when she has a half dozen peas in the pod. Gradually, his stutter receded.

I nodded and said, "Oh really?" at appropriate intervals, watching Beaulah all the while. She rolled Obadiah in his wheelchair back and forth, back and forth on the terrace. After a few minutes, it seemed that Obadiah had nodded off. Beaulah parked him facing the house. She slunk down the terrace steps, across the lawn, and into the hedge maze.

"—and so it is ever so important to give your bitch plenty of water," Hermie said.

"I beg your pardon?" I asked. "Oh—yes, of course."

Hermie checked his gold wristwatch. "I must step inside for a moment, for I am supposed to t-telephone the funeral home regarding arrangements for poor Muffy's—p-poor M-muffy's s-service."

"Mind if Cedric and I look about the garden? I adore roses."

"Not at all." Hermie went toward the house, Bitsy strolling at his side in a proprietary fashion.

20

....

Once Hermie went inside, I made for the hedge maze into which
Nurse Beaulah had gone. Cedric dawdled, sniffing the grass.
I stepped inside the maze and turned right. There was Beaulah, all
alone on a bench. Legs crossed, smoking, a tin of Lucky Strikes beside her and a magazine propped on her knee.

She looked up and lifted a penciled eyebrow. "Whatcha lookin
for?" she asked, spouting smoke. "The butler said you can't use the
lav in the house, didn't he? Well, this isn't a good spot. I think I saw
some poison ivy, plus there are all these danged golf balls."

It was true: dozens of golf balls littered the maze path. "Um,"
I said.

"It's the next-door neighbor," Beaulah said. "Always whacking golf
balls over the property line. Butler said he comes over to get the ones
on the lawn, but I guess he doesn't know about all these in the maze.
Anyway, if you gotta go, try the bushes out behind the garage. Lotsa
privacy there."

"Actually, I wished to speak with you," I said.

"Me? Wait. You do look kinda familiar."

"I was briefly booked into Willow Acres. When Muffy Morris was killed. My name is Lola." I left out my surname since I have the misfortune of sharing it with Chisholm—i.e., Beaulah's boss. No need to put her hackles up.

"Okay, Lola . . . so whatcha doing in the Inchbalds' hedge maze?"

"I am investigating the death of Muffy Morris—"

"A lady detective? Well, ain't that something!"

"—and I'd like to ask you a few questions."

"I already talked to the cops about a hundred times, but okay. . . ." Beaulah closed her magazine. The brand-new issue of *Thrilling Romance*. Lucky duck.

"Perhaps there is something you could tell me that the police won't listen to," I said. "I am familiar with the way the police pooh-pooh a lady's version of things."

"And how!" Beaulah said. "They kept trying to make it out like I gave Mrs. Morris that rum or something." Beaulah's eyes bubbled with tears. "Like me, Beaulah Starr, would try to hurt some lady I didn't really know."

My breath caught. "*You* were on duty in the East Ward the night Muffy Morris died?"

"Yep."

Finally.

Beaulah met my eyes steadily. "And I didn't see *nothing* funny. Did my job the way I always do. Exactly. Didn't see a *single thing* outa place."

Why was Beaulah so adamant? Was she hiding something, or was she merely defensive as a result of having been roasted over the coals? "Why did the police think you did it?" I asked. "What motive could you possibly have?"

"That's what I said!" Beaulah spread her scarlet-tipped fingers. "Police are just lookin' for someone to blame."

"Someone to blame? Then you believe Mrs. Morris was murdered?"

Beaulah's expression closed. "No, I don't—I just meant that if a rich lady like that dies, even if it's an accident, people want to have a scapesheep or whatever it's called."

"I happen to know the vial of medicine wasn't what killed Mrs. Morris. There was another vial. A vial given to Muffy by someone inside the East Ward. It seems to have contained arsenic."

Beaulah crossed and recrossed her legs, studied the ash at the end of her cigarette, and tossed it into the hedge.

"Is there something else," I said, "something to do with . . . a man?" A stab in the dark, but with us ladies, it is so often to do with a man. I pointed to her copy of *Thrilling Romance*. "A man like Bill Hampton in 'Hello, Darling,' perhaps, who stomps on ladies' hearts?"

Beaulah's eyes brightened. "You been reading 'Hello, Darling'?"

"Of course I've been reading it. Although I haven't yet read Part Two, so don't—"

"Listen to this—this is at the abandoned cottage across the lake from the lodge, where Bill Hampton went looking for Thelma during the big rainstorm." Beaulah flicked through the magazine and then read aloud, "'As fast as lightning, Bill swept Thelma into his arms, captured her mouth with unnerving, swift violence, and kissed her. "Oh, I—I despise you!" Thelma cried, slapping him. "You're a beast! Now, kiss me again!"'"

"Thelma?" I said. "Bill Hampton is kissing *Thelma*? What about Maude?"

"What about Maude is right." Beaulah slapped the magazine shut and corked a fresh cigarette in her lips. "Fellas are all just a bunch of stinkers, and just because a fella's rich and famous and everything don't make him less of a stinker."

"Bill Hampton isn't exactly famous," I said. "No one knows about his dukedom in England except his valet."

"I'm talking about my fella. Well, my former fella."

"Who?"

Beaulah preened a little. "Winfield."

"Winfield *Morris?*" I asked.

Beaulah nodded. "My precious monkey-angel. Well, he was a monkey-angel. Now he's just a monkey."

Oh. My. Word.

"Where did you meet him?" I asked.

"Here at Inchbald Hall. Obadiah is his father-in-law, see."

"You were working here in the capacity of Obadiah's nurse. . . ."

"Uh-huh. And Winnie followed me into this very maze, matter of fact. Said he was watching me, wanted to get me alone." Beaulah giggled.

Ugh. Creepy. "How romantic."

"He used to be romantic. Now he's just a skunk."

"Really?" I leaned in with a Confidential Girl Chat tilt of the head. "What did he do?"

"He might've started seeing another girl! I said, I'm the ice cream sundae, mister, and there aren't no extra scoops." An inchworm had appeared on Beaulah's bench. She coaxed the inchworm onto her tin of Lucky Strikes. "Course, he denied the whole thing."

"They always do." I watched as Beaulah gently set the Lucky Strikes on the ground. The inchworm undulated to the edge of the tin.

"*There you go, little fella,*" Beaulah whispered to the inchworm when it made it onto a blade of grass.

Right then and there I made up my mind: Beaulah couldn't be a murderer. Murderers don't treat inchworms like royalty.

"Did Senator Morris ever mention anarchists to you?" I asked. "Anarchists out to get him?"

"No. Those are foot doctors, right?"

All of a sudden I had the crawly feeling that someone was eavesdropping on our conversation. We were in a hedge maze, for Pete's sake; ten people could be crouched within earshot. But I didn't want to stop Beaulah, now that I had her talking.

"I'm real irked," Beaulah said, "because Winnie told me if anything was ever to happen to his wife, he was gonna marry me."

My mouth fell open.

"But this is what really steams my clams," Beaulah said. "As soon as Muffy kicked the bucket, Winnie jilted me! When I tried to see him at his house yesterday, his gatekeeper turned me away and said I wasn't to ever show there again. I even called Winnie up this morning when I knew he'd still be in bed, and I told him—I told him—I told him what I had . . ." Beaulah broke off and rubbed her nose.

"What did you tell him?" I asked.

"Nothing. He hung up on me. I don't even get an explanation."

"Fellows never provide explanations. Did you happen to tell any of this to the police?"

"Naw."

"Well, you probably shouldn't."

"Why not?"

"Because it gives you a motive for having murdered Muffy Morris."

Beaulah gasped. "I hadn't even thought of that! As if I'd kill a lady just to marry her husband?"

Was Beaulah really so dim? Funny thing was, my gut told me she was. Of course, my gut had also recently requested two pastrami sandwiches.

"It appears that Senator Morris may very well have attempted to frame you for murdering his wife," I said.

"But Winnie wasn't even at Willow Acres that night."

"Someone could have been working on his behalf," I said. "Don't you see? What if Winfield told you he'd marry you if something should happen to his wife in the hopes that you'd go and tell that to someone? Someone who would remember it once something *did* happen to Muffy. Someone who'd stand up in front of a courtroom and testify against you."

"That bastard!" Beaulah yelled. "I'm gonna sock him one!"

"Don't do anything rash," I said. "Winfield is powerful and wealthy—"

"I don't care. I'm gonna go see him! I was thinking about it and thinking about it, 'cause I saw in the newspaper he's gonna give a speech at a Coney Island beauty pageant this afternoon. Well, this settles it. I'm going to Coney Island. Pageant's at four o'clock, I saw it in the newspaper. I wanna stop home and change real quick. I hate Winnie's guts, so I have got to look my best, you know—"

I nodded. I knew.

"—but I gotta be quick because I might have to take the train if my friend Harriet—she's got her own motorcar—can't take the afternoon off from her cashier job at the feed store." Beaulah tossed aside her cigarette and stood. "Say, Lola, you've been so nice, warning me, why don't you borrow this?" She held out her copy of *Thrilling Romance*.

"Really? Thank you!" I took it.

"Just drop it off at my place when you're through. I'm at seven-oh-three Oak Street in Hare's Hollow. It's a boarding house and the landlady won't let you in, but if you give the magazine to her, she'll give it to me."

"Seven-oh-three Oak Street," I said.

"Mrs. Woodby?" Hermie's voice called. "Mrs. Woodby, are you in the maze?"

Beaulah narrowed her eyes. "Mrs. Woodby? Say, you some relation of Dr. Woodby's?"

I swallowed. "Well, yes, but Chisholm and I—"

"You stinking rat!" Beaulah snarled. "Give me my magazine back."

"But I—"

"I don't lend my *Thrilling Romance* to sneaks." Beaulah snatched it and stormed away.

"There you are, Mrs. Woodby," Hermie said, emerging from around a hedge with Cedric at his ankles. "What are you doing in here?"

Could he have been eavesdropping?

"Only exploring, and then I spoke with Nurse Beaulah a bit," I said.

"You can't hire good help these days, can you?" Hermie said. "But Father refuses to fire that chit. He's a filthy old beast. Now, then. It occurred to me that we haven't discussed Cedric's diet at all."

"His diet?" To be honest, Cedric looked like he was wearing a thermal waistcoat. "I'll put it this way, Mr. Inchbald: he has the appetite of a Newfoundland dog."

"It is a good thing that you don't intend to show him, then."

21

....

I excused myself from Hermie as quickly as I could, and motored
to the spot where I'd dropped off Berta earlier outside the Morris
estate.

No sooner had I parked than Berta exploded from a hedge,
crossed the road, and climbed into the passenger seat. She carried
her handbag and a soft-bound book. "Goodness me," she said, picking a leaf from her dress. "This heat is dreadful."

"Aren't you going to ask me what I discovered at Inchbald Hall?"
I asked, accelerating onto the road to Hare's Hollow.

"It cannot possibly be as important as what *I* have discovered."
Berta waved the book. "The *Institut Alpenrose Alumni Directory*, 1922
edition."

"Wowie. How did you manage it?"

"I posed as a cleaning woman—recall the apron borrowed from
Mr. Demel. I entered by way of the conservatory and traversed the
house unseen. However, just as my hand was upon the doorknob of
Muffy's room, a thuggish man in a suit appeared—"

"Buster?"

"Another one just like him—and a most unsettling exchange transpired, in which the man seemed to take me for one of—" Berta coughed. "—one of Senator Morris's assignations."

"Really? You in your apron?"

"There are men who find aprons exciting, Mrs. Woodby. Thinking swiftly, I decided my best course of action would be not to disillusion the man."

"Berta!"

"At any rate—knowing how you tend to dillydally, Mrs. Woodby—after I located the directory, I examined it on the premises and found each American woman who had attended the school in the years 1890 through 1895, of which there were ten. I then proceeded to telephone these women."

"From where?"

"From Muffy's boudoir telephone, of course. I got through to three—the others were either not at home, or they would not take my call."

"Who did you say you were?"

"A detective. Of the three I spoke to, only one was kind and womanly. The others were rather obstructive and rude, and one threatened to call the police. At any rate, we are to meet with a Mrs. Dun—Margaret Dun—at eleven o'clock tomorrow at the Imperial Ballroom on Forty-second Street. She suggested that she has something to relay about the schoolgirl scandal rumor that might interest us a great deal—goodness, Mrs. Woodby, look out for that squirrel!"

I swerved to miss a squirrel scampering across the road.

"Where are you motoring to in such a hurry?" Berta asked. "I would very much enjoy an iced beverage, you do realize. I have been trotting about like a pig to market."

"No time for a beverage," I said, rolling through a stop sign and turning right. "We're going to Nurse Beaulah's boarding house before it's too late."

"Too late? Nurse Beaulah?"

I told Berta about how Beaulah was the night nurse in the East Ward and how she'd been Senator Morris's twist-and-twirl. How he'd promised to marry her if something ever happened to his wife, and how he'd jilted her right after something *had* happened to his wife. "I think Senator Morris might have set Beaulah up as his scapegoat to take the fall for Muffy's murder."

"But he hired us to look into his wife's death," Berta said. "Why would he have done that if he is responsible for her murder?"

"I don't know."

"Ah. *I* know," Berta said grimly. "Such a scenario befell the novice gumshoe Brett Wallins, Thad Parker's young protégé."

"That fellow with the hook for a right hand?"

"It is his left hand, but yes. In *Parisian Peril*, the villain Marceau Dumonde hired Brett to investigate *his own crime*. Dumonde believed Brett would bungle things, you see, while at the same time exonerating himself by having hired someone to investigate."

"You're saying that Senator Morris hired us to investigate because he thinks we're . . . incompetent?"

"In a nutshell, yes."

"*Bastard.*" I pressed harder on the gas.

Berta straightened her hat. "However, I must add that Brett Wallins ensnared Marceau Dumonde in the end, after a thrilling chase to the top of the Eiffel Tower."

I slammed to a stop in front of a tall clapboard house on Oak Street with a picket fence and 703 on the mailbox. "This is Beaulah Starr's boarding house. We're motoring her to Coney Island in order to see for ourselves what happens when she gives it to Senator Morris hot and strong. The truth might all come out, and I want to

be there if it does." We got out, and I left the windows open for
Cedric. Poor peanut.

A landlady with a sharp face and a pendulous bosom opened the
door to my knock. "Yes?" She gave Berta and me a disdainful north–
south.

"We're here to visit Miss Starr," I said.

"No visitors allowed."

"What is this, a nunnery?" I said, trying to see past her.

"I do not like your tone," the landlady said.

"I must return a magazine," I lied, shaking my handbag as though
it contained a magazine. "The new issue of *Thrilling Romance*."
Surely even the stoniest woman could, at least secretly, sympathize
with that.

But the landlady's lip curled. "My niece reads that lurid publication. Nothing but detailed instructions on how a young girl might
lose her virtue."

"I do agree," Berta cut in, "but Miss Starr requires the magazine
for other, more moral purposes. You see, the most recent issue of
Thrilling Romance happens to contain an advertisement for a mail-
order teach-yourself-piano at-home course, and Miss Starr would
very much like to learn how to play the piano."

"No music in my house. Go away." The landlady slammed the door.

"Should we shout for Beaulah?" Berta whispered.

I shook my head. "The landlady might telephone the police. Let's
sneak in."

Berta sighed. "After this, no more sneak-ins for me for the rest
of the day."

"I'm afraid I can't guarantee that."

We motored away in case the landlady was watching, parked
around the corner, and crept down an alley to the backyard of the
boarding house. Laundry drifted on a clothesline.

"Look—there's an open window in the cellar," I whispered.

"I am not certain we will be able to fit through."

The open window was one of those smallish, ground-level affairs. "We might not. But let's give it a try."

We tiptoed through the laundry to the window. Berta went through feetfirst and although it was a tight fit, she made it. I went next. Also, alas, a tight fit.

"See?" I whispered to Berta. "Kid's stuff." I looked around the dank cellar.

"You have ruined your buttons."

"Buttons?" I glanced down. My dress gaped where the window frame had tugged two buttons loose on their threads. "Phooey. I think I have safety pins in my handbag. I'll fix it up later. Come on."

We went up the cellar stairs and peeked through the door at the top. The kitchen. A pot simmered on the stove, but no one was there. We rushed through the kitchen and stopped again at a doorway onto the main entry hall. Ah—and there were the stairs. We went up as quickly and quietly as we could and found ourselves in a long upper hallway.

"Which room?" Berta whispered.

"No notion." We went down the hallway, softly rapping on doors.

When I rapped on the fourth door, someone called, "Yeah?" The door popped open. Beaulah. Her eyes went hard. "Oh. You again. What do you want? How'd you get past Mrs. Beecher?"

"Miss Starr, may we come in?" I asked.

"Fine, but only because I'm too busy getting ready to try and get rid of you. I've got just enough time to get to Coney Island, and I'm not gonna let that lying scumbag get away this time." Beaulah went into her room, and Berta and I followed. I shut the door.

Dresses, nylon slips, wadded stockings, and brassieres were flung across the bed, on chair backs, and over the mirrored wardrobe door. The windowsill held a vase of dead roses. Romance and beauty magazines lay on every flat surface along with, oddly, three of Violet Wilbur's home décor books.

"Whatcha staring at?" Beaulah stood inches away from the wardrobe mirror, going to town with heated curling tongs.

"I wouldn't have pegged you for a Violet Wilbur fanatic," I said.

"She gives some real good advice about pillow tassels. What? I'm not gonna live in a dump like this forever. Someday I'm gonna have a big, beautiful house. I've got aspirations. So. Whatcha want?"

"First of all," I said, "I would like to tell you that, although Dr. Woodby is my brother-in-law, I am in no way allied with him."

"She detests him, dear," Berta said to Beaulah in a soothing voice.

"Then you're really a lady detective?" Beaulah asked.

"Yes," I said. "And this is my detecting partner, Mrs. Lundgren."

"Hi," Beaulah said to Berta.

"We'd like to motor you to Coney Island," I said.

Beaulah's hands froze mid-wave. "How come?"

"We are investigating Senator Morris," I said. Well, it was true as of ten minutes earlier, wasn't it?

"Okay," Beaulah said, "because I hate to bug my friend Harriet at the feed store. But I'm not going anywhere with you two dressed like that."

"Like what?" Berta said in an offended tone.

"Like a couple of church ladies," Beaulah said. "And you lost a couple buttons, Lola. Coney Island's a place of style on a hot summer day like this. You gotta look pretty. It's okay—you can borrow some things from me."

I would have protested, but I had two dangling buttons.

"I do not believe I shall fit into one of your dresses, Miss Starr," Berta said.

"Sure you will. My figure goes up and down like a seesaw. I always slim down when I'm working for months at a health farm, but whenever I go home to see Mom, something comes over me and I go at the honey ham like there's no tomorrow. Mom makes the best honey ham with those pineapple slices stuck all over, you know?"

My mouth watered.

"Your mother must be very proud," Berta said.

Ten minutes later we were on the road to the city, with Beaulah and Cedric sharing the backseat. Berta and I were wearing cheap and lightweight summer dresses. Berta had chosen a roomy yellow number with a white sailor collar and white buttons. Mine was red-and-white gingham and a size too small. It never would have buttoned up all the way if I hadn't happened to be wearing my most robust girdle. As it was, my bosom wasn't fully stashed away.

Good thing we were going to Coney Island.

22

....

When we at last arrived in Brooklyn, I parked the Duesy at the curb on Surf Avenue—a possibly illegal spot, but we were in a hurry—and switched off the engine. The entrance to Luna Park was just across the street, with towers and flapping flags and, beyond, a roller coaster. Faint screams floated on the breeze.

Beaulah climbed out of the backseat. "Thanks, girls. Maybe I'll see you there." She bolted down the crowded sidewalk, her white handbag swinging.

I clipped on Cedric's leash, and Berta and I hurried after Beaulah to the long boardwalk. Beaulah's pink dress and barmaid's sway in the crossbeam were easy to keep track of.

"She seems to know where she's going," I said to Berta.

We snaked through merrymakers with their ice cream cones, screaming kids, and sunburns, past hot dog stands, cigarette shops, dance halls, and nickel exhibits. Seagulls squawked and calliope music burbled. Down in the sand and surf, people swarmed in bathing suits.

Halfway down the boardwalk, a huge sign arched over a stage: CONEY ISLAND MERMAID QUEEN. Beyond the sign, the ocean glittered.

"Where is Beaulah?" I said.

"There." Berta pointed. "Up near the front. Do you see her straw hat?"

A crowd pressed thick around the stage, and onstage, girls in dresses paraded stiffly. Each girl had a number pinned to her dress and a frozen smile. Photographers snapped pictures, and a couple of journalists scribbled on notepads.

I picked up Cedric, and Berta and I plowed through the crowd toward the front.

"Where is he?" Beaulah was demanding of no one in particular. "Where's the senator?"

"Shut up, we're trying ta watch the beauties," a stocky man growled.

Beaulah grabbed the man's hat and tossed it in the air. "Watch that, dough boy."

A splatter of applause as one contestant exited the stage and another entered.

"It smells quite intensely of underarm in this crowd," Berta said.

"*Berta*," I whispered, "is that—is that *Grace Whiddle* onstage?"

"Oh my. Yes, it is. She is standing up straight for a change."

Grace had made up her face and bobbed her blond hair. She'd also chucked her eyeglasses, which probably explained why she bumped into a wooden support before she disappeared behind the curtains.

"Forget Beaulah and Senator Morris," I whispered to Berta. "Let's catch Grace! Maybe Mrs. Whiddle will pay up after all." More tantalizing than getting paid was catching Grace before Ralph Oliver did.

Berta nodded.

We inched sideways through the crowd and found a gate in front of a curtained-off backstage area. I glimpsed pageant contestants dashing to and fro back there.

The gate was blocked by a fellow with forearms like a bricklayer. "Contestants only," he said.

Berta stiffened. "We *are* contestants."

"That so? Then I suppose you know that it's the bathing suit contest next?"

"Oh." Perspiration sprang up on my hairline. Bathing suit? With *photographers* in the crowd? I took a step back, hugging Cedric.

"We are going to be late," Berta cried. "Now, please, allow us through!"

Popeye shrugged and opened the gate.

I said, "On second thought, Berta, I think maybe I ought to go and keep an eye on Beaulah after all." I took another step back. "And Cedric probably shouldn't—"

"Weak as a kitten!" Berta glared at me before pushing through the gate.

"You coming?" the guard asked me.

"Um, no," I muttered. I slunk back to the audience. But really! A *bathing suit*? Don't misunderstand, I'm not a prude, but wearing slinky underthings in the dim—and preferably pinkish—light of one's own boudoir is not the same as exposing every soft, white inch to the merciless light of the afternoon sun.

I'd just positioned myself where I could see the stage when someone said, "Well, hello there, angel. Smashing dress."

"Why, Mr. Hathorne!" I said. "Hello. Coney Island is just about the last place I would've expected to see you."

"What about me?" Hermie Inchbald poked his head out from Raymond's other side.

"Mr. Inchbald!" I said. "Nice to see you again so soon."

Hermie Inchbald was rashy and damp-looking in his black wool suit and hat. Raymond Hathorne looked tall and cool in fawn-colored flannels and a straw boater hat with a navy blue band.

Raymond said, "I motored down to investigate soda pop sales and consumption patterns here on Coney Island—what better place?—and I brought Inchbald along to give him an airing."

"It was all very sudden," Hermie said, dabbing his forehead with a handkerchief.

"No sense in him moping at home in a pile of poodle fur," Raymond said.

"Actually, poodles have hair, not fur," Hermie said. "And they don't shed, so—"

"Inchbald has just lost his sister who was, by all accounts, his best friend." Raymond spoke to me as though Hermie weren't there. "He could crack up staying at home by himself. Don't get me wrong, I know exactly what he's going through."

"You do?"

"I lost my own sister years ago. She was my best friend, too."

"I'm sorry," I said.

"Sure, back when she died, I was fit to be tied—like Inchbald here is now, I suppose you could say. But it passed. Oh, we also stopped by Willow Acres on the way and picked up Mr. Tibor Ulf. You know, the vigorology instructor? It's his day off and I remembered him saying he wished to see the real America. I suppose this is it." Raymond looked around the crowd with a lofty, bemused expression. "I don't know where Ulf has taken himself off to, though. Probably doing calisthenics on the beach. What are you doing here, Lola?"

"Oh—I'm here to listen to Senator Morris's speech. And the ice cream here is second to none."

"Ah." Raymond's eyes glittered.

I would've liked to ask Raymond to explain why Hermie had heard a woman's giggles emanating from his room at Willow Acres the night Muffy died. Alas, I couldn't bally well do that right in front of Hermie. The poor egg was already as twitchy as Charlie Chaplin's mustache. "Did you happen to notice that Grace Whiddle is competing in the pageant?" I asked both men.

"Is she?" Raymond said. "How amusing."

Hermie was frowning. "Grace has a lot of explaining to do. Where is she?"

"You'll see her," I said.

We turned our attention to the pageant. Toothy, lipsticked girls preened in bathing suits that crept dangerously close to the fork in the road.

Two young bucks squeezed between Raymond and me, and then Hermie squirmed through the crowd to stand on my other side. "Mrs. Woodby," he whispered, "since you seem to be cultivating a friendship with Raymond Hathorne, I feel it is my duty to warn you that he isn't who he says he is."

"Whatever do you mean?"

"He didn't buy the Pitridge estate. He's only letting it. I know this absolutely, because I spoke with the leasing agent just before Mr. Hathorne took up residence last month. And there is no such thing as Fizz-Whiz soda pop. *No one* has heard of it."

"Nobody knows about anything made in Canada, Hermie. And Raymond told me he purchased his house. He said he's going to repair it."

"Pulling the wool over your eyes," Hermie said. "He is n-not a nice man, Mrs. Woodby. N-not at all."

"Why, Mr. Inchbald, what did he do?"

"I s-s-see it in his eyes. C-cold. I'd bet he's one of those g-g-gentleman adventurers, l-looking for a w-wealthy lady to s-support him. I only c-came along today because he w-was s-s-so v-very insistent. But h-he's slippery. He's a t-trained actor, you know. He t-t-told me he h-headed up the Shakespearean S-s-society at c-college."

I could picture Raymond in Hamlet tights. But Raymond an adventurer? No. That couldn't be correct. Mother had vouched for Raymond's good family and substantial fortune, and Mother could be relied upon when it came to such things. Hermie must've had some sort of axe to grind with Raymond . . . or perhaps Hermie was attempting to divert attention away from himself.

Berta was the tenth contestant to parade across the stage. When she emerged in a black, scratchy-looking Edwardian bathing suit—where had she gotten that?—in all her stout, ladylike dignity, the audience erupted in cheers and hoots. When she posed center stage with hands on hips, cameras clicked wildly. Berta spotted me in the crowd and sent me a dark look.

More contestants paraded past, and then a man in shabby evening clothes burst from behind the curtains. "Ladies and gentlemen, thank you for attending the first Coney Island Mermaid Queen Pageant!" he cried.

The crowd clapped, although now that the half-naked girls were gone, a lot of men were peeling off. I'd lost track of Hermie and Raymond, and I couldn't see Beaulah anywhere, either.

"And now, it is my profound pleasure to introduce to you, ladies and gentlemen, New York State Senator Morris!"

Winfield strode onstage to lackluster applause. His suit was dark and expensive-looking and his hair was oiled back from his little forehead. "Good afternoon, citizens of New York. It will be my great honor to crown Coney Island's first Mermaid Queen. But first, I have a few words I would like to convey to you, my fellow Americans." He looked around the crowd with a soulful expression. The lady next to me took a huge bite of hot dog, catsup squirting. "Like so many of you," Winfield said, "I long to return to a simpler age. An age of apple pie and grandmother's knitting, of mother and father at the fireside, ringed round with the rosy cherubs of their devotion—"

A man in the crowd yelled, "Hey! It's Schlump!"

Schlump?

Senator Morris made shushing gestures. Except the crowd didn't require shushing; everyone was silently goggling at a fellow at the edge of the crowd in a bushy beard, a big-brimmed hat, and green-tinted sunglasses.

"It *is* Schlump!" another man yelled.

Someone reached out and gave the fellow's bushy beard a yank. It sagged and sprang back on elastic strings.

"Whaddaya doin here, Schlump? Studying the beauty queens to figure out how to throw like a girl?"

"Already throws like a girl!" someone else shouted.

"Like a girl?" yet another person screamed. "He throws like a goddam baby in diapers!"

The irate crowd surged around Pete Schlump.

Pete was obviously there at the boardwalk to see his girl Grace Whiddle compete in the pageant. And why he was in disguise, well, that was pretty obvious, too. A runaway train isn't as terrifying as a disappointed Yankees fanatic.

Someone threw a punch. Grunts and squawks. More punches. A soda pop bottle went whistling through the air. I was knocked to my knees by a man eager to join the brawl. I clutched Cedric to my chest. Mustard splattered down my arm. Panic careened through me and I struggled to get to my feet, but other people's blurry legs churned all around me. I was knocked forward, and I braced my fall with my free hand on the wooden planks of the boardwalk. Cedric squirmed in my other arm. Then a woman I couldn't really see in the jumble trod on the back of my hand with a small, pointy high heel. I yelped.

A huge, wrinkled, suntanned hand appeared in front of my face. I grabbed it. Someone pulled me to my feet and steadied me.

"Mr. Ulf!" I said, my voice thick and quavering. "I almost didn't recognize you in—in ordinary clothes. Thank you."

"But of course, Mrs. Woodby," Ulf said, taking Cedric from me. Ulf still gripped my hand, for which I was grateful. I'd gone fluff-headed and rubbery.

A gunshot cracked through the bellows and hoots and cries. Then a heavy, hollow sound, like a sack of potatoes hitting a wooden floor. Except—I sucked in a breath—that was no sack of potatoes up there on the stage.

That was Senator Morris.

"Someone's shot the senator!" a lady shrieked. "Someone's got a gun!"

"Anarchists!" another woman screamed.

"It's the anarchists!" a man yelled.

The crowd stampeded in all directions.

Ulf wrapped his arm around me and kept me on my feet until most of the crowd had dispersed. In Ulf's other arm, Cedric yawned with anxiety, his little ears slicked back.

Onstage, two men knelt over Senator Morris. "He's a goner," one of them said, shaking his head. "Straight through the heart."

23

A policeman elbowed through the throng and bent over Senator Morris's body. Gawkers flocked. I clung to Ulf and we both stared, speechless, at the chaos twirling around us. The sun beat down, but I felt ice cold, even after Ulf had placed Cedric in my arms.

More police roared up in paddy wagons, and they made everyone clear the area in front of the stage. An ambulance blared through the throng a little after that. I stood on tiptoe and looked around, but with so many people licking ice cream cones and pointing at the corpse, I couldn't spot Berta, Beaulah, or Grace. Raymond and Hermie seemed to have evaporated, too.

"We must speak to the police," Ulf said. "It is our civic duty to do so."

"Did you see anything?" I asked him.

"I did not see the shooter, but perhaps there is something else we have not thought of yet."

"Look. They've found something over there," I said, pointing. Two policemen crouched in front of the stage. One of them held a small thing up, and it glinted metallic in the sunshine.

"A spent cartridge," Ulf said. "Then it seems that the killer stood just in the crowd. Not far from where you and I were standing, Mrs. Woodby."

I looked at the back of my hand. A round purple welt pulsated where the woman had trod upon it. Could the shooter have been that woman?

Up on the stage, a policeman draped Senator Morris's body with a shroud. How quickly life flicks out. It's terrifying.

"Ah, I see Mr. Hathorne and Mr. Inchbald are giving their statements to the police," Ulf said to me. "Come, Mrs. Woodby. We should, as well." He guided me with a chivalrous air to the haphazard crowd of people waiting to speak with the police near the paddy wagons and the ambulance. By the time we got in line, I'd once again lost track of Raymond and Hermie.

"I tell you, it was an anarchist!" a lady was shrieking to a cop. Her hair looked like she'd just stuck her finger in an electrical outlet, and she wore a mangy bathrobe. "They're everywhere, those horrible Reds!"

Ulf and I exchanged a knowing glance: *Whew. She's cuckoo.*

But as Ulf and I waited fifteen or twenty minutes to speak to the police, people started looking at Ulf funny. They'd heard his German accent. Next came the hostile whispers. Then angry stares. Someone snarled to Ulf, "We don't want your kind in this country."

Then it was my turn to give a statement. I told two policemen all about what I'd seen and how Ulf had been helping me up—I pointed him out—when the shot was fired. One policeman took notes and the other one looked bored. I gave them my Longfellow Street telephone number. By the time I was through, Ulf was surrounded by an angry mob of people babbling about European Reds and anarchists, and a lot of people were throwing the term *assassination* around.

The cuckoo lady in the bathrobe popped up again, telling the police "It was him!" She pointed a vibrating finger at Ulf. "He did it! I saw him pull the trigger!"

"No!" I cried. My pipes were dry. Nobody heard me. The mob closed around Ulf, and the next I saw of him, he was in handcuffs and being pushed by a cop into the back of one of the paddy wagons. Doors slammed and the paddy wagon rolled away down the boardwalk.

"Good riddance," a skinny man with a sunburned nose said to no one in particular, and took a swig from his soda pop bottle.

I simply stood there slack-jawed, following the paddy wagon's retreat down the boardwalk. Berta, back in her dress and hat and arm linked firmly through Grace Whiddle's, marched out from the backstage area.

"But I must find Petey!" Grace was wailing. Tears and makeup streamed behind her glasses. She wore a sundress over her bathing suit.

Berta said, "My dear, if Pete has even an ounce of sense, he is in a taxicab speeding away from here. Those men wished to tear him limb from limb. You may telephone him from my apartment." Berta saw me, and her expression cooled. "Oh. Hello, Mrs. Woodby. As you can see, I have apprehended Grace."

"Oh. Congratulations. Hello, Grace."

"Hi," Grace said, her voice cracking. "Isn't it just awful about Senator Morris? I hated him, and he would've made the rottenest father-in-law, but golly, didn't he look like a big dead hairy woodchuck up there on the stage?"

"Mrs. Woodby," Berta said, "I do realize you prefer not to wear bathing suits, but it seemed to me that you might have sacrificed a *little* of your pride for the sake of our—"

"They've arrested Tibor Ulf for shooting Senator Morris," I said. "He's been accused of being an anarchist assassin."

Grace said, "That muscly old man from Willow Acres? But how could he hide a gun? He's always wearing those really small white shorts."

"Mr. Ulf?" Berta said. "I would not have thought it of him. Anarchists always seem to smoke a great deal and eat unwholesome foods out of tins."

"It *wasn't* him," I said. "I'm dead certain. Grace, would you excuse us for a moment?"

Grace shrugged.

Berta said to her, "I have my eye on you, young lady, and if you attempt to bolt, I will fell you like a little tree."

Grace pouted. "Don't worry, I've got blisters on my heels from these shoes. I'm not going anywhere."

I led Berta over to the boardwalk railing for privacy. I told her in hushed, hurried tones how I'd been knocked down in the boardwalk brawl, how a lady had stepped on my hand with her pointy shoe—I showed her the purple welt—and how Ulf had been helping me up when the shot was fired. "I told the police all of this," I said. "Should I go back and tell them again?"

"Goodness no," Berta said. "What is the point? You already gave them your statement that should have exonerated Ulf. Arresting a European makes the police appear heroic to the public, does it not? Protecting Americans from crazed Continental communists and so forth. I imagine they would sooner have their teeth pulled than release him."

"But he could go to the electric chair!" I cried.

A lady in a loud floral sundress looked at me askance. Grace was all ears, too.

I lowered my voice to a whisper. "I know that our sole employer is dead now, so we're not going to get paid for any of this, but we must find out who murdered the Morrises. It's the right thing to do. I can't sit back and watch an innocent man go to the electric chair."

"I do agree," Berta said. "We have no choice in the matter."

"Now we're working for justice, not money," I said. I felt good about this. My pocketbook did not. "How we are going to pay our bills is another problem entirely."

"I have no doubt that we will sort it all out with great speed," Berta said, "since it is patently obvious that Beaulah Starr is the murderer."

"Beaulah? Why do you sound so certain?"

"You must be jesting, Mrs. Woodby. Beaulah had a perfect motive for killing Muffy Morris—clearing the way to become the second Mrs. Morris—and, that plan having failed, she killed Senator Morris in a fit of passion. Beaulah must have had a gun in her handbag. And—" Berta gestured to my bruised hand. "—her shoes were rather pointy, I happened to notice."

I thought of the inchworm Beaulah had rescued with her Lucky Strikes tin. Yet I couldn't tell Berta that I believed wholeheartedly that an inchworm cleared Beaulah from suspicion. It sounded too soft-boiled. "Okay," I said, "then should we tell the police our suspicions about Beaulah?"

"Certainly not."

"Why?"

"Because *you* motored her to Coney Island, Mrs. Woodby. You may have aided and abetted a murderess."

"I may have? What about you?"

"You were behind the wheel."

Oh golly.

"We must find Beaulah and obtain a confession," Berta said, "or else gather some harder evidence against her. Matching her gun to the one used to kill Senator Morris would do very nicely. Now. We cannot stand about on this boardwalk forever. Grace has agreed to return with us to Washington Square, where I will feed the poor child, for she tells me she has dined upon nothing but strawberries and champagne for the past two days while—" Berta coughed. "—during her stay with Pete Schlump. Pete has, of course, fled the irate Yankees fanatics."

"Wait." I stole a glance at Grace. She was somehow chewing gum and yawning at the same time. "Could Grace have shot Senator Morris?"

"No. She was backstage with me at the time."

"Why was she competing in the pageant, anyway?"

"Just as her friend Josie Van Hoogenband told us, Grace dreams of becoming a burlesque dancer or a motion picture star. She theorized that winning a beauty pageant would be the first step to that end. Pete Schlump was only too happy to assist her in the endeavor."

I threw one last look at Winfield's shrouded body, now being loaded onto the ambulance like a casserole into an oven. "Let's go," I said.

I made a stop along the boardwalk to purchase chocolate ice creams for myself and Grace.

"Is that a business expense?" Berta demanded. "If so, you must log it in the book."

"Sure," I said, waving my fingers.

While Grace was licking her ice cream and crying to Berta about the missing Pete some more, I slipped into a telephone booth, slid in a coin, and asked the operator to put me through to Hare's Hollow. The Hare's Hollow exchange girl put me through to Clyde's Bluff.

"Yes?" Sophronia Whiddle said when I had her on the line.

"This is Lola Woodby. The Discreet Retrieval Agency has located and captured your daughter, Grace."

"WHAT? Where is she? Is she harmed? Where are—?"

"She's quite fine, and we'll tell you the rest when you come to collect her at our Longfellow Street office. Oh—and cash or check will be fine."

Sophronia did a spot of heavy breathing and then said, "I shall order my chauffeur to take me directly. I'll arrive in no more than an hour and a half—and do not allow anything else to befall her!" She hung up.

"Who was that?" Grace asked me as we set off once more down the boardwalk.

"Oh, no one," I said.

24

Back at the apartment, Grace collapsed fully dressed on Berta's bed and fell instantly to sleep. She'd slept in the Duesy on the way back from Coney Island, too—I guess she'd had quite a tuckering time with Pete Schlump in his apartment—so Berta and I would have to wait till she woke up to interrogate her about the murders. She was, strictly speaking, still a suspect at least in Muffy's death.

Berta and I went to the stuffy kitchen. I opened the window, kicked off my shoes, and fed and watered Cedric. Berta assembled a pot, a wooden spoon, and a cutting board.

"You're going to cook in this heat?" I said.

"Yes, and I am certain you will eat what I make." Berta poked her head into the icebox. "Oh dear. We are out of butter. I meant to make a pot pie, but I can't make the crust without butter."

I thought of Berta's flaky golden pastry crust. It seemed that my life would go from problematic to blissful if only I could eat some of that crust. "I'll go with you to the shop. It's so stuffy in here."

"What about Grace? If she escapes, Mrs. Whiddle will not pay us."

In fact, Mrs. Whiddle probably wasn't going to pay us, anyway. Telephoning her had been wishful thinking on my part. After all, she'd fired Berta and me. Still, I hoped she'd be so overjoyed to have her daughter back that she'd get lavish with the checkbook.

We peeked into the bedroom. Grace was sprawled and snoring.

"She won't be waking up anytime soon," I said. "But we can lock her into the apartment, if that's any consolation."

"All right. We will not be gone more than ten minutes, anyway."

Berta and I left Cedric snoozing on his pouf in the kitchen and walked out into the soft summer evening.

Along the way, we passed a newsstand. The proprietor was just closing up.

I stopped. "Excuse me, but do you have the latest issue of *Thrilling Romance?*" I asked him.

He laughed. "Do you know how many birds have asked me just that question today?"

I sighed. "Thanks anyway—"

"Why the long face? I got a few copies left."

Yippee!

The cover featured a girl in golf togs getting a kiss from a gorgeous fellow. Since I hadn't brought my handbag, Berta paid for the magazine and I rolled it up and stuck it in the pocket of my dress.

At the market around the corner, Berta purchased a half pound of butter, and we set off toward home. We rounded the corner and stepped out into the street in order to cross.

A shiny black motorcar thundered toward us.

I froze. Berta grabbed my elbow and yanked me back to the curb.

The motorcar squealed to a stop. It was a Chevrolet with a smashed front fender. The rear door fell open.

"Gee, that's some real fancy footwork for a couple of overfed dames," Baby Doll Mallone chirped from the shadowed interior.

"Hello, Miss Mallone," I said coolly, even though my heart was throbbing. Eggie—aka Mr. Egghead—was crammed beside Baby Doll. The chauffeur was a mere silhouette behind the wheel.

"Enough with the chitchat," Baby Doll said. "We got business to take care of." She shimmied out of the motorcar. I happened to notice, even in my fog of panic, that her shoes were the bee's knees: red kid leather with a curvaceous, teetering-high heel.

Eggie held an enormous pistol across his thighs.

"*Gun,*" I whispered to Berta.

"*Run!*" Berta whispered back.

"Don't even think about running or we'll shoot you down like a couple a Easter Bunnies," Baby Doll said.

"You'd shoot the Easter Bunny?" I cried. "You're sick!"

Baby Doll smiled. "I know. Ain't it grand? Get in."

Eggie lumbered out and grabbed Berta. Berta swore in Swedish and kicked, but Eggie stuffed her into the backseat.

Baby Doll jammed what felt like a gun barrel into my ribs and then somehow I was in the backseat, too. Doors slammed. Keys rattled. Eggie and Baby Doll got in beside the chauffeur, and we were off.

I jiggled the door handle. Locked. "What does Mr. Van Hoogenband want from us, anyway?" I demanded. Could this really be all about protecting his spoiled daughter, Josie?

"Beats me," Baby Doll said.

Berta leaned forward. "You will not get away with this," she said. "You cannot simply muscle people about."

Baby Doll peered back at us, only her eyes visible between the top of the seat and the brim of her cloche. "Course we can. Do it all the time! Where you been living, lady? Inside Mother Goose's nursery rhymes?" She gave a tinkling laugh.

The chauffeur grinned and Eggie gurgled.

....

The Van Hoogenband house was one of the few freestanding old city mansions left over from the last century. Many had been razed to make way for apartment buildings, and only the really, *really* Big Old Money still had mansions surrounded on all sides by gardens and iron fences. The Van Hoogenband place was stone and redbrick with all sorts of spiny turrets and pointed windows, and every last window shone yellow.

The chauffeur pulled through a gate and parked at the side of the house. Baby Doll and Eggie urged Berta and me out of the backseat with their pistols—Berta had no choice but to leave her handbag and her butter behind—up stone steps, and inside.

As we passed through a corridor, I happened to glance up at a large oil painting. I blinked.

It was the same painting that I'd seen delivered to Chisholm's house yesterday: The Heyliger still life with the lobster and the wine-glasses and lemons. Maybe Chisholm had objected to the booze in the picture and passed it off to Van Hoogenband.

I elbowed Berta. She saw the painting and her eyebrows lifted, inquiring.

"*I saw the same painting at Chisholm's house,*" I whispered.

"Put a sock in it," Eggie said.

We were shown through rooms with more fancy millwork, flocked wallpaper, and Tiffany lamps than a crazy lady's dollhouse. In a half-lit library, Eggie shoved us down on a couch and tied our hands to-gether at our backs.

"You gottta tie their ankles, too, you dumbbell!" Baby Doll said.

Eugene Van Hoogenband strolled in. Baby Doll and Eggie hur-ried over to the wall, where they stood like guards.

Van Hoogenband wore evening clothes, and pomade glossed his

dark hair. He stood before Berta and me, hands behind his back, looking thoughtfully down.

I fought the urge to say something cute about the weather.

"At last we meet," Van Hoogenband said. "You have given me a great deal of trouble, you know. You live up to your name, I am loath to admit. *The Discreet Retrieval Agency*. Discreet, indeed. Wily, I would even venture to say."

He didn't sound sarcastic.

"Say, Mr. Van Hoogenband," I said, "did Violet Wilbur happen to decorate this house of yours recently?"

Van Hoogenband narrowed his eyes. "Yes, but I can't think why you'd mention that now."

"She has a terrible habit of straying from the main topic," Berta told Van Hoogenband.

That settled it: Violet Wilbur dealt in forged paintings. The sneak!

Van Hoogenband said, "First, you break into my country house and confront my innocent young daughter, leaving her *this*." He extracted the business card we'd given Josie, the one blotched with mascara. "Taunting me with the blacked-out street number, blacked out with some infernal substance that even the most careful procedures could not remove."

Tell me about it. That mascara wouldn't budge in a hurricane.

"Then—taunting me again—you evaded my helpers not once but twice, first with a sudden maneuver with your motorcar that caused rather costly damage to mine, and then, convincing those fools—" Van Hoogenband threw a dark look at Baby Doll and Eggie. "—that you were residing in a yacht in the Hare's Hollow Marina. I went there. What did I find? A ghost ship! No sign of you!"

Berta and I were silent.

"Must I convince you to talk?" Mr. Van Hoogenband said.

"Because I do have ways to make people talk. My family didn't get where it is today by sitting back and allowing others to decide our fates. No, the Van Hoogenbands are leaders. Doers."

Berta said, "What was it you wished to discuss, Mr. Van Hoogenband?"

"What is it I wish to discuss?" Van Hoogenband threw back his head and laughed. "Playing dumb?" He shoved his face close to Berta's. "We're a bit beyond that stage, don't you think?"

"That depends," I said.

"Foxes!" Van Hoogenband swung around and paced across the carpet, scowling.

"If he wants to believe we are wily foxes," Berta whispered to me, "who are we to stop him?"

"*No*," I whispered, "this could be dangerous! Don't—"

"Silence!" Van Hoogenband roared. He came toward us again, dark eyes glittering. "Where is the diary?"

The diary? Oh. Things came into sharper focus. Van Hoogenband wanted the diary. So *that's* why he'd sicced Baby Doll and Eggie on us. Miss Cotton had said that Van Hoogenband perused the diary in her office at the academy. So it looked like Van Hoogenband knew exactly what was in the diary . . . and it was something that made him vulnerable or even incriminated him.

"Grace Whiddle's diary," Van Hoogenband said. "Tell me where it is. In a safe, perhaps? Or hidden in your secret lair?—by the by, where is it that you two hide out on Longfellow Street? No, never mind, for soon it shall not matter in the slightest. I want that diary. I shall have it."

"Why do you think we have it?" I asked.

"Because that absurd lady newspaper columnist Ida Shanks telephoned and told me that you, Mrs. Woodby, had linked me not only to the Morris deaths, but to Grace Whiddle's diary."

Ugh. I'd known that was dumb, dumb, dumb.

"*You told Miss Shanks all that?*" Berta whispered to me furiously.

"I very much hope, then," Van Hoogenband said, "that you either have the diary or that you know where it is."

I said, "We don't—" but Berta kicked my ankle.

"The diary is in a safe location," she said.

Okay, Berta was going to bluff. I hoped this wasn't the Highway to Regret. Or worse.

"But," Berta went on, "we are well aware of how valuable the diary is to you, Mr. Van Hoogenband, and we simply could not part with it . . . unless . . ."

"What is your price? My checkbook is in the desk just over there."

My mouth went sour. The problem with Berta's little impulse to extort Van Hoogenband—even it was simply to buy time—was that we didn't actually know where the diary was.

"We don't know where the diary is," I said. "We've never laid eyes on it."

Van Hoogenband's eyebrows shot down. "Oh? But your friend here says that you know of its value to me."

I swallowed. "Well, yes."

"Then you know what is written in the diary?"

"Oh. Um. In a manner of speaking." Why, oh, why couldn't I lie more convincingly?

"But you do not have it, nor are you capable of retrieving it for me?"

"Ah . . ."

"Well. This rather changes things, doesn't it? You have quite suddenly gone from being the two people I was most interested in to simply being two meddling old tabbies who know too much."

"*Old?*" I said.

"We know nothing!" Berta cried.

"Get rid of them," Van Hoogenband said in a bored voice to Baby Doll and Eggie. "Make it clean—the Miller's Creek bridge site should do nicely. The concrete supports are scheduled to be poured in the morning, so that would be quite suitable."

Then Baby Doll and Egghead were prodding Berta and me with their guns back through the mansion. And there wasn't a dratted thing we could do about it, since our hands were still tied behind our backs.

We passed the lobster painting, the potted palms, and the grand staircase. My mind was a white blank of horror.

25

Outside Van Hoogenband's mansion, the Chevrolet was waiting, but the chauffeur was gone. Berta and I were shoved and slammed inside by Eggie. I didn't even try to resist. I was numb. Berta cursed and elbowed to no avail.

Eggie got behind the wheel. Baby Doll circled around and climbed in beside him. And I do mean climbed. She would've benefited from a portable stepstool.

"Wait a minute," Baby Doll said. "We oughta blindfold 'em, just in case."

"In case a what?" Eggie said. "They ain't comin' back."

"Just do it."

Eggie got out, opened the rear door, and tied handkerchiefs around our eyes. I was frozen with fright, too confused to even recoil. Then he slammed himself into the driver's seat, and the motorcar rumbled to life.

We drove a long time, leaving the stops and starts and buzz of the city behind, and after an hour or more, we were on a winding road and I smelled the freshness of the countryside. Beside me, Berta softly snored. How could she sleep? I was so scared, I feared I would wet myself.

The motorcar turned onto a bumpy road. I caught a whiff of pine trees, and after a few minutes we came to a stop.

"Golly, Eggie, could you have driven any slower?" Baby Doll said in a whining voice. I heard a door open.

"I ain't no chauffeur," Eggie said. "I'm an expert in my field."

"Well, then expert to your heart's content and wake up those two hens in the backseat. And don't go and fluster 'em either."

The door beside me opened. "Get out," Eggie said.

"Would you take off this blindfold?" I said.

"Nope."

"But we've arrived at our destination, haven't we?"

"Sure."

"Then it's okay if I can see."

"She's right, you know," Baby Doll said.

Eggie tore off my blindfold.

At first, everything was pitch black. Cool wind whipped up from somewhere. My eyes adjusted and I saw trees towering up into a starry sky. The moon shimmered through the branches.

"Unhand me, you great oaf," Berta was saying, and then she was next to me, her blindfold off, too. She gazed around, blinking. Her big black handbag dangled from her arm. Baby Doll and Eggie didn't seem to care about the handbag.

Berta saw me looking at the handbag. She made the tiniest of nods.

Hope bloomed in my chest, because I knew what Berta sometimes carried in her handbag.

"Get a wiggle on, girls," Baby Doll said. "You first." She circled behind us, and both she and Eggie had their guns pointed at our backs. "Into the trees."

We marched off the dirt road and into the forest. The ground was soft and slippery with layers of pine needles. An owl hooted and tree boughs murmured. I attempted to communicate telepathically with Berta. I wished to tell her that even though our hands were tied and we were being herded by professional thugs who had a couple of loose screws and a loaded gun each, maybe we ought to make a break for it. Especially if Berta had what I thought she had in her handbag.

No dice. Berta stared stonily at the ground as she went. She was having a tough time keeping upright, as a matter of fact, what with the slippery pine needles and her old-fashioned boots. Not that my shoes were much better. And I was willing to bet that Baby Doll in her cute-as-a-button red pumps wasn't exactly comfy, either.

The ground abruptly sloped down, and I heard gushing water. I tripped, fell on my tokus, slid a couple feet, and hit the trunk of a pine tree.

I panted for a moment. My too-small dress had popped a couple seams, pine needles were poking into my undercarriage, and I realized that the rolled-up issue of *Thrilling Romance* was still in my dress pocket. What a thing to carry to your grave. "I'm sorry, but if you want us to keep walking, you must unbind our hands," I said.

"Oh, all right," Baby Doll snapped. "After all, we've got the guns. Eggie, untie 'em."

Eggie untied our hands. "Now, keep goin'," he said.

Berta and I led the way down the slope, keeping ourselves upright by grabbing tree trunks and low branches. The gushing water grew louder and louder, and at the bottom, we found ourselves on a riverbank. Moonlight bounced off the rapidly flowing water, and jutting rocks made foamy breakers.

If I dived in, would I be able to keep my head above water? What would happen if my head dashed against one of those rocks?

"Thataway," Eggie said. He pointed with the snout of his gun.

"The bridge?" Berta asked.

"Get a move on," Baby Doll said. "I need my beauty rest. I'm going to the pictures with a gorgeous feller tomorrow and I don't wanna look like no raccoon with circles under my eyes. I'm hoping he'll come up for coffee."

The bridge was wide enough for one motorcar lane, but the funny thing was, there wasn't a road leading up to it. It was simply an unfinished steel bridge in the middle of the woods.

We walked onto the bridge. There was a railing on only one side; the other side dropped to the gushing river. I could jump, and provided I didn't land on a rock, well, I'd plunge out of sight underwater and be carried downstream. Baby Doll and Eggie probably wouldn't be able to see well enough in the dark to shoot me. The wild card was Berta. Would she jump? Even now I could hear her wheezy breathing, and her footsteps were uneven. She hated heights.

"Don't even think about jumping," Baby Doll yipped at me. "Water's only a foot deep down there. You'd pop like a piñata on them rocks." She darted close and ground the gun barrel into my spine.

"Piñata, Miss Mallone?" I said. "How very cosmopolitan."

"Went to Mexico City for a job once. Stayed for the Latin lovers."

"I'll bet you did," I muttered.

"Whatcha mean by that?"

"You're no bluenose, Miss Mallone."

"You ain't no nun yourself, lady. I can just picture what sort of cootchie-cooing you and Ralph Oliver get up to."

"*What?* No, we do *not*." Well, not anymore. And now that I was about to be fogged, never again. A lump gathered in my throat.

"Yeah, sure, whatever you say. Ralph's just buggy about you, you know. Jeez, I couldn't make him shut up about you down in Cuba—"

Really?

"—going on and on about your warm heart and your knockout figure. I don't see it myself. If I saw you in a crowd, I woulda guessed you're a farmer's daughter with a bad apple pie habit. Especially in that gingham dress you've got on now. Holy cow."

"Then why did you lead me to believe Ralph and you were, you know—"

"Just yanking your chain, lady. You shouldn't make it so easy."

Was it possible? Ralph was innocent of any kind of Jack the Lad indiscretions and I hadn't given him a chance to explain and now it was . . . curtains?

We'd walked all the way across the bridge, but no one had shot Berta and me or shoved us into the river. Then I saw the huge wooden boxy things lying on the ground. Van Hoogenband had said, *The concrete supports are scheduled to be poured in the morning.*

"All right, girls," Baby Doll said, waving her gun at the boxy things. "Upsy-daisy. Climb in."

"In there?" Berta said. "Good heavens, no. Why would we do such a thing?"

Since my throat was sticking to itself, I let Baby Doll do the explaining.

"Didn't you hear what Boss said? We're puttin' your bodies in them things since the concrete boys are coming in tomorrow to pour the supports."

Berta frowned. "Supports?"

"For the bridge," Baby Doll said with an impatient sigh. "Once the concrete dries, they put 'em in the water. That's what holds up all those steel thingums."

"And you mean for our bodies to be encased inside those blocks like the jelly inside of a doughnut?" Berta asked in an affronted tone.

"That's the plan."

"It is revolting!"

"I don't make the rules. Now, hop in. Let's make this short and sweet."

Berta and I looked at each other. The gush of the river seemed to crescendo.

Again, Berta made a tiny nod. I made a tiny nod back. I wasn't sure what we were about to do, but we were about to do *something*.

I said to Baby Doll, "By the way, since I probably won't have another chance to tell you this—I simply adore your shoes."

"Thanks, honey. Splurged on 'em at Wright's just the other day." Baby Doll shifted her weight from side to side and rotated her ankles so we could admire the shape of her shoes in the moonlight.

"Oh no!" I said. "Did you—? Why, Miss Mallone, it looks like you've dinged up the heel of your shoe. Did you get it caught in a subway grate?"

"Are you kidding me? I always louse up my new shoes!" Baby Doll twisted to peer at her heel.

I shoved her. She went down as easy as an underfed duckling. Her pistol bounced out of her hands and I dived for it. The feel of that cold metal in my fingers was sheer bliss. I barely felt the pang of my skinned knees, and I didn't care that *Thrilling Romance* had fallen out of my pocket.

Out of the corner of my eye, I caught a flash of Berta pulling her .25-caliber Colt from her handbag.

"You dumb broad!" Baby Doll screamed, snatching at my ankles.

I staggered to my feet and away from her.

Berta aimed her Colt at Eggie's chest. He didn't look especially concerned, considering that *his* pistol was pointed at *her* chest. And his pistol was quite a bit bigger.

Baby Doll was crawling toward me.

Eggie's eyes lit up. "Hey. What's that? That the new issue?" He waved his gun at *Thrilling Romance*, its pages fluttering in the breeze.

I darted over and snatched it up. "Why, yes," I said. "Yes, it is. Hot off the press. You're dying to know what happens in 'Hello, Darling,' aren't you? Well, it's like this: Thelma gets caught in a rainstorm in an abandoned cottage across Big Trout Lake—"

"Shaddup!" Eggie bellowed.

"—and Bill Hampton—he was in an awful rage at Maude—went and found Thelma and—get this, he kissed Thelma—"

"NO!" Eggie howled, covering his ears with both hands. His pistol dangled from one finger.

Berta wound up and smacked Eggie's noggin with her handbag. He staggered sideways, and his pistol sailed into the river. He stared blankly after it.

"Let's tie them up," I said to Berta. "Keep your gun on Eggie. Here, Eggie, read this." I tossed him *Thrilling Romance*. Then I kicked off my shoes, unclipped my stockings, and rolled them down with one hand, keeping an eye on Baby Doll all the while. Baby Doll glared, but she didn't try to take off. How could she in those shoes? I used one stocking to bind her wrists behind her back and the other to bind her ankles out in front.

"Ow!" Baby Doll yelled.

Next, Berta disappeared into the shadows, leaving me with the gun trained on Eggie.

He was thumbing through *Thrilling Romance*, squinting to make out the print in the dark. "I just hate that Thelma," he said. "She's a sneaky little number, but Maude's sure got a problem always going after them baddies."

"Is Bill Hampton a baddie?" I asked.

Eggie shook his head. "You dames never can see 'em coming."

Berta emerged with her wool stockings draped over her arm. Together we tied Eggie's ankles and bound his huge wrists. He managed to keep hold of the magazine the whole time.

"The motorcar key," Berta said.

"Good thinking, Watson," I said.

"Sherlock, if you do not mind."

"Where's the key, Eggie?"

"Trouser pocket."

I dug it out and slid it into my brassiere for safekeeping.

"The concrete men will find you tomorrow," I said to them.

"Boss is gonna kill you!" Baby Doll shrieked. "And I'm gonna be a mess for my date tomorrow!"

"Ready?" I asked Berta.

"Ready."

We set off over the bridge. I stopped and called over my shoulder, "I wasn't lying when I said I adore your shoes!"

"Go to hell!" Baby Doll yelled back.

We made it to the motorcar and piled in.

I was so jittery, I crashed the front and then the rear fender into trees while getting turned around on the dirt track, but soon we were out on the main road.

"Where are we?" I said. "There's nothing but forest."

Berta was rummaging in the glove box. "Keep driving until we see a sign. Ah. Here is a road map of New York State—do you suppose we are still in New York State?"

"No idea."

I kept driving although I had to blink hard to keep my eyes focused. It couldn't be past midnight, but some sort of post-fright lethargy was oozing over me.

Presently we came to a small town with a sign reading WELCOME TO PERRYTOWN, POP. 1,672. Berta located Perrytown on the map— we were up the Hudson Valley. We found the highway and set off toward the south.

26

....

We arrived back in the city at around two o'clock in the morning. My eyelids felt like they had sand stuck under them. Berta was dying to use the bathroom, but she insisted she could wait until we got back to our apartment. I suggested that we park the Chevrolet across the street from the Van Hoogenband mansion.

"It is sheer madness to return to that villain's house," Berta said. "Besides which, Mr. Van Hoogenband probably has a dozen motorcars, if this is due to a misplaced sense of—"

"It's not that," I said. "It's just, well—what if those concrete-pouring fellows don't show up? Baby Doll and Eggie could get pneumonia or get eaten by wild animals and I couldn't sleep at night with their blood on my hands."

Berta heaved an annoyed sigh. I took it as a yes.

The Van Hoogenband mansion was dark. We parked his Chevrolet across the street, left the key in the glove box, and legged it to Fifth Avenue, where we flagged down a taxicab.

Our second-floor windows were lit up when we arrived at Long-fellow Street. Someone—yes, Ralph—leaned out an open window. "Thank God you're all right!" he called.

Something unfamiliar bubbled up in my chest at the sight of him. Something warm and skittish and joyful . . .

I was in love with Ralph.

With Ralph, who wasn't a Jack the Lad but a horribly misunder-stood, gallant darling who thought I had a warm heart and a knock-out figure.

Berta paid the cabbie with a handful of change. He muttered something unkind under his breath and chugged away.

Upstairs, Ralph let us in. His hair tufted and his eyes were bleary. "I've been worried sick about you two," he said. "Sorry I had to pick the lock. When I arrived, Grace Whiddle was sound asleep." He passed me the wiggling, whining Cedric, and I buried my nose in his fragrant fluff. I blinked back tears.

Berta rushed off to the bathroom.

"Where's Grace?" I asked Ralph, feeling shy all of a sudden.

"Left with her mother hours ago."

"Rats!" Berta and I had missed our chance to thoroughly ques-tion Grace about the murders.

"I stuck around because it seemed funny that you and Mrs. Lund-gren left Grace and Cedric alone," Ralph said. "Oh—Mrs. Whiddle cut me a check for finding Grace."

"She cut *you* a check?"

"Don't worry. I'm signing over the whole kit and caboodle to you and Mrs. Lundgren."

You see? He was such a gentleman. "Is that why you're here?" I asked, pulling off my dirt-caked shoes. "Sophronia Whiddle tele-phoned and told you we'd caught Grace?"

"That's right. Say, you haven't told me where you've been, and judging by the smudges on your cheeks and the way that muscle under your eye is twitching, I can tell it wasn't to take in a musical comedy. Hold still." Ralph picked something out of my hair. A pine needle. "Well?"

I longed to tell Ralph how I felt about him, how I'd been childish and blind, to twine my arms around his neck—

"You all right, kid?" Ralph asked. "You look a little dizzy. Need to sit down?"

"No—yes." I turned and walked toward the sitting room sofa.

"Whew, kid, your whole caboose is just covered with dirt," Ralph said behind me. "What've you been doing? Tobogganing without a toboggan?"

"What?" I twisted around. Ugh. My bottom looked like a mud pie. I sat quickly on the sofa to hide it, Cedric on my lap.

"Could I fix you a drink?" Ralph asked.

"No booze in the house."

"Teetotaling?"

"Hah. Broke."

"Tell me what happened." Ralph sat down next to me. He picked a twig off my sleeve. "What's next? A whole family of badgers crawling out of your brassiere?"

My heart was brimming and Ralph glowed like a ginger-headed god to me, but I knew he wouldn't let up until he had answers. So in a rush I explained how Baby Doll and Eggie had kidnapped us and taken us to Van Hoogenband's mansion in the city, how he thought we had Grace Whiddle's diary, and how, when he realized we *didn't* have the diary but still believed we knew what was written in it—thanks to me and my big mouth—he ordered his thugs to take us out to a bridge site in the middle of nowhere and murder us. "Obviously, we got away." I petted Cedric to hide the way my hands shook. "Baby Doll and Eggie are still out there, I suppose."

"A bridge site?" Ralph said.

"Yes. Why do you look so excited about a bridge site?"

"And you say Van H did all this because of what's written in Grace Whiddle's diary?"

"Yes."

"The diary!" Ralph was on his feet and pacing. I'd never seen him so agitated before. "Well, then, there's nothing doing. I've got to get my hands on that diary."

I stared at him. "Mind telling me why? Because the last thing I knew, you were only trying to find Grace. For her mother. What do you want with her diary?"

Ralph looked at me like he'd forgotten I was in the room. "Where *exactly* did Van H's goons take you, by the way?"

"It was about five miles outside of a town called Perrytown up in the Hudson Valley—but you haven't answered my question. Hold it. You're investigating Van Hoogenband, aren't you? That's why you were slinking around at Breakerhead the other night. You lied to me!"

Ralph sat down again and took my hand in his big, warm, rough one. "Listen to me, kid, and listen hard. I'll never lie to you, and I never have. If there's something I can't tell you, I simply decline to comment."

"Does that make it better? Is 'declining to comment' different than lying?"

"That's the best I can do."

"Why are you investigating Van Hoogenband?"

"It probably doesn't have any bearing on your investigation."

"Tell me."

Ralph sighed. "All right. Long story short, it looks like Van H may have been bribing people he shouldn't have. I've been hired to get the goods on him. If he's so hot and bothered about Grace's diary, well, I'm thinking that diary may contain the evidence I need to clinch my investigation. If only I'd known he wants the diary earlier this evening when I had a chance to talk to Grace."

"Who are you working for?"

"I have to decline to comment on that one, sweetheart."

Okay. That was annoying. But my heart was still brimming—if a little less than before—and Ralph still looked like a ginger-headed, well, demigod. This was the Magic Moment, our hands clasped, our eyes locked. "Ralph. Listen to me. I've got to get something off my chest. . . ." My voice trailed off.

Ralph was not gazing poignantly into my eyes; he was inspecting a gaping-split seam in the side of the borrowed gingham dress. My sad, wrinkly gray underpants were so exposed, they may as well have been flying on a flagpole.

I grabbed a sofa cushion and hid myself, blushing hotly. Hadn't Ralph seen the yearning in my eyes or heard the winsome catch of my breath? Jeez.

"You did have a rough time of it, didn't you?" Ralph said in a bemused voice. "That dress of yours is so kaput, you're lucky you weren't driving all the way back to New York City in nothing but your skivvies. Why's that dress so tight? Now, what was it you were saying to me? Something you need to get off your chest?"

"Off my chest? No. Nope. I said I need some rest. This has been the longest day of my life; I'm so bushed, I'll fall asleep if I blink too long; and unfortunately, at night this sofa serves as my bed." I cleared my throat.

"Course." Ralph stood, looking a little confused. "As soon as you and Mrs. Lundgren are finished with the bathroom, I'll sleep in the tub, all right? You two might sleep more soundly knowing there's a man in the place."

"Fine."

I slept on the sofa behind a folding screen with my face mashed between Cedric and a cushion. Cedric's belly gurgled all night. It's funny, but those gurgles were comforting. Amid all that anxiety and uncertainty in that apartment that wasn't really mine, they were the sound of home.

I was conscious of Ralph's presence in the apartment, too. Not that he snored or anything. It was more like there was a constant hum of humiliation in the back of my mind. Because maybe Ralph did think, as Baby Doll had said, that I was warmhearted and the proud owner of a knockout figure. But we certainly weren't on the same page romance-wise. I might've jumped to the juicy parts in the middle of the book, but Ralph had stuck the bookmark in Chapter Two.

It could've been worse. I could've told him how I felt.

27

When I woke in the morning, stuffy heat had already seeped into the apartment. I lay still for a minute or two, disoriented. Wait. Van Hoogenband. The bridge. That horrible black roiling water . . . I bolted upright, panting for breath.

Berta and Ralph's voices wafted from the kitchen along with the aromas of coffee and bacon. I got up, folded my sheets, and stowed them in the foyer closet. Then I washed, did my hair and makeup in the bathroom, stuck fresh plasters on my skinned knees, changed into a pink silk dress with a boat neck, a dropped waist, and plenty of wiggle room—no more split seams for me, thanks—and went into the kitchen.

"Good morning," I said.

Cedric's tail whapped on the floor.

"Morning, Lola," Ralph said, drinking coffee at the table. Hair slicked and fully dressed, he looked too good to have slept in a bathtub. True, his jaw glinted with gold stubble, but as far as I was concerned, that was the icing on the cake of his handsomeness.

Darn him.

"How are you, Berta?" I asked. Although her bun was perfect and her dress looked crisp, wrinkles creased her forehead. Berta never looked wrinkly. Last night's kidnapping had taken its toll.

"Well, it would feel rather nice not to wonder if thugs were about to burst in at any second," she said, standing at the stove and poking at frying bacon with a fork.

"Van Hoogenband doesn't know our exact address, because of that blotch of mascara on the card." I sat. "He said we have a lair."

"He did?" The corner of Ralph's mouth twitched.

"But we do not have a lair, do we?" Berta said. "It is merely a stroke of luck that he has not been able to find us here. Do not forget that we were kidnapped on this very street last night."

A chill slithered down my back despite the warmth. Berta was right. Someone could be watching our apartment now.

"Look at the front page," Berta said, tapping the newspaper on the table.

I looked.

FOREIGN ANARCHIST ASSASSINATES SENATOR!

Berta passed me a cup of coffee. Her lips were grim. "Mr. Ulf will never get a fair trial. We must act."

I skimmed the article. A spent Luger Parabellum cartridge had been found near the boardwalk stage. This was the same pistol widely used in the German army, and Tibor Ulf admitted that his sons had served in the German army during the Great War.

I tried to sip my coffee and spilled it. Brown droplets sank into the newsprint. "This is awful," I said. "What should we do?"

"Locate the true murderer, Beaulah Starr, of course," Berta said. She cleared her throat. "By the by, I made it to the sixth page."

"What do you mean, you made it?" I flipped to page six. "Oh."

In a small photograph, Berta posed, hands on hips, in her black woolen bathing suit. The caption read, *Bathing beauty Mrs. Lundgren, head detective of the Discreet Retrieval Agency and oldest pageant contestant.*

"Geewhillikins," I said. "Is there no end to our . . . fame? And— head detective?"

"I thought it sounded better. Now, then. About Beaulah Starr—"

"Yes, about her," I said. I told Berta and Ralph how I'd witnessed Beaulah rescuing an inchworm with her cigarette tin. "So you see, she can't be the murderer. Murderers don't pamper bugs. Murderers squish bugs."

Ralph hid a grin in his coffee cup.

"What is so humorous?" I asked.

Berta stared stonily at me for a full five seconds, holding a plate of bacon aloft just to torture me. At last she said, "I do believe that is the most frivolous thing that has ever escaped your lips, Mrs. Woodby. Why, just this morning I swatted two houseflies here in the kitchen. Does that make me a murderer?"

"No," I mumbled. Berta set the plate of bacon down and I dug in. Honestly, I did suspect that Beaulah hadn't told me everything she knew about Muffy's death. She had been so shifty when we spoke in the hedge maze. But I was also convinced she wasn't the murderer. After a few bites of bacon, I said, "Even if Beaulah is our top suspect, well, we should still continue to investigate Raymond, Hermie, Pete, and Grace. They were all at Willow Acres *and* Coney Island. That can't be a coincidence. One lead we have is Mrs. Dun from Muffy Morris's Swiss finishing school, remember? We still have our appointment to see her this morning at eleven o'clock."

"I had forgotten all about that," Berta said, ladling pancake batter onto a griddle. "However, first things first. You should begin by ringing up Beaulah Starr's boarding house and Willow Acres and inquiring as to her whereabouts."

"*I* should?"

"I am cooking pancakes. Or did you not wish to have pancakes, Mrs. Woodby? They are buckwheat."

I went quickly to the telephone in the hallway, ignoring Ralph's chuckles. He could chuckle all he wished, but I knew if it came down to the wire, he'd do handstands for Berta's buckwheat pancakes.

"Hello," I said when I was put through to Beaulah Starr's boarding house in Hare's Hollow. "Could I please speak to Miss Starr?"

"That harlot?" the landlady squawked. "Gone. She stopped in last night only long enough to pack a suitcase in a hurry."

"Did she say where she was going?"

"Who did you say you were, young lady?"

"Oh, her—her sister."

"You sound like a harlot, too. Your mother didn't raise you girls right!"

"Beaulah packed a suitcase," I said. "Did she say anything about where she was going and why?"

"I asked her about next month's rent that's coming due, and she yammered on with some crazy talk about someone trying to kill her—"

"Kill her?"

"Are you deaf, too? A deaf harlot! Last thing this world needs! I don't have time for this. I'm making pickled carrots." The landlady hung up.

My heart beat fast. Someone trying to kill Beaulah? That was a monkey wrench. I dialed 0 and had the operator put me through to Chisholm's office at Willow Acres.

"Yes?" Chisholm said coldly.

"Hello, Chisholm darling," I said. "Nurse Beaulah—is she in?"

"Lola, is that you? No. Nurse Beaulah missed her shift yesterday and then had the audacity to telephone and say she wouldn't be in until further notice because someone is attempting to murder her."

Uh-oh.

"I had not noted any paranoia in her behavior before," Chisholm said. "It must be a recent development, doubtless the result of her excessive fondness for ham. I am pleased that you telephoned, Lola, because I have just spoken with your mother about your peculiar visit to Amberley two days ago, and we both—"

I hung up so fast, the ringer clanged.

Back in the kitchen, I told Berta and Ralph how Beaulah was on the run from someone trying to kill her.

"So she says," Berta said. "I would warrant that it is a ruse—a smoke screen, you see, to deflect attention from her own nefarious actions. Every dime novel villain employs such a strategy."

I looked at Ralph.

"I'll stay out of this," he said, glugging blueberry syrup on pancakes. "I'm only sticking around for the grub."

"And the diary," I said.

"And the diary." He *almost* appeared nonchalant.

"I wonder where Beaulah has gone?" Berta said. "How will we find her now? She could be anywhere."

"Hopefully she isn't dead in a ditch," I said.

"Do not be melodramatic, Mrs. Woodby."

"I hope you're correct about the smoke screen." Coffee and bacon curdled in my stomach. "I'm going to telephone Raymond and Hermie to ask about what they saw at Coney Island yesterday. Who knows, one of them may have even seen Beaulah."

But there was no answer at Raymond's house in Hare's Hollow—funny that not even his servants were picking up—and the butler at Inchbald Hall told me that Hermie was "most uncharacteristically" still abed. "I was forced to give the poodle an airing myself," the butler said in a sour tone, and then restrained himself from revealing more, despite my prying.

I hung up. Hermie Inchbald had had a rough night. How come?

I reported all this to Berta and Ralph, but neither was too interested. Berta was still pondering how to locate Beaulah, and Ralph said, "Would you call up the Whiddle house, kid? Find out if we can see Grace about her diary?"

"*You* telephone Grace," I said crossly. "I've earned my buckwheat pancakes by now. Ask the operator for Clyde's Bluff."

Ralph took his turn with the telephone, and in what seemed like one minute he returned. "A maid told me that Grace and her mother will be at—" He checked something in his notebook. "—Antoinette G. Lovell's Bridal Shop on Fifth Avenue at one o'clock."

Of course Ralph had gotten a maid to spill the beans.

"So we'll head to the bridal shop together, like one big happy family," Ralph said.

Peachy. Berta, Ralph, and I had three separate agendas. Berta only wished to hunt down Beaulah Starr. I wished to follow up on all the other suspects. And Ralph? All he cared about was finding out if Grace Whiddle's diary contained the evidence he needed to bust Van Hoogenband for bribery.

It promised to be one zonker of a day.

We finished eating and cleaned up the kitchen. Ralph went outside with the Duesy keys and drove it around to the other side of the block in case Van Hoogenband was still searching for our lair. Meanwhile, Berta, Cedric, and I sneaked out of the building through the rear basement entrance, hurried down an alleyway, and found Ralph idling at the curb. We climbed aboard and motored off into the hot city to meet Mrs. Dun.

28

The Imperial Ballroom stood on jostling Forty-second Street. We couldn't find a parking space, so Berta said she would wait in the double-parked motorcar while Ralph and I went in.

"But this is our investigation, Berta," I said.

"Yes, but Mr. Oliver is so persuasive with ladies. Besides, what has Mrs. Dun to do with our chief suspect, Beaulah Starr? Nothing. You are wasting your time."

I didn't want to argue either point with Berta. Besides, she was minding Cedric.

Ralph and I went upstairs, through a pair of tall doors, and found ourselves in a cool, silent ballroom. Crystal chandeliers hung unlit, the dance floor gleamed, and the orchestra dais held nothing but empty chairs and music stands.

"You must be the detectives," a woman said, coming toward us. She wore a sequined dress and high-heeled dancing shoes. Her dyed orange hair was tucked beneath a feathered headband. Bags puffed under her eyes.

"Mrs. Dun," I said, holding out my hand, "I am Lola Woodby of the Discreet Retrieval Agency. This is my, um, assistant, Mr. Oliver."

"He's your assistant?" Mrs. Dun shook my hand in a hurry in order to move on to shaking Ralph's. "Do you enjoy ballroom dancing, Mr. Oliver? We suffer a chronic shortage of gentlemen here at the Imperial. Stop by anytime you like, and I'll give you a discount."

"Say, thanks," Ralph said. "I just might take you up on that, if my boss here ever gives me a day off." He winked at me. "She's a slave driver."

"You look like you'd be just velvety on your feet," Mrs. Dun said.

"Let's get down to business," I interrupted, "for I know you must be very busy, Mrs. Dun. My partner, Mrs. Lundgren, tells me that you attended Institut Alpenrose the same time as did the late Muffy Morris, and that you knew something of a scandal attached to her."

"I did attend Institut Alpenrose, yes. I know what you're thinking— why would a dancing instructress have had such an education?" Mrs. Dun smiled bitterly. "A finishing school education is perfectly useless if one doesn't marry well, as I have spent the last two decades learning. Mr. Dun is in the upholstery trade. And the scandal? Yes. Well, no. I mean to say—I did not like to speak of this on the telephone because it's so indelicate, but there was a scandal, yes—all of us girls were aware of it to one degree or the other. But it wasn't Muffy. It was Violet Wilbur."

I frowned. "Miss Wilbur told me the scandal was Muffy's."

"Well, she would, wouldn't she? Deflecting attention from herself, probably."

"What did Miss Wilbur do?" I asked.

"Carried on with the horseback riding instructor during her final year at the school. A German man. Married with two small children. Well, he lost his job, of course, and Violet was very nearly expelled. So was Muffy, now that I think of it."

"Muffy? Why?"

"She aided Violet in the whole deception. Lied for her, that sort of thing, in order for Violet to sneak off to the stables for her assignations."

"But the girls weren't expelled?"

"No. In the end, the headmistress decided—this is only what I heard, I don't know for certain—she decided that Violet had in fact been victimized by the man."

"Because he was older than she?"

"That, and because it turned out he was some sort of criminal. A burglar. Stole silverware, paintings, that sort of thing, from the villas about the lake when their owners were not there. So everyone suddenly began boo-hooing for poor, frail little Violet having been seduced by a scoundrel, and—you've met her, yes?—so then you can imagine how smug she was about *that*."

"You don't suppose she was a victim?"

"Oh no. She was a thrill-seeker, particularly when it came to boys. She preferred the baddest boys in the village. Then I believe even those boys bored her, and that's when she started working on a grown man."

"You fancy Violet seduced him?"

"Well, I would not go that far. But mark my words, Violet Wilbur is no victim. How can I put this? She sort of thrives on the energy of bad men, gulps it down like, oh, like Nosferatu sucking blood— did you see that picture? Women like her—we've met them before, haven't we?—when men mistreat them, it seems to make them feel delicate and feminine. Didn't you see that little scandal about Violet published in the papers about, oh, five years ago? She'd been carrying on with a dashing fellow who was smuggling naughty books into the country."

This didn't sound like the Miss Priss Violet Wilbur I knew. "And this horseback riding instructor," I said, "what was his name?"

"I don't recall."

"Was it Tibor Ulf?" Ralph asked.

Mrs. Dun tipped her head. "Tibor Ulf? It could have been, I suppose."

I knew Ulf was innocent of shooting Senator Morris, but it was possible, by a stretch, that he was Violet Wilbur's former lover. Although Ulf didn't strike me as capable of either burgling villas or seducing schoolgirls. Despite the muscles and the postage stamp–sized shorts, he had a courtly, old-fashioned air.

"Was anything of this scandal published in the Swiss newspapers at the time?" I asked.

"Oh no. The school kept it all very hush-hush. Now, that is all I know, so if you haven't any more questions, I must begin preparing for my eleven-thirty Beginning Viennese Waltz class. I must move everything against the walls. Last week one couple crashed into and destroyed the Victrola in the middle of 'By the Beautiful Blue Danube.'"

"I think that is all for now, Mrs. Dun," I said. "Thank you, and if you think of anything else, please do telephone the agency." I rummaged in my handbag for a card but remembered too late I didn't have one. Ralph scribbled my telephone number on the back of one of his cards.

"Good-bye," Mrs. Dun said, her eyes latched longingly on Ralph.

Not that I could blame her, but gee whiz.

"Quick," I said to Berta as I climbed into the Duesy's passenger seat. "Pass me the Alpenrose directory."

Berta, in the backseat, was flushed for some reason, and Cedric's leash was clipped on. Berta handed over the directory. I flicked through and found Violet Wilbur's address and rattled it off to Ralph. He fired up the engine and we were off.

"Would you please tell me what is happening?" Berta said.

I told her how Violet, according to Mrs. Dun, had had an affair with the German horseback riding instructor at Institut Alpenrose. "Maybe it was Tibor Ulf," I said. "Maybe Violet is still in love with him now. She said something to the effect that she'd do anything for the man she loved—oh yes, that she'd 'walk the plank' for him."

"That is very intemperate," Berta said. "Do you suggest Violet Wilbur murdered the Morrises to somehow benefit Mr. Ulf? Have you forgotten he is in jail?"

I shrugged. "Maybe her plan backfired. It's only a half-baked theory."

"Half-baked?" Berta sniffed. "It is still batter in the bowl."

"What's your plan if you find Violet at home?" Ralph asked me.

"Confront her and hope she cracks?" I said. "She does have fragile nerves."

"I made progress in the investigation while you were in the Imperial Ballroom," Berta said.

I swiveled in my seat. "I thought I saw a glint in your eye."

"Beaulah Starr mentioned that she has a friend who works in a feed store, so Cedric and I walked to a public telephone booth and rang up the Hare's Hollow feed store."

"You left a double-parked motorcar empty?" Ralph asked. "It could've been towed."

"One must take great risks to make great strides," Berta said. "And I did make a great stride. Beaulah's friend—described as her best friend by the man I spoke with on the telephone—is named Harriet Klipper, and she will be in to work at the feed store at three o'clock this afternoon. I shall telephone again then, and I expect to discover Beaulah's whereabouts. I do hope you will not utterly exhaust us dashing to and fro for no reason until then, Mrs. Woodby."

"No reason?" I cried.

"We must not forget your little problem of straying from the topic," Berta said.

"Just because I'm not ready to dismiss all our other suspects yet doesn't mean——"

"Ladies, ladies," Ralph said. "It's okay to go sniffing down two different trails. That's what it's like working with a partner."

A pause. Cedric panted and traffic clamored past.

"Have you ever worked with a partner, Mr. Oliver?" Berta asked.

"Nope. And you two are reminding me why."

Violet's town house on the Upper West Side was a trim white stone affair with topiaries on the porch, one block away from Central Park. Somebody was in the process of moving in next door: Two movers' vans half blocked the street, and sweaty men in coveralls carried furniture through the front door. Ralph parked at the curb behind the movers' vans.

Violet wasn't at home, her maid told Ralph and me as we stood on the porch. Berta had once again elected to wait in the motorcar with Cedric.

"Miss Wilbur is giving a lecture this evening," the maid said. "At the Xavier House Hotel. You could see her there."

"What time?" I asked.

"Seven o'clock, I think, because this morning Miss Wilbur's gentleman told . . ." The maid fell silent and she bit her lip. She'd been instructed not to blab.

"Gentleman?" I prompted.

"I spoke out of turn, ma'am. I really can't say." The maid glanced over her shoulder into the entry hall.

Ralph and I traded a look.

"Is Miss Wilbur's gentleman still here?" I asked the maid.

She pinched her lips and blinked. "Never said that."

Violet's gentleman was inside. I was sure of it. This confirmed that Violet's gentleman couldn't possibly be Tibor Ulf, since he was in jail.

Why did I suddenly feel like a hound sniffing blood?

"Well, thank you," I said.

The maid shut the door.

Ralph and I walked toward the Duesy.

"I want to go in the house," I said in an excited whisper. "I'm perishing to find out who Violet's gentleman is. This is important. I just know it." I stopped on the sidewalk next to the Duesy. "I'm going to march right back up to the front door and demand that the maid let me in. I'll say Violet borrowed something from me—a piece of jewelry—and I urgently need it back."

"I've got a better idea," Ralph said. "See that balcony on the second story?"

"Yes."

"And see how the town house next door has its own second-story balcony?"

"You don't mean—"

"Why not? There's a parade of moving men going in and out. We can say we're real estate agents if anyone asks, go upstairs, out onto that balcony, and climb over to Violet's balcony. Piece of cake."

"Monkey business," Berta said out the Duesy's open window. "I shall continue to wait in the motorcar."

29

Sneaking into Violet Wilbur's town house really was a piece of cake. At first. The next-door moving men didn't question Ralph and me as we went inside and upstairs. I would've liked to think this was because of my dazzling smile or Ralph's masterful stride, but it was probably because the moving men were too hot and wheezy to talk.

In the front-facing room upstairs, Ralph unlatched the balcony windows and we went out. Ralph climbed easily over the thigh-high railings and onto Violet's balcony, and then lent me a hand over. Only when I was safe on Violet's balcony did I dare look down. No gawking passersby. No moving men shaking fists. Only Berta and Cedric watching us from the Duesy.

I wondered if Berta was impressed by my lithe cat burglar abilities.

"Violet's window is open, thanks to this heat," Ralph said in low tones, "so all we've got to do is, nice and easy, take a peek in the—*Lola!*"

I blatted like a baby elephant as I tumbled through the window in a tangle of curtains. I landed in a heap on the floor.

Ralph stepped silently inside and helped untangle me from the curtains. "You okay, kid?" he whispered.

"Never been better." I wiggled my shoe back on and stood. We were in a bedroom that was only dimly lit because all the curtains were drawn. The door was shut.

"Good thing no one's in here," Ralph whispered. "I myself generally like to do a little recon before I go barging into a place. Just in case."

"Well, *I* don't," I whispered back, although naturally, I hadn't meant to fall through the window. I'd lost my balance in my tippy T-straps. "And let me make something clear, Ralph: This is *my* investigation, not yours, so I'm in charge. No muscling in."

"You got it." Ralph sauntered away. "Well, well. Lookee here." He picked up a bottle from the night table and tipped it upside down. "French champagne, and not a drop left."

"Two champagne glasses. And the bed's a mess." My cheeks grew warm when I saw slithery mauve garments tangled in the sheets.

"Somebody had some fun last night," Ralph said. "No doubt about it, there's a boyfriend in the picture."

Yes. But who?

As I was scanning the items on Violet's vanity table—kohl and lipsticks and French perfume, all brand-new—footsteps sounded overhead.

"Someone's walking around on the third floor," Ralph whispered.

"The maid?" I tipped my head. "Scratch that. Listen. I hear dishes clattering downstairs. The maid is in the kitchen. That is Violet's gentleman walking around up there." I headed for the door.

Ralph caught up to me and put a hand on my shoulder. "Are you nuts?"

"That's what they say."

"This could be dangerous."

"I know how to handle men." I shrugged Ralph's hand off my shoulder.

"I won't argue that point with you, kid."

"Good." I didn't actually have a plan, but geewhillikins, I wasn't about to tell Ralph he was correct. I sashayed out the door, down the hall, and tiptoed up the carpeted stairs to the third story. Ralph was right behind me. We looked through an open door.

Tall south-facing windows flooded the spacious room with light. Easels displayed paintings in progress. A table held brushes, cloths, smeary palettes, and crunched metal tubes of oil paint. A man in a seersucker suit and a boater hat was stuffing some of the painting supplies into a leather satchel. He hummed in a reedy tenor as he worked.

"Golly. It's Gil Morris," I whispered almost inaudibly to Ralph, who hadn't to my knowledge met Gil before. "I must speak with him."

"How are you going to make him talk?"

"Oh, I don't know. The Friend and Foe tactic?"

"Where'd you learn about that?"

"From a book." A trashy dime novel, to be exact. In this tactic, one policeman acted nasty toward their subject, and the other acted sympathetic. According to Thad Parker, hero of my favorite series, it was a crackerjack strategy for getting villains to yap. "I'll be the Foe."

Gil spun around, crying, "Who's there?" His eyes bulged when he saw Ralph and me in the doorway. "What on earth—?"

I strolled into the room. "Well, well, well. Mr. Morris. What, no mourning attire? I'd have thought you'd be in head-to-toe black after losing both of your parents in such quick succession. It's almost as though you're pleased they're toast."

"I am pleased." Gil eyed Ralph. "Who are you?"

"Ralph Oliver, private detective."

"You brought along an Irish hooligan to rough me up?" Gil said to me.

"No. I'm the tough one. Ralph's as mushy as my aunt Dorinda. Tell me, Mr. Morris, why are you stealing Violet Wilbur's painting supplies?"

"*Violet's* painting supplies?" Gil scoffed. "Violet can't even paint her own lipstick on straight."

"That's a bit like the pot calling the kettle black, isn't it?" I said. "Your own paintings—well, have you ever considered visiting the eye doctor? Or perhaps—your atrocious painting of the farm animals is still giving me nightmares, you know—a mental sanatorium would be the ticket."

"Ouch," Ralph murmured.

I pointed to one of the paintings on an easel. "Look. This painting here doesn't look like one of yours, Mr. Morris." The canvas depicted a woman in an Elizabethan collar that made her head look like it was on display in a cake shop window. It wasn't quite done—the collar was only half painted—yet it had been made with great skill. "Nor does this one." The exact same painting stood on the adjacent easel—except it was finished. "No googly eyes in sight. Violet Wilbur made these, didn't she?"

"I know nothing," Gil said, setting his jaw.

"I don't believe you," I said.

"You can't make me talk."

"Actually, I can." I stepped over to the table with all the painting supplies and picked up one of the paintbrushes.

"Aw, Lola," Ralph said. "Not the paintbrush tactic!"

"Yes," I said coolly. "I'm afraid it's come to that." I wondered what to do with the paintbrush. Tickle Gil's nose until he cracked? I held it up and advanced toward him.

"Flossie!" Gil shrieked toward the open door. "Flossie, can you hear me? Telephone the police! Hurry!"

"Who is Flossie?" I asked.

"The maid. She will telephone the police, you know."

And I was just getting warmed up with this Foe business. "I knew Violet Wilbur was selling forgeries, but I didn't know she made them, too." I gestured with my paintbrush in what I hoped was a threatening manner. "Who knew she had such skill? These paintings are absolute dillies. Did Violet learn to paint in finishing school, or, no, they're so fine, she must have had training in—"

"Shut up!" Gil screamed, clutching his cheek. "*Shut up!*"

"What?" I blinked.

Ralph was trying hard not to laugh.

Then it hit me.

Gil had made the forgeries. "*You* made these?" I asked.

"Quite obviously!" Gil resumed dumping painting supplies into his satchel. "Flossie! Are you telephoning the police?"

"Wait a minute," I said. "Why do you produce those hideous paintings that hang in people's bathrooms when you can make things like this?"

"To put all of you off the scent."

"Is that why you were painting the day we met you at your father's house?"

"Yes. Dad told me you were coming. I wished to keep up the ruse for your benefit. I'm not stupid, you know." Gil stuffed paint tubes into his satchel.

"A touch risky, isn't it, peddling multiple copies of the same paintings?"

"Saves me some effort, and no one has ever noticed before. Dingdongs."

"I saw Violet Wilbur collect a delivery of fake Dutch old masters at Chisholm Woodby's house. I suppose that was you driving the delivery truck?"

"I need not answer your questions, you interfering nitwit."

I was still holding the paintbrush, so I grabbed a tube of oil paint—black, excellent—squirted it on a palette, and dipped the paintbrush. "I know," I said. "I think I'll try my hand at painting, too. How about a nice, fat, black mustache on Mrs. Elizabethan Collar here? Perhaps some curls at the tips?" I went up to one of the paintings, paintbrush aloft.

"Stop!" Gil screamed.

I turned.

"That painting took me absolute eons, you dumbbell. You wish to know about Violet and the copies? Suit yourself—but get that black paint away from my work! There. Oops, you've gotten paint on your lovely pink dress."

Phooey.

"Violet's decorating business provided me with a never-ending list of buyers," Gil said. "Now that the paterfamilias has kicked the bucket, of course, I needn't bother anymore. I've just been to see the family lawyers. I inherited everything. I'm free. I need not marry Grace Whiddle anymore. I was only marrying her birthing hips so Mummy and Dad wouldn't cut me off. But now, I can travel Europe as a free man."

"What about Violet?"

"What do you mean?"

"Isn't she your, um, paramour?"

Gil didn't answer; he was going toward the door, satchel in hand.

"Violet prefers baddies," I called after him, "and with this forgery racket, it seems that you're a baddie. I wouldn't have thought it of you, Mr. Morris—all the seersucker quite put me off—but now I see that you're just the sort of enterprising criminal Violet would walk the plank for."

"You're insane," Gil said. "An insane busybody." He was in the doorway now.

"Who do you believe killed your parents?" I asked.

"Oh, I don't simply believe. I know."

"Who?"

Gil turned. "That man-eating floozy in a nurse's uniform, Beaulah Starr. You really aren't very good sleuths if you haven't figured out that she was involved in an affair with my father."

"We knew that," I said.

"Yet you don't suspect her? Good Lord. She has the oldest motive in the book."

"Did you tell your suspicions about Beaulah to the police?"

"Why would I? She did me a favor in bumping off the folks. It was her, though. She has a gun."

"Go on," I said with a sinking stomach.

"She was carrying on with Father for several months, you know, even at the Long Island house when Mother was away in France this spring. Naturally, I was a bit curious as to who Beaulah was— although God knows it wasn't the first time Father had a bit of tart on the side—so once, when Beaulah had left her handbag on the carpet in the library when they'd gone up to the bedroom, I had a look. Saw her driver's license and her Willow Acres identification card. And, of course, I saw her gun. A foul little Luger pistol—one of those German things. Ah, I see from your expressions that you've read how it was a Luger that killed Dad? Yes. That nurse merely committed two sordid crimes of greed and passion. So very blah."

Was it really so simple, after all? Beaulah Starr, double murderess? How could I have made such a duff about the inchworm and all that? Berta would never allow me to live this down.

Gil slipped away down the stairs. A siren keened somewhere nearby.

Uh-oh. Flossie had summoned the fuzz.

"We'd better skate," Ralph said.

We rushed down the stairs, to the front bedroom, and out onto the balcony. No police in sight. Ralph climbed over to the next-door balcony and helped me over, and then we were inside the house that was crawling with furniture movers.

"Was that your first time playing the Foe?" Ralph asked as we went down the stairs.

"Yes, and this is the last time I'll be wearing this dress." Smelly black oil paint streaked across the skirt.

Ralph grinned. "Well, you did all right."

We looked out a downstairs window to see a paddy wagon swing to a stop in front of Violet's house.

"Oh no," I whispered. "Where is Berta?"

"There." Ralph pointed.

Berta had moved the Duesy to a spot up the block in front of the movers' vans. She was at the wheel.

Ralph and I walked calmly out the front door, up the sidewalk, and got into the Duesy, Ralph in front and me in the back.

Berta started the engine and pulled into the street. "When I heard sirens approaching, I suspected you would require a getaway car," she said.

"You're a lifesaver." I gathered Cedric onto my lap and looked back. Gil and the maid were speaking with a police officer on Violet's front porch.

Crumb cake.

"Well?" Berta said. "What occurred in there?"

I told her how we'd found Gil Morris, of all people, clearing out his painting supplies, and how he was Violet Wilbur's accomplice— and the artistic talent—in a forgery scheme.

"But is he also Violet's gentleman?" Berta asked, steering carefully through a busy intersection.

"Well, actually, I'm not sure," I said. "He didn't admit it, but it all seems to line up, doesn't it? Oh, and Gil is throwing Violet over in order to sling off to Europe. However, it doesn't matter much, Berta, because you were correct about Beaulah Starr." I swallowed. "Gil confirmed that Beaulah was, um, making whoopee with his dad, Senator Morris, and that, ah, he once saw a Luger pistol in her handbag."

"*Aha!*" Berta cried, almost clipping a parked motorcar. "I told you so. At three o'clock, when I telephone the feed store and discover where Beaulah is hiding out, this matter will be nearly sewn up."

It sounded too good to be true.

Ralph checked his wristwatch. "Well, time to head over to the bridal shop to see Grace Whiddle, ladies."

"About her diary," I said darkly.

"Yup."

30

Four lanes of motorcars, buses, and delivery trucks rumbled in both directions on Fifth Avenue. Ladies with parcels and men in bowlers hurried on the sidewalk in front of Antoinette G. Lovell's Bridal Shop. The shop windows displayed fussy gowns of silk, satin, and embroidery.

Ralph parked half a block away and studied the shop. "I'm pretty sure fellows aren't welcome in that joint, so I can't see how I'm going in, short of slapping on a wig and some lipstick."

"You'd probably need to shave, too," I said.

"I guess I'll wait here with the pooch," Ralph said, "so I'm counting on you two to get the lowdown."

"You look like someone's sticking pins in you," I said.

"Daggers, kid. I like to gather my own info. Now, listen. All you need to do is ask Grace where her diary is."

"That's it?"

"Sure. That's all I need to know. How tough can it be to pinch a diary from a debutante?"

"You'd be surprised," I said. "But all right."

Berta and I got out. Berta was more convinced than ever that Beaulah Starr was our woman, but she required the lavatory. I was keen to ask Grace Whiddle what she might've seen or heard at Willow Acres and Coney Island, and to try to suss out if she was a murder suspect or not. Berta had been with Grace backstage at the Mermaid Queen Pageant when Senator Morris was shot, but she didn't have an alibi for Muffy's death.

Inside the bridal shop, powder blue carpet muffled the noise of the street. Snooty-looking plaster mannequins on podiums displayed wedding dresses and shoes. Sophronia Whiddle perched on a pouf in the middle of the shop, her back to the door. A schoolmarmish lady in gray hovered near her.

"Have you an appointment, mesdames?" Schoolmarm trilled.

Sophronia turned. Her eyes flared when she saw Berta and me.

"No," I said, "but I was in the neighborhood and thought I'd pop in for a browse."

"Mrs. Woodby," Sophronia said nastily, "I am afraid you are no longer eligible to wear a white wedding gown."

I beamed. "No, silly me, I ought to have mentioned it—remember dear Lillian will be wed soon. I'm looking for her. By the way—is my mother about?"

"No, I dropped her at her home on Park Avenue," Sophronia said. "And I was certain Lillian was having her dress made at Worth's. In Paris."

Why did Sophronia Whiddle know that and I didn't? I was a rotten sister. "Yes, well, she's had a change of heart. Brides do, you know. Jitters, et cetera."

"Excuse me," Berta said to Schoolmarm, "but would you happen to have this in my size?" She touched a mannequin in a cylindrical flapper's gown with a daring V neckline.

Schoolmarm's jaw dropped.

"I am to be married in a fortnight," Berta said, "and I have not a stitch to wear. Mind you," she added with a twinkle, "my fiancé does not mind that a bit."

Sophronia gasped.

"I'll just go look in the back," Schoolmarm said in a tight voice.

"I shall wait in privacy," Berta said, toddling toward the dressing rooms. "These boots are ever so difficult to remove in this heat. My feet swell up like pot roasts." She gave me a pointed glance over her shoulder.

"Oh," I said. "Yes. Allow me to help you with your boots, Mrs. Lundgren."

We passed through an archway to find ourselves in a hallway of dressing rooms. Five of the six doors were wide open.

I knocked on the closed door. "Grace?"

Rustles inside. The door opened. "Oh. The snitches—yes, Mother told me all about how you telephoned her yesterday. What're you doing here? Don't stare. It's Mother's gown—at least it *was*, until Madam Lovell added an entire *bolt* of fabric to let it out for me."

Grace's sleeves poofed at the shoulder and then hugged as tightly as banana peels from the upper arm to the wrist. Her head—thick glasses and all—seemed balanced on top of the high lace collar.

Berta said, "My dear girl, you look as though you are being devoured by that gown."

"You could fit an entire three-ring circus under this skirt," Grace said.

"Is there something the matter, Miss Whiddle?" an attendant asked, popping up behind Grace's shoulder like a startled rabbit. I hadn't noticed her back there.

"Of course there is," Grace said. "This gown weighs about a thousand pounds and it's making me thirsty. I want some lemonade. Now."

The attendant squeezed past Grace's dress, Berta, and me and scuttled away.

"Well?" Grace said. "Come to spy on me some more? Or maybe to laugh at me in this monstrous thing?"

"I . . . I really don't know what to say about the gown," I said.

"How about it was the height of fashion in 1897? Unbutton me, will you? Golly, I can't even breathe." Grace turned, and Berta started picking at a long row of satin-covered buttons.

"We'd like to speak to you some more about the Morris deaths," I said, "and about your diary."

"Can't. I'm just leaving." Grace stepped out of the dress, leaving it mountained on the floor. Her torso was embalmed in one of those S-bend corsets the Gibson Girls adored. "I'm going to keep this awful corset on because it would make me about an hour late if I tried to unlace it. Anyway, my waistline doesn't look half bad in it."

"Late for what?" I asked.

"I still wear a corset," Berta said. "Those modern girdles offer no more support than a bath towel."

Grace was tugging on a fashionable blue cotton dress with a dropped waist and a wide sash. She smoothed her golden bob, put on a low-brimmed straw hat, and picked up her handbag. "Sorry. I must dash."

"But where are you going?" I asked.

"I'll kill you if you tell Mother."

"We won't," I said.

Grace lowered her voice. "Yankee Stadium. It's Petey's first game since his nerve treatment. If you wish to talk, you'll have to come along—would you like tickets to the game? Petey told me a bunch would be waiting for me at the ticket office. He said the seats were right behind the dugout, whatever that means."

"Oh my," Berta breathed.

"You're sneaking off to see Pete Schlump?" I said. "I was under the impression that you planned to go ahead with your marriage to Gil Morris."

"Never! I'm just playing along to keep Mother from shipping me off to her family in Philadelphia. Petey was hiding out at the Plaza till things blew over, but he telephoned just before Mother and I left for the city this morning and asked me to come to the game. Said it's ever so important that I see him play and that he's got something he wants to ask me. And then, well, I suppose we'll run away together after that. I've got big dreams to be a star, and Petey's going to help me." Grace gave a dramatic sigh. "Poor, sensitive Gil. Maybe he'll cut off his ear for me like Van Gogh did for his patootie."

I guessed Grace was in the dark about Gil, Violet, and Gil's plans to travel to Europe.

"We could go to the game if you'll answer some questions," I said. Besides, this could be our chance—finally—to talk to Pete Schlump. He was the one suspect from the East Ward whom Berta and I hadn't yet grilled. "We could offer you a ride, too."

"Ducky!" Grace said. "I'm no good at flagging down taxicabs."

After Berta made a quick stop in a lavatory off the stockroom, the three of us left Antoinette G. Lovell's the back way.

"Hot dog," Ralph said as we piled into the Duesy. "You snagged Grace again." He started the engine. "Where to?"

"It's funny you mention hot dogs," I said, "because we're going to Yankee Stadium."

Ralph glanced in the rearview mirror. "Jiminy Christmas." He hunched down.

Sophronia Whiddle was trundling down the sidewalk toward us, yelling.

"Gas it, won't you?" Grace cried. "Mother really scares me when her hat feather does that quivery thing."

Ralph angled into the stream of Fifth Avenue traffic.

"She'll tell Mother about seeing me," I said.

"You society girls and your mothers," Berta said. "It is time to cut the apron strings."

"All right, Grace," Ralph said over his shoulder, once Sophronia had receded to the size of a tick. "Where's your diary?"

Grace had removed her glasses and she hunkered over a mascara compact, wetting the brush with her tongue and laying it on thick. "What's it to you, mister?"

"He's a detective," I told Grace.

"Oh, is that supposed to explain everything?" Grace rolled her eyes, nearly stabbing her eyeball with the mascara brush in the process. "If I'd known a whole herd of detectives would be snooping after that diary, I would've burned it."

"Where is it?" Ralph repeated.

"It's gone. Someone stole it from my room at Willow Acres."

Ralph groaned. "When?"

"The last afternoon I was there, sometime after Mrs. Woodby and Mrs. Lundgren were in there looking around. It was Muffy who nicked it. I'm positive. Petey said he saw her tiptoeing out of my room while I was having my hydropathic treatment that afternoon."

"Okay," Ralph said, "and why do you think someone like, oh, I don't know, someone like Eugene Van Hoogenband might want to get his hands on your diary?"

"Oh, I know exactly why."

Ralph would have seemed as cool as a cocktail shaker if it weren't for the way his knuckles on the steering wheel turned white.

"It's because of what happened last winter," Grace went on. "Well, not exactly *because* of what happened last winter, but because I wrote it down. It's about him, you see. In a way."

"Go on," Ralph said.

"Josie Van Hoogenband is my best friend—she's a mean little cat, of course, but she's always up for some fun—so I spend a whole lot of time at her family's houses. Last winter, sometime in January, I was at Breakerhead and I couldn't sneak a ciggy in my usual spot in the rose garden, because it was snowing outside."

"That is a filthy habit, young lady," Berta said.

Grace took a lipstick from her handbag and uncapped it. "Well, Josie and I were playing backgammon and I was dying for a smoke so I sneaked off to her father's study because it always stinks like cigars in there so I figured no one would notice if I smoked in there, too. Halfway through my ciggy, I heard men's voices, so I stubbed it out in the ashtray and hid behind the curtains. Three men came into the study. Mr. Van Hoogenband, Senator Morris—I recognized his voice, since he's Gil's dad—and old Obadiah Inchbald in his wheelchair, Gil's grandfather. Once he pinched my bottom at the horse races."

"The three founding members of the Titan Club," I said.

"That's right." Grace was smearing on lipstick, so her consonants were a little garbled. "They meet regularly, I guess—that's what Josie told me. They like to keep tabs on everyone and, I don't know, sort of plan out how to run the show in New York. In business, mostly. Well, they talked and talked until I was just freezing from being against the cold window with that blizzard outside."

"What did they talk about?" Ralph asked, keeping his eyes on the road.

"All sorts of things." Grace capped the lipstick. "Mr. Van Hoogenband was all riled up about something his younger brother Fizzy had done with a hotel manicurist—gotten married and had a baby with her even though he's already married—and then there was something about how Obadiah Inchbald's clothing company became filthy rich back in the Civil War—I don't know why ancient history like that matters, but they all had kittens about it."

"You wrote all of this down in your diary?" Ralph asked.

"I write everything down. I have a great memory for conversations as long as they're fresh. They start fading after a day or two. I could be one of those ladies who record things in courtrooms. If I knew how to type, I mean."

"If Muffy stole the diary," I said, "it would be in her personal effects taken from her room at Willow Acres. Gil might have it."

"He doesn't," Grace said. "I telephoned him last night to ask. He was given a box of his mother's things, I mean, but he said the diary wasn't there."

"He could've been lying," I said.

"What else can you remember about that entry, Grace?" Ralph asked.

"Nothing."

"Think," Ralph said.

"Oh, I never do that. It gives you wrinkles."

31

I hadn't yet been to the brand-new Yankee Stadium in the Bronx—nor the old one. It looked quite like the Colosseum in Rome. We collected tickets reserved for Grace at the ticket office and joined the throngs streaming through doorways. The vast sunlit sweep of the stadium smelled of fresh paint and sod, roasted peanuts, hot dogs, and several thousand overwrought men. Blue sky arched overhead. The white and green of the field dazzled my eyes.

Berta, Ralph, and I followed Grace to the bottom of the bleachers. Voices hummed and I kept hearing "Schlump, Schlump, Schlump." Grace made a beeline around the lower perimeter of the seats until we were within a stone's throw of what I took to be the Yankees dugout. Players in their striped uniforms, caps, and knee-high socks loitered around, gabbing and spitting. Pete Schlump, smaller than the rest of his teammates by a head, stood to one side. Ostracized from the herd.

With the game starting any minute, I figured I'd have to wait until the intermission—or whatever they called it—to grill Pete about the murders.

Grace leaned over the railing. "Petey!" she yelled. "Hey, Petey!" She waved wildly.

"Why don't you get off the railing, Grace?" I said. "You aren't wearing your glasses. You could fall."

Pete looked over and his face brightened. Grace blew him a kiss and Pete pretended to catch it.

Ah, the folly of love.

Speaking of which, I wound up sitting in the aisle seat next to Ralph. He cracked roasted peanuts from a paper bag on his lap and tossed them into his mouth.

I flicked him a glance. "Don't take this the wrong way, but if Grace doesn't know where her diary is, then why are you still sticking around? Shouldn't you be off tracking it down?"

"Nope."

My stomach cartwheeled. Maybe he was sticking around because he couldn't bear to part with my sparkling personality and distinct ankles.

"Don't you get it, kid?" Ralph said. "If the diary was stolen from Muffy's room at Willow Acres and it wasn't in her personal effects, that means the murderer has the diary."

Oh. Yeah.

"I've got to hand it to you and Mrs. Lundgren," Ralph said. "I think you're hot on the trail and I want to be there when you bag the murderer." He cracked another peanut. "That's why I'm sticking around."

Did I mention how pleased I was that I hadn't told this thick-headed, single-minded, gorgeous gink that I was in love with him?

"If the murderer has the diary," I said, "then that means the murderer has been leaking those scandalous stories to Ida Shanks at the newspaper."

"Uh-huh," Ralph said. "Smells like an act of vengeance to me."

Berta leaned over. "I do agree, Mr. Oliver. Perhaps Beaulah Starr was at one time or another slighted by Obadiah Inchbald—and we know very well why she loathed Senator Morris." She glanced at her wristwatch. I knew she was counting down the minutes till three o'clock, when she could call the Hare's Hollow feed store and speak to Beaulah's friend.

And perhaps that would be the end of it. Too bad Violet Wilbur couldn't have been the murderer. I sort of liked Beaulah.

"HOT dogs!" A vendor yelled, coming down the steps. "Get yer HOT dogs! Pipin' hot! Mustard, relish, onions, catsup! HOT dogs! Get yer HOT dogs!"

"You take the works on your hot dogs, don't you, kid?" Ralph said to me, digging for his wallet.

How did he know? "I'm not hungry," I said primly. But who was I kidding? I'd missed lunch and I'd kill for a hot dog with the works.

Ralph bought two hot dogs with the works, all for me. "Got you some soda pop, too," he said. "Ginger ale. I'll hold it till you have a free hand."

"You're a knight in shining armor." I bit in.

The game began. Apparently, since it was Yankee Stadium, this meant that the other team—the Boston Red Sox—went to bat first. And this meant that Pete Schlump was on the pitcher's mound.

He got on the mound to a smattering of applause mixed with a rumble of boos. But silence hung thick over the stadium as he wound up his first pitch. The ball bulleted toward the batter, a huge, lanky man who Berta had claimed was "Dy-no-mite." Which sounded good . . . but Mr. Dynamite swung and missed.

"Strike!" the umpire yelled.

The crowd roared.

Pete had the ball in his hand again, and he twiddled it around as though getting the perfect grip. Mr. Dynamite waited, knees bent, neck taut. Pete threw; Mr. Dynamite swung wildly.

"Strike!"

The crowd erupted. Men nearby started chanting "Schlump's back! Schlump's back!"

"Well, I'll be," Ralph said.

I was more interested in my hot dog than the game—where had they gotten that divine pickle relish?—but Thomas Edison would've classified the air in the stadium as *electric*.

Pete pitched again, and Mr. Dynamite struck out. Then another batter was up, and he struck out, too, and so did the third batter. The crowd was in ecstasy. Grace screamed, "I love you, Petey!"

The teams shuffled around for the second half of the inning. Pete had his back thoroughly slapped by his teammates. Newspaper photographers jockeyed for shots. I bit into my second hot dog. A little pickle relish dripped onto my lap. Sigh.

The baseball game went on and it wasn't especially exciting, because every time Pete was on the pitcher's mound, not a single batter could hit the ball. The crowd was in deafening ecstasies.

Berta crowed insults and directed raspberries at the umpire, who, despite calling strike after strike for Pete, was also occasionally obliged to call a strike for a Yankees batter. "The man is a monster," she huffed.

At last there was a break in the game, which Berta referred to as the seventh-inning stretch. Grace hung over the railing, yelling for Pete, who was waving to the crowd and posing for cameras. Berta and I joined her. Ralph stayed back. He liked to keep a low profile.

"Grace, honey!" Pete called, coming over. "About that question I wanted to ask you!"

"Yes, Petey?" Grace said breathlessly.

"Wait." I stopped Grace with a hand on her arm. I leaned over the railing and spoke in a stage whisper so the newspaper report-ers over by the dugout wouldn't hear. "Mr. Schlump, I have a few questions for you regarding the deaths of Muffy and Winfield Morris."

"*Waste of time,*" Berta murmured.

"Questions?" Pete took off his baseball cap and scratched his head. "Kinda funny time to be asking, dontcha think?"

"You've been unavailable," I said.

"Of course, Mr. Schlump," Berta said, "we know you are terribly busy and we do not wish to impose—"

"We *do* wish to impose." I jabbed Berta with my elbow. "Now, tell me. Why were you at Coney Island yesterday when Senator Morris was shot?"

"Watchin' this sweet little doll here compete," Pete said, smiling at Grace.

"Do you own a gun?" I asked.

"The only shooting I do is with this puppy," Pete said, flexing his right arm.

Grace giggled, and so did Berta.

Gee whiz. "And what about the night Muffy Morris died at Willow Acres?" I asked. "Do you have an alibi?" The newspaper reporters were heading over. I hoped Pete wouldn't notice.

"Oh, I've got an alibi, all right," Pete said with a suggestive grin.

"*Petey,*" Grace whispered.

"I was with Grace," Pete said. "All night. We couldn't have killed Muffy, because we were too busy."

The newspaper reporters clustered around Pete, snapping photographs and scribbling in notebooks. No way was any of this going to be kept secret.

I turned to Grace, who was blushing but also preening a little for the cameras. "Grace," I said, "I, um, happened to look into your room that night and I saw you sleeping. Alone."

"I wasn't asleep. I knew you were coming for my diary. Pretty obvious after you tried to nick it off my nightstand that afternoon—

and so after you rattled my doorknob and found it locked, I pretended to be asleep while Petey hid under the bed. I heard you sort of grunting, Mrs. Woodby, as you climbed along the ivy outside my window and peeked in."

I heard Ralph chuckling behind me and I chose to ignore it. Anyway, I didn't recall any grunts on my part. But I did recall the way Grace's head had tossed from side to side on her pillow and how she'd muttered incoherently. She hadn't been dreaming; she'd been pretending to dream.

"I've got a question!" Pete shouted. "Will you marry me, Grace Whiddle?"

"Yes!" Grace screamed. The stadium erupted in hoots and cheers. "Catch me, Petey!" Grace swung her legs over the railing and jumped.

Pete spread his arms, but honestly, Grace probably outclassed him in the weight department. She flattened him on the turf.

The crowd roared. Pete and Grace kissed. The photographers crouched and tippy-toed, angling for shots.

"I think we need one-way tickets to Timbuktu," I said to Berta over the din of the crowd, "for when Sophronia Whiddle learns about this turn of events. My gut tells me that Grace and Pete are telling the truth about being together that night at Willow Acres, so that eliminates them as suspects." Grace and Pete were the first suspects to be eliminated, actually. I felt that I deserved something made out of chocolate.

"I told you Pete could not have killed anyone, Mrs. Woodby," Berta said. "Oh, look at the time. Three o'clock at last. It is time to ring up the feed store."

We found a pay telephone booth just outside the stadium. Berta fed it a nickel and rang up the Hare's Hollow feed store. At length she had Harriet Klipper on the line. I crammed inside the telephone booth, too, and got my ear as close to the earpiece as I could. Ralph was left outside with Cedric. How he managed to look suave while holding the leash of a teddy bear–sized dog is anyone's guess.

Berta said, "Miss Klipper, I am searching for Beaulah Starr and I understand you are her dear friend. Do you know where I might find her?"

"Beaulah Starr?" Harriet's voice was guarded. "Yeah, I know Beaulah."

"Have you seen her in the last day? Is she all right?"

Silence. Then, "I'm not sure if I should go telling you anything—who did you say you were?"

"Her friend. Mrs. Lundgren. We met at Willow Acres."

"Oh. I'm only checking because Beaulah said someone was trying to kill her. I guess it's okay to speak to you."

Yipes. Harriet was the kind of friend who'd tell you it was okay to fly a kite in a lightning storm.

Harriet went on, "She went to the city to go shopping, see, after last night."

"What occurred last night?" Berta asked.

"Listen, I feel funny about this. How about you ask her yourself? She's gonna be at some book lecture thingum in the city this evening. Tried to drag me to it, but I don't put on airs like she does, and anyway, I'm working overtime." Harriet hung up.

Berta and I popped out of the telephone booth and told Ralph what Harriet had said.

"Thank goodness Beaulah is safe and sound!" I said. "I can't begin to guess why she's out shopping when someone is trying to kill her—"

"That was a smoke screen, Mrs. Woodby," Berta said.

"—but I *can* guess where she'll be at seven o'clock: at Violet

Wilbur's lecture at the Xavier House Hotel. Remember how she had bunches of Violet's books in her room at the boarding house? Berta, it's our lucky break. Your favorite suspect and my favorite suspect are showing up in one place. How do you like that for convenience?"

32

Berta, Ralph, and I killed the hours until seven o'clock at the counter of a Midtown coffee shop that didn't seem to mind Pomeranians as long as they ordered the roast chicken. We read newspapers and magazines, ate sandwiches, drank too much coffee, and stared at a wall clock that seemed to have arthritis.

At one point—blame it on the coconut layer cake I was digging into—I started feeling extra glowy toward Ralph. When Berta went to the lavatory, I took another stab at a confession.

"You know, Ralph," I said, "there is something I've been meaning to discuss with you."

"I thought there was." Ralph put down his newspaper.

"Really?"

"Sure." A pause. "Go on. You can tell me."

I looked shyly down at my half-eaten cake. Poetic genius struck. "The thing is, Ralph, there are ladies who love all sorts of icing on their cake—chocolate fudge, buttercream, even plain old vanilla. But the problem is, well, I've got a bit of a cake dilemma." I lifted my

eyes to Ralph's. "I'll put it like this." I swallowed. "I, well, I love coconut frosting and *only* coconut frosting."

Ralph's gray eyes twinkled. "Ditto, sweetheart."

I waited for him to say more, but . . . he didn't. He signaled the
waitress, ordered a slice of coconut layer cake and a cup of coffee,
and turned back to his newspaper. The faintest smile played on
his lips.

Oh, jeez. My hairline broke into a sweat. He hadn't understood.
Or . . . had he? Ralph was either a shameless lady-killer or a hope-
less lunkhead. Which was worse?

At last, it was time to go to the Xavier House Hotel.

In a room off the rose-scented lobby, Ralph, Berta, and I accepted
programs and squeezed into gilt cane chairs at the rear. The audience was mostly made up of ladies in hats and pearls. I settled Cedric on my lap and studied my program. It read,

GOOD TASTE:
What It Is and How One Might Acquire It
A Lecture Series in Twelve Parts by Miss Violet Wilbur.
July 19, 1923
Lecture XII: Good Taste in the Boudoir

"Good golly, these ladies have already stuck it out for eleven lec-
tures so far?" I whispered.

"Hnn." Ralph slid lower in his chair and adopted a stoic
expression.

Berta was scanning the audience. "I do not see Beaulah Starr
anywhere."

"Maybe she's running late," I said. "Oh. Look. Raymond Hathorne.
Third row. What's he doing here, I wonder?" Raymond was the only

man in the audience besides Ralph. He wore a pale blue suit and a boater hat. "I must speak with him about the giggling Hermie Inchbald claims to have heard coming from his room at the health farm. Back in a twinkling."

"Don't feed the sharks," Ralph said.

"Why, hello, angel," Raymond said when I sat down next to him. He closed his program and smiled, but I could've sworn something like panic flitted across his eyes. Perhaps he was embarrassed to have been caught at such a feminine venue. "What a surprise. You look smashing."

Actually, I didn't. It had been a footslog of a day. My hair drooped, my skin felt gritty, I had black oil paint and pickle relish on my dress, and I would've sold my soul for a toothbrush and some Colgate's.

"How is the Ritz treating you?" Raymond asked. "Isn't that where your mother told me you've been staying?"

"Yes. Oh, you know. Noisy pipes and simply dreamy service. Last night when I telephoned down for some kibble for Cedric, they brought up caviar on a Sèvres saucer. What are you doing here? I didn't know you and Miss Wilbur were friends."

"Oh, we're not. Not really. But I happened to bump into her this afternoon and she convinced me to come and hear her speak. Told me it was my last chance since she's off to Europe in a day or two."

"She's off to Europe? Did she say why?"

"She has received an offer to redecorate an entire castle in the Rhine Valley."

I smelled baloney. Gil Morris was taking off for Europe, too. Up until then, I hadn't been completely sure if Gil was Violet's gentleman or not, but that clinched it.

"If I wasn't up to my elbows in work for Fizz-Whiz," Raymond said, "I wouldn't mind a European holiday myself."

"You know, Mr. Hathorne, a reliable source told me that a woman's giggles were heard coming from your room at Willow Acres the night Muffy died. My source also told me that you're only renting your house and that there is no such thing as Fizz-Whiz soda pop. Care to explain?"

"Did Hermie Inchbald tell you all that? Because I wouldn't call him a reliable source."

"Well . . ."

Raymond leaned in. "Let me tell you something, Lola. Inchbald has had it in for me from the get-go. Spreading lies. And he's forever staring through the hedges at me, too. Damned unnerving, if you want to know the truth."

Staring through the hedges? *Oh.* "You live next door to Inchbald Hall?"

"That's right. In the old Pitridge place."

Raymond had told me this already, but I hadn't realized the Pitridge place was just next door to the Inchbalds. What had Beaulah said about Hermie's next-door neighbor when we talked in the hedge maze? Something about him whacking golf balls over the property line, wasn't it?

Foreboding squirmed deep inside me. I was forgetting something. But what?

"Now, listen," Raymond said, leaning still closer. "Hermie's not right in the head. But since you're such a brain, angel—really inquisitive, aren't you?—I'm going to tell you the truth. Here's the thing. I spun that tale about the Fizz-Whiz company because I wished to fit in here in America, fit in with all these captains of industry who run New York. Americans don't like aristocrats."

I raised my eyebrows. "You're an aristocrat?"

"After a fashion," Raymond said. "The fact of the matter is, I inherited all my money. Queen Victoria knighted my grandfather and bequeathed to him a huge tract of land in Quebec. We're aristocrats, practically, but who likes to talk about that? So yes. Fizz-Whiz is a sham, and I'm only an idle playboy. It's embarrassing, really. But say—" Raymond smiled. "—if maple-flavored soda pop means so much to you, we could go into business together. Breathe life into that silly idea."

A lady's voice at the front of the room said, "Good evening, ladies and gentlemen."

The crowd hushed.

"Thank you for attending." The speaker was Violet in a lavender suit and bulbous pearls. "Good taste. What is it? How might one acquire it? Good taste depends upon refined distinctions that are nearly imperceptible to the eye. It is my wish—some might even say my duty—to magnify for the masses these distinctions and to thus elevate the current state of society."

Excited murmurs, rustling programs, bobbing hats.

"The topic this evening is good taste in the lady's private boudoir," Violet said, "a shamefully overlooked topic. And for those of you who have purchased my recent volume, *The Tasteful Abode,* I shall autograph books at the conclusion of the lecture."

Titters of excitement. The lady on my left had two copies of a green book protruding from her handbag. The spines said THE TASTEFUL ABODE in gold. I looked around. Almost every lady was holding a copy.

Violet went on and on about airy rooms and why footstools must be round, not square. Now and then, she lost the thread of her speech. At one point, she called a mahogany lowboy a *manly lowboy.* And another time, she blushed when describing how to plump up sofa cushions properly. Violet had romance on the brain, all right.

However, most of the lecture was as dull as dishwater . . . which gave me plenty of time to decide to confront Violet about fleeing to Europe with her lover and forgery accomplice, Gil Morris. I'd need a book for Violet to sign, though, to keep Raymond off the scent.

The lady next to me was busy speaking with someone on her other side, so I leaned over, slid one of the green books from her handbag, and slid it into my own. I would return it after I'd quizzed Violet. After a few minutes, the lady noticed one of her books was gone and looked under her chair.

"Let's go for a walk," Raymond said to me over the applause when Violet finally concluded her lecture. "Beautiful evening."

"No," I said. "I would like Miss Wilbur's autograph." I waved the stolen book, plopped Cedric in Raymond's lap, and stood. "Back in a jiffy."

"Wait a minute," I heard the lady next to me say. "That's *my*—"

I edged through the crowd to the front of the room.

I'm not one to cut in line, but time was of the essence, so I took advantage of the haphazard and chatty line and made my way to Violet's signing table. Her large alligator handbag sat at the side of the table. I've always felt there is something hideously wrong with ladies who carry alligator handbags.

It was my turn. Violet still hadn't looked up at me as I placed the stolen book in front of her.

She thumbed to the title page. "Whom should I make it out to?"

"Why don't you make it out to, 'Did you murder the Morrises to cover up your hand in the forgery business, or was it to assist your lover Gil in getting at his inheritance ahead of schedule?'"

"What's this?" Violet looked up with slitted eyes. "Mrs. Woodby? Your brother-in-law warned me about you. How dare you come here and—"

"Skip the soapboxing and answer the question."

"You leave Miss Wilbur alone," a familiar voice said.

I turned to see a woman in a smart suit and a low-brimmed cloche hat with a dotted veil. "Beaulah Starr?" I said. "Is that you? It is you. I'm so glad to see you're all right."

"*Pipe down!*" Beaulah whispered, looking nervously around. She was going incognita in that hat and veil, then. Did that mean someone *was* trying to murder her? Or that she was a murderer herself?

"There she is!" someone shrieked behind me. "She's the one who stole my book, right out of my handbag! She's the only one who could've done it!"

Violet smirked. "Stealing, Mrs. Woodby, is in such poor taste."

"She is a thief," Beaulah said. She turned to me. "You haven't returned my gingham dress."

"When could I have possibly—? Never mind. I'd like to speak with you privately, Miss Starr."

"No way! You're nothing but trouble. Keep away from me." Beaulah took a step back.

"I want my book!"

All hell broke loose. A stout lady in periwinkle grabbed the stolen book from the tabletop, and someone else grabbed the handle of my handbag. I craned my neck, looking for an escape route, but every way seemed to be blocked by frilled blouses, heaving bosoms, and jeweled brooches. Why weren't Ralph and Berta springing to my aid?

The lady-sea parted and a couple of chairs toppled. I made a feint toward the door, and a lady shoved me. I staggered back, knocking over Beaulah. She screamed and thumped to the carpet. Her handbag cracked open and disgorged its contents. My hips crashed into Violet's table, the table fell over, and I sprawled on my back. Violet's alligator handbag landed a few feet away. Its contents scattered.

I sat up and swayed. Tweeting cartoon birdies made figure eights in my head.

"Lola!" Ralph called from somewhere. "Kid, are you all right?" Berta cried, "Heavens to Betsy, Mrs. Woodby!" But I couldn't see Ralph and Berta. All I saw were T-strap pumps and legs in stockings.

Beaulah was on her hands and knees, gathering up her belongings and stuffing them into her handbag: green book, powder compact, coin purse, peppermints . . . and a pistol.

"I hate you, Lola Woodby," Beaulah sobbed. "Someday soon,

you'll be sorry. You don't know who I am." Then she was on her feet and rushing away.

Everyone stared at me for a breathless moment. I struggled to my feet and made a break for it.

Raymond joined me halfway across the lobby. "Care to tell me what's happening?" he asked, striding beside me with a writhing Cedric in his arms.

"Beaulah," I said, breathing hard. "Beaulah Starr. I can't let her get away." She was absolutely terrified of me, and that spelled one thing: *guilt*. There was no time to wait for Ralph and Berta.

Beaulah glanced over her shoulder as she swung through the lobby doors. When she saw Raymond and me, her mouth slackened with horror. She bolted. Raymond and I burst out of the doors to see Beaulah heading in the direction of Central Park.

"You've terrified the poor girl," Raymond said, slowing. He passed Cedric to me and shoved his hands in his pockets. "What am I missing?"

"No time," I said, breathless. "Are you coming with me or not?"

"My curiosity is piqued."

I supposed that meant he was coming. Holding Cedric tightly, I dashed after Beaulah.

33

Raymond and I tailed Beaulah one block along Sixty-fourth Street, past stately stone row houses and lush trees. At Fifth Avenue, she darted into traffic. A delivery truck veered, horn beeping, and a taxi screeched to a stop. The cabbie hollered, shaking his fist out the window. When Beaulah reached the opposite curb, she threw another glance over her shoulder, saw Raymond and me, and dashed through a gate into Central Park.

I went more cautiously than Beaulah into the Fifth Avenue traffic, but I wasn't going to let her get away. I burned to ask her what she'd meant when she said I didn't know who she was, and I wished to know how she'd paid for those new glad rags. The hat alone could've covered my rent.

I'll hand it to Raymond, he was a trouper. He dodged through the beeping, swerving motorcars, taxis, and trucks right alongside me.

"Where has she gone?" I said when we'd made it into the park.

"Why don't we let it alone, angel?" Raymond said. "Say, I'll buy you an ice cream, how would that be?"

"There she is!" I broke into a jog; Beaulah was at the zoo ticket booth, fumbling with her purse.

She'd already pushed through the zoo turnstile by the time Raymond and I reached the ticket booth. Raymond paid for our tickets, saying wryly, "Well, if we don't get arrested for hounding that poor girl, I'd love to know what this is all about."

I plucked a ticket from his fingers. "Tell you later." I shoved through the turnstile.

"Hey, lady!" the man in the ticket booth shouted through the hole in the glass. "No dogs allowed in the zoo! It'll spook the animals!"

I kept going.

The evening was warm and midsummer-bright. Crowds of children and their adults still lingered around the sea lion pool. Colorful rubber balloons bobbed against the sunset-rosy sky. Ice cream carts lured children. Above the trees, the city skyline was black. Laughter, splashing, the croon of peanut vendors. Cedric kicked and whined, so I set him on his paws. No time to clip on his leash.

Where was Beaulah? I turned in a slow circle.

There. By the elephant pen. I dashed over, Cedric frisking alongside me.

Beaulah had squeezed herself into the crowd around the elephant's cage. The elephant stood dully in a patch of soiled straw. By golly, zoos are depressing.

I drew up behind the crowd. "Miss Starr," I called. "Miss Starr, I only wish to speak with you." Raymond pulled up beside me.

Beaulah turned, her hat veil trembling. "Leave me alone!" She took off again, but her expensive pumps were wobbly. She tripped behind the crowd at the tiger's cage, stumbled, and fell. No one really noticed, because the tiger was doing something amusing; people snapped its photograph and *oohed*.

Raymond went to Beaulah and held out a hand. Beaulah refused it, her face scrunched. She stood shakily, breathing in raspy little squeaks.

Was I really so scary?

"Miss Starr," I said, nearing them, "an innocent man is in all likelihood destined for the electric chair. How could you live out your days with that on your conscience?"

Beaulah's shoulders wilted. A distant carousel warbled calliope music. A confession was at hand—I could taste it.

Beaulah wiped tears with the back of a finger. "I won't let nobody louse up my plans! You hear? Nobody!" She swung her head in panic, veiled hat askew, and then malice hardened her mouth. She bent, picked up Cedric, and elbowed through the crowd.

"No!" I screamed, lunging. I trod upon shoes and might've sent a tyke sprawling, and when I reached the front of the crowd, Beaulah had already wedged Cedric between two bars of the tiger's cage. Cedric twisted and squealed. Beaulah was trying to stuff him through.

Inside the cage, the tiger's amber eyes lit with interest.

"Monster!" I screamed, grabbing Beaulah's collar and yanking her back. She staggered but did not fall. She clawed at my arms. A blueberry-sized diamond winked on her finger. Surprise relaxed my grip on her collar.

Beaulah wrenched free, her handbag hit the ground, and she once again took off running. She'd left her handbag on the ground.

I tried to gently dislodge Cedric from the bars of the cage. He wouldn't budge. His tender middle was wedged snug and his legs kicked in the air, two inside the cage and two out. "Don't worry, peanut," I sobbed. "Mommy will get you out."

The tiger stalked nearer, tail swishing.

"Someone help!" I cried, making shooing motions at the tiger.

"The dog's stuck!" a man yelled.

Someone took a photograph of Cedric.

"Is the tiger going to eat him, Mommy?" a child asked.

"Don't look, Timmy," the mother said.

"Should we telephone the fire brigade?" a man said.

"Someone notify a zookeeper!" a lady shrilled.

More photographs were snapped.

The tiger was only two prowls away.

"Allow me," Raymond said. Very gently, he held Cedric's sides and seesawed him, and then Cedric was free and in my arms.

"Peanut!" I said, tears dripping. "Poor little peanut. It's all right now. Mommy's here."

"Awwwwwww," the crowd around me said. Lots more photographs were taken. Raymond took my arm and drew me away.

"I don't know how to thank you, Mr. Hathorne," I said. Hugging Cedric, I stood on tippy-toe and kissed Raymond full on the mouth.

He kissed me back with cool dry lips. He smelled of balsam shaving lotion, just like Alfie used to wear. This was wrong. Wrong, wrong, wrong.

I pulled away, confusion spinning through me, my cheeks pulsing-hot. Ralph and Berta were a few paces off, watching—when had they arrived? Ralph's eyes were hidden in the shade of his fedora, but Berta's eyes and lips were round.

"Don't thank me just yet," Raymond said. "I'm going to go catch that crazy nurse for you, all right? She won't get away with this."

I nodded.

Raymond strode away in the direction Beaulah had fled. Hermie had called him a liar, but I'd seen the steely look of determination in Raymond's eye. He was going to hunt Beaulah down for me. Well, for my dog, anyway.

The crowd dispersed. The excitement had passed.

I sank onto a zoo bench. My knees were jellied.

"Mrs. Woodby!" Berta said, arriving next to me. Her own handbag was slung over her right forearm, and Beaulah's handbag dangled from her left.

Ralph sauntered over more slowly. "Lola, are you all right? And the pooch?" His voice, though charitable, wasn't exactly warm.

"I think he's all right." I cradled Cedric. "He might be bruised."

"Aw." Ralph gently scratched Cedric behind the ear. "Poor little fella."

Cedric wagged his appreciation.

"Say, where did Hathorne take himself off to?" Ralph asked me.

"To catch Beaulah."

"You're sure? Because the look on his face reminded me of a guy who'd just had a narrow escape."

"Don't be silly. What would Raymond be escaping from?"

Berta had seated herself next to me on the bench and was inspecting the contents of Beaulah's handbag.

"Beaulah was wearing a big diamond ring," I said. "I'm pretty sure it was the real McCoy, too—and did you see her fancy new clothes? She's gotten herself engaged to someone rich. But she was trying to lie low in that hat with the veil. I think you were correct all along, Berta. I think she's the murderer."

Berta pulled out Beaulah's copy of *The Tasteful Abode* and set it on the bench. "Do not feel too badly about yourself, Mrs. Woodby. You were only attempting to be thorough." She took out Beaulah's powder compact, coin purse, peppermints, and—gingerly—the pistol. "Aha. Here it is. The weapon used to murder Senator Morris."

"Hold on," Ralph said. "Let me see that." He took out a hankie, wrapped it around the handle of the gun, inspected it. Then he looked at Berta. "I hate to say it, Mrs. Lundgren, but this isn't a Luger Parabellum."

Berta gasped. "Are you certain?"

"Yep. It's a Luger, all right—Gil Morris wasn't lying about that—but it's an Alphabet."

"But what does this mean?" Berta asked in a small, lost voice.

"For one thing, it blows your theory about Beaulah Starr being the murderer out of the water," Ralph said.

"But—"

"That's the breaks, Mrs. Lundgren. Been there myself." Ralph placed the gun on top of the pile of Beaulah's purse contents. They weren't balanced properly, and they all crashed to the ground.

Berta and I bent to retrieve the items, hands outstretched. We both froze. The book had landed open to a middle page, and a red ribbon bookmark curled from its spine like a lick of blood.

"But this isn't—this book is filled with *handwriting*," I said. I picked it up and thumbed through. Page after page of round, girlish handwriting. "I think this is Grace Whiddle's diary."

"Well, I'll be," Ralph said. "There it is."

"But why on earth was Grace's diary in Beaulah's handbag if she is not the murderer?" Berta said.

"Beaulah might have gotten Grace's diary from Violet Wilbur's handbag," I said.

"I beg your pardon?"

"During the scuffle at the hotel book signing. Don't you see? Beaulah could've picked up the book by mistake after both of their handbags fell open, thinking that it was her own copy of *The Tasteful Abode*."

"There were a whole heck of a lot of green books flying around in that lecture room, you know," Ralph said. "This diary could've even come from somebody else."

I swallowed. "This investigation won't end. I feel sick."

"There is no time to feel sick, Mrs. Woodby," Berta said. "We must go and see if Violet Wilbur is still at the hotel."

"What about Cedric? He should be looked over by a veterinarian."

Berta waved a hand. "Just look at Cedric. He is as fit as a fiddle."

Cedric was scarfing down a smashed ice cream cone he'd found under the bench.

I looked at the diary in my hands. I looked up at Ralph. "And . . . what about you? I suppose all you wish to do is read this diary?"

"Well, sure. But first things first. You've got to apprehend Violet. I'll come with you in case you need backup." Ralph held my gaze a smidge too long.

I glanced away, ashamed for kissing Raymond Hathorne and hopelessly confused about coconut icing. I stashed the diary in my handbag, picked up Cedric, and plucked a shard of ice cream cone from his mouth. We hurried after Berta.

When we reached the lecture room at the Xavier House Hotel, it was empty except for a bellboy swabbing the carpet up front.

"Wait here," I whispered to Ralph and Berta. I left them in the doorway.

"Excuse me," I said when I reached the bellboy, "is Miss Wilbur still on the premises?"

"No, madam." The bellboy didn't take his eyes off his swabbing. "She left in a hurry. A deranged woman—an obsessive fanatic is my guess—stole books and knocked over the table. Miss Wilbur was frightened half out of her wits." The bellboy glanced up and his face clouded. "Say, aren't you—?"

"Thanks ever so much!" I returned to Ralph and Berta. "She's gone. I'll telephone her house. It's not far from here, and she's had plenty of time to reach home."

We found a bank of telephones in a marble corridor off the lobby. Berta recited Violet's street address, I gave the address to the operator, and after a moment she put me through.

I got the maid.

"I'm very sorry," she said, "but Miss Wilbur is not in."

Phooey. "When do you expect her to return?"

"Well, she's going abroad—"

"Yes, I've heard. But those ships bound for Europe always leave in the morning."

"Oh! Are you the woman who broke into the house this morning? I told the police—"

I disconnected and turned to Ralph and Berta. "She's not home, and it sounds as though she's leaving for Europe in the morning. What next?"

"Let's have a look in that diary before we make another move," Ralph said. "That thing could be packed with clues."

I glanced out into the swanky lobby. "Here?"

"Why not?"

Berta, Ralph, and I sat in a row on a velvet couch, and I took the diary from my handbag. The concierge was looking at me hard from his desk. I tugged my hat down to hide my eyes, just as Ralph always did. I opened the diary on the portion of my lap not occupied by Cedric, and we started perusing.

"Lots of moaning and groaning about her mother," I said.

"Where does she get that purple and green ink?" Ralph said.

"Her horrid mother gives her such an awful time about her figure," Berta said. "Goodness! In my village in Sweden, it was always the thin girls who despaired over their figures."

"Times have changed," I said. "Now we're all supposed to look like number-two lead pencils." I turned a page. "Grace said that it was wintertime when she overheard that conversation in Eugene Van Hoogenband's study, right? She said it was snowing outside."

"January, I believe," Berta said.

I found January. The first days were cluttered up with grumblings about her mother and unemotional notes on Gil's courtship, and then—a long entry dated January 7, 1923.

34

It was all there in the January 7 entry of Grace Whiddle's diary. Inchbald & Sons, Fine Clothiers' war profiteering. Fizzy Van Hoogenband's second wife and kid. Even details about Muffy's tipply problem.

"There's more," I said, pointing to the next passage.

What about Hermie? Said Mr. Van H. What of the revolting little shrimp? said Senator M.

Mr. Van H said Well, he has that skeleton in his closet, you know, from France. Oh you mean the girl? said Senator M. Yes the girl, and goddammit how can you be so ~~blahzay~~ blasé about it? Old O said It was a war for God's sake. These things happen in wartime.

"'Old O' must mean Obadiah Inchbald," I said.
Ralph and Berta nodded.

*Senator M said there is no proof of any of that. No proof? Said
Mr. Van H There were witnesses, the girl's family and that
private from Inchbald's own regiment—Yes but that private
died, didn't he? I tell you, as long as Hermie keeps his sorry trap
shut and leaves off bragging about that goddam Silver Citation
Star at every turn no one will ever know about this.*

Berta said, "I would wager that Hermie got a French girl in trouble during the war."

"Hermie, a father?" I said.

"Mrs. Woodby, has it escaped your notice that even the most putrid men sire children with great frequency? And soldiers, well, they
are thought dashing by silly young girls."

"There isn't anything else about France," I said. "See? The subject changes to something about steelworks."

"Where?" Ralph tensed.

"Here." I tapped the page.

*The men were getting up to go and then Mr. Van H said to
Senator M that he sure as hell hoped the steelworks contracts
were all cut and dry because he wished to begin work on twenty
new bridges by summer, and Senator M said Oh, I nearly
forgot, good news, Eugene, the legislation passed and you are
sitting pretty, but don't you go forgetting your promises to me.
The old battleship has her heart set on a diamond necklace from
Tiffany and you know how she is if she doesn't get her ~~bobbles~~
baubles.*

After that, a new entry started, all about Gil's bad breath and Gil's
girlish hands.

Ralph let out a long, low whistle. "Jackpot." He grinned.

"I don't understand what this last passage means," I said, "other than that Senator Morris planned to buy Muffy a diamond necklace."

"That's not the important thing," Ralph said. He glanced around the lobby and lowered his voice. "The important thing is, it's proof that Senator Morris was in Eugene Van H's pocket. Senator Morris passed legislation to make sure that all state bridge-building contracts used V. H. Steelworks—that's Van H's gig. This is what I've been looking for, what I was hired to find. Do you know what a crime it is for Van H to have bribed a politician like that? To set up a sweet deal that favors his own company, a deal that excludes the usual competitive bidding for government contracts? Van H is headed for the lockup."

"Oh, thank goodness," Berta murmured.

"I mean, Van H *ought* to go to prison," Ralph said, "but who knows what'll happen at trial."

"With any luck, Van Hoogenband will have forgotten all about Berta and me by then," I said.

"He won't have any reason to go after you as soon as my client has this diary in their possession," Ralph said. "Say, could I borrow it for a few hours? I'll need to show it to my client. I'll return it."

I looked at Berta. She nodded.

"Who is your client?" I asked, pushing the diary into Ralph's hands. "Or are you still going to keep your lips buttoned about that— and about every single other thing that might be of the slightest interest to me because Ralph Oliver, Private Detective, absolutely must keep as cool as an icicle every minute of every day?" Whoops. Probably shouldn't have blurted that.

Ralph tucked the diary in his inside jacket pocket. His eyebrows lifted slowly.

"Oh dear," Berta murmured. "I will just pop away to make a telephone call." She scurried off.

"Let me tell you something, Lola," Ralph said in a low, impassive voice, "and listen hard because I'm only going to say it the once—"

"Ralph—"

"Let me finish." Ralph's voice had gone rough.

I shut my trap.

"If you stick with this agency," Ralph said, "I can promise you that there will come a time when your safety, or Mrs. Lundgren's safety or my safety or, heck, your dog's safety, will depend on you keeping mum about your work. I've only been doing my job, and I've been trying to do it right. I can't be blamed if it knocks you a little sideways when I won't sit, roll over, and beg for you, okay?"

"Well, I *never!*"

Ralph kept going. "What I think, Lola, is that you haven't really come to grips with your life. You're stumbling forward, and sure, changes are tough, and the gumshoe trade, it's real tough. But one of the reasons you're stumbling is because you're looking over your shoulder the whole time. That's your business, not mine. But you and me, kid, well, the reason we can't quite get started might be, like you said, partly because I've got to keep details about my work under wraps a lot of the time. And sure, maybe it's also because in general you blow a little hotter than I do, or that you like to talk about coconut icing when I prefer to just taste it—"

Oh. Gosh.

"—but another reason we can't get started is because you don't really *want* us to get started."

"That's not true." My indignation drained away. "I love being with you, Ralph."

"Oh yeah? Then why do I get the feeling you're playing games with me? One minute you're calling me Ralph and looking all mushy at me with your big blue eyes, and the next thing I know, you're petting that damned pretty boy Hathorne and calling me Mr. Oliver."

"I'm not playing games with you." I studied my dinged-up shoes.

"What about *you* coming clean to the world? Your job is a secret, I'm a secret . . . I've got too much pride to be some lady's dirty little secret, Lola. I'm a grown man, not some—some chew toy. I have to insist on being treated with respect, so if you're ever ready for that, well, let's talk. Till then, go ahead. Go back to your ritzy world." Ralph swept a hand around the hotel lobby. He stood. "Me, I'm done."

"You're only leaving now because you have what you wanted!" I blurted. "Go on, take the stupid diary!"

Ralph looked down at me for a long, steady moment. Then he sauntered across the lobby while Cedric whined and tried to jump out of my arms to follow him. Ralph pushed through the doors and disappeared into the summer evening.

My bottom was glued to the sofa cushion. My tongue felt like a chalkboard eraser. I stroked Cedric to calm myself, to keep the tears dammed up.

I heard Berta's boots tap-tapping toward me. "I am finished with the agency," she said, stopping a few paces away.

My heart faltered. "What?"

"You heard me."

"But why?"

"Where to begin? Is it because you refuse to keep track of your business expenses in the log? Is it because you refused to don a bathing suit in order to collar Grace at Coney Island? Well, is it?"

I made a limp shrug.

"No!" Berta cried. "No, it is not."

The concierge looked up sharply. He picked up his telephone.

Berta went on, "I was willing—goodness knows why, upon reflection—but I was willing to overlook your slapdash way of doing business because, in spite of everything, you are a rather fine sleuth."

"And because we're friends, too," I said meekly. "Right?"

Berta sniffed. "What I am not able to overlook, Mrs. Woodby, is that you turned down Ida Shanks's offer to trade information regarding her informant in exchange for giving her an interview."

"Um," I said.

"I have just spoken with her on the telephone."

No.

"I wished to ask her, one last time, to divulge information about her informant," Berta said. "Well. Ida told me, to my great surprise, that she had already offered to divulge what she knew about the informant to you, and you had refused."

"Yes," I said, "but did she tell you what she wanted in return?"

"An interview, Mrs. Woodby! Merely an interview. And you refused."

"Ida means to humiliate me, Berta," I said.

"But it is not the threat of humiliation that concerns you, is it?" Berta said. "I am not blind. I understand quite well that what you wish to avoid is your mother learning about your new occupation. Your mother—oh, never mind. I am more than sixty years of age, and I no longer have the inclination to beat my head against brick walls. I hereby terminate my employment with the Discreet Retrieval Agency."

"We haven't caught the murderer yet," I said lamely.

"Yet you could. You have seen what is the diary. Give Ida the interview, put two and two together, and you will crack the case. The crux of the matter is, you have not done your utmost to solve the case. I, Mrs. Woodby, only wish to work with persons who do their utmost." Berta turned and walked toward the lobby doors.

I scurried after her, carrying Cedric and my handbag. "Where will you go?"

"As you know, I received an offer of employment as cook at an estate in Gloucester, Massachusetts, last week. I have just telephoned the household to tell them I have decided to take the post. They requested that I start immediately."

"You mean you're leaving for Massachusetts . . . now?"

"Of course not. I am going to my friend Myrtle's bed-sit. I will take the first train to Boston in the morning."

"What about Mr. Demel at the bakery?" I asked, bargaining for time. "Don't you wish to say good-bye to him?"

"I might easily do that over the telephone."

"But I thought you—?"

"I had hoped that going against type, as it were, would furnish a refreshing change, but it seems that there was no . . . suffice it to say that Mr. Demel's baked goods, in the end, turned out to be a bit dry."

"And you still miss Jimmy the Ant," I said.

Berta waved a hand. "You are attempting to distract me. None of that is any of your affair."

"What about your things at the Longfellow Street apartment?"

"I shall send funds for you to box them up and forward them to me in Gloucester. I do not own much, at any rate, and nothing I care about." Berta's hand fluttered to her locket. "I will not expect you to do that until this case has blown over. I shall keep abreast of the case via the newspapers. It is terrible, of course, that poor Mr. Ulf is still in jail, but surely that will sort itself out."

"We were supposed to sort it out, Berta!"

"Yes," Berta said sadly. "We were."

"What if Van Hoogenband finds you in Massachusetts?"

"If Mr. Oliver is to be believed, that matter will be resolved in short order. Good-bye, Mrs. Woodby."

"Don't go!"

"I really must." Berta pushed through the lobby doors and was gone.

The concierge was coming my way with an officious stride. "Excuse me, madam," he said. "I recognize you from that appalling fracas in the lecture room earlier, and I have just telephoned the police—"

Clinging to Cedric, I hoofed it out of there.

35

Outside, Berta had vanished and night had fallen. I buried my nose in Cedric's fluff as I went along the sidewalk. The night was still warm, but it had grown blustery. The air smelled of motorcar exhaust, perfume, and cooking meat. Taxicabs honked and balled-up newspapers fluttered in the gutter.

When I reached the place I'd parked the Duesy hours before, it was gone. Stolen, maybe, but probably towed.

Would I ever see it again? I found myself not really caring. With Ralph and Berta gone, well, what was a missing motorcar?

The walk to my parents' Park Avenue apartment took nearly twenty minutes. By the time I rang my parents' gold-leaf doorbell, I'd come to a decision.

Their butler, Chauncey, who knew me although I suspected he wished he didn't, told me that Mother was in her bedroom, dressing for an evening soiree.

I stopped in her open doorway and knocked.

"Lola!" Mother cried, swiveling on her vanity stool. "I've been worried sick about you! Why, you look like something the cat dragged in. You've lost a little weight, I see. No, it doesn't suit you, not a bit. It's done nothing for your ankle concern."

"Hello, Mother."

"Sophronia Whiddle telephoned earlier. She said you and that Swedish cook woman kidnapped Grace from the bridal shop? And now it seems Grace has eloped with a baseball player—"

"We didn't kidnap Grace," I said. "We merely gave her a lift."

"It's reprehensible. And where have you been staying? Do not even attempt to convince me that it's at one hotel or another, for I've telephoned each and every one a dozen times. Is it—" Mother's earrings trembled. "—are you living in . . . sin? Because although Mr. Hathorne does, admittedly, possess a modern streak—"

"No, Mother, I'm not living in sin."

"Thank goodness, although I was beginning to wonder if perhaps it isn't a good match after all, because Mr. Hathorne does adore golf and you take after your aunt Pauline in the way your hips in golfing skirts—"

"About Mr. Hathorne and golf," I said. "You're certain he said he'd been golfing in Scotland when you met him on the ocean liner?"

"Why yes. Scotland. Or was it Deauville? Was it both?"

I frowned. "Deauville? Are you quite certain?" Had Raymond met Hermie and Muffy in Deauville? Because that's where they had spent their spring holiday. I was too tired to untangle that knot.

"Oh, I can't remember," Mother said. "The point is, here you are, and I do hope you're home to stay, because—"

"I have something to tell you."

Mother blinked.

I took a big breath and told her about the detective agency and the Longfellow Street apartment, and I told her to forget about pairing me up with Raymond Hathorne or the Prince of Persia or anyone else, because I was in love with Ralph Oliver, Private Eye, and I was very sorry if that jiggered up the family name and prospects.

Mother's mouth fell open. It closed slowly, like a sea anemone. Then slowly, it opened again and a long, thin shard of a scream poured out. My eardrums rattled. Perfume bottles vibrated on the vanity.

Chauncey appeared beside me. "Madam?" he said.

Mother kept screaming.

"She'll be all right," I said to Chauncey. "Oh—and I'll be staying in the guest bedroom tonight."

As soon as I woke up the next morning, I rang for the maid and asked her if my mother was about.

"No, ma'am. Mrs. DuFey has gone out to attend her Lady Friends of Chamber Music breakfast, although I told her she ought to stay home because she sounded ever so hoarse."

Excellent. "Oh, and would you be a dear and take Cedric for a walk?"

"Yes, ma'am."

After the maid had left with Cedric, I picked up the telephone beside my bed. I asked the exchange girl to put me through to my veterinarian and arranged for him to make a house call to check on Cedric. Park Avenue veterinarians do that sort of thing. Then I telephoned the offices of *The New York Evening Observer*.

Naturally, Ida Shanks was happy to chat.

"Hello, Duffy," she said. "I've been expecting your call ever since I spoke to your Swedish sidecar yesterday evening. Ready for your interview?"

I unclamped my teeth. "Yes."

"Oh good."

"Now?"

"Of course. This is the newspaper business. Time is of the essence. Let's see—it's only quarter till ten. I'll be able to squeeze you into today's edition. You're used to squeezing into tight fits, aren't you, Duffy?"

"Do you promise that you'll tell me everything you know about your informant the very moment we're done?"

"Pinky swear."

Ida's promises were as valuable as wooden nickels, but what choice did I have? "All right," I said.

Ida interviewed me over the telephone for about fifteen minutes. I described my former position in high society, my financial ruin after Alfie's death, how Berta and I had subsequently begun a detective agency, and how we'd cracked our first case. I heard a couple gasps and chewing-gum snaps that told me the exchange girl thought it was pretty gripping stuff.

"But you haven't exactly been discreet, have you?" Ida said.

"All I can say is, we do our utmost," I said. "Make sure you publish that. Now it's my turn."

"He has a stutter," Ida said.

My breath caught. "Say that again?"

"My informant. It's a he, and he has a stutter. That's all I know, but a stutter's a doozy, don't you think? Got to go, Duffy dear. This thing's hot." Ida hung up.

My hands shook as I hung up. A stutter. Ida's informant was Hermie Inchbald! How could I have been so blind? At every turn, there Hermie Inchbald had been. And yet, because he didn't stand to inherit the Inchbald bucks just because Muffy had died, we'd written him off.

But what if he'd had a different motive? France had cropped up time and again, but only now did I see that France was smack-dab in the middle of everything. What if Hermie had killed his sister and brother-in-law because they found out he'd put a bun in a French girl's oven? What if Hermie had leaked those scandals from the diary in an attempt to intimidate or even destroy the other people—his father, Obadiah; Eugene Hoogenband—who knew his terrible secret?

I stared at nothing for a long while, thinking. The bedside clocked ticked. My nerves cried out for coffee and my stomach chimed in with a polite request for an omelet. And despite all that commotion, my mind finally fit together two crucial pieces of the puzzle: *Hermie Inchbald and Raymond Hathorne must have known each other before Raymond arrived in America.* That was the only explanation for why Hermie was so intent on sandbagging Raymond. And judging by what Mother had said last night, they'd met in Deauville.

Why Violet or Beaulah had had the diary in her handbag when Hermie was the one leaking those high-society scandals to the press, well, one of them must be engaged to marry Hermie.

There was only one thing to do: Corner Hermie Inchbald and make him sing.

I picked up the telephone again and had the operator put me through to Inchbald Hall. No answer. I dialed 0 again and was put through to Raymond Hathorne's house. He lived next door to Hermie, so if he was home, well, perhaps he could help. I wondered if he'd ever caught up with Beaulah last night. Not that any of that mattered anymore.

Raymond himself answered after only one ring. "Lola, angel," he said, "how are you? Nerves settled down after yesterday's little fiasco at the zoo? I've always hated zoos. By the way, I lost Beaulah Starr last night after a bit of a chase, and when I returned to the zoo, you were gone."

"Never mind that. Mr. Hathorne, I'll be blunt. Did you—well, you knew that Hermie Inchbald got a French girl in the family way during the war, didn't you?"

"Why, no. What do you mean?"

"You do know, don't pretend. I saw what Hermie did written down—"

"Written down?"

"In a girl's diary, actually."

"Oh. I see. Whose diary?"

"I've put it all together—how Hermie and you knew each other previously, perhaps in France—you never did mention you'd served in the Canadian military, that would've made things so much simpler!—and the way he kept trying to warn me off of you, suggesting you're a liar. Well, I see it all now. You two recently encountered each other after many years, perhaps in Deauville this spring."

"You're right. I was a solider, and I did briefly know Hermie during the war in France. When we met again by chance in Deauville, well, I'm afraid things came to light that he had hoped he'd buried for good. That is why he has been so intent on slandering me, you see. To turn people against me just in case I happened to tell anyone about his past sins."

I knew it. "Raymond, I suspect Hermie murdered Muffy and Winfield Morris in an attempt to cover up his past. I must confront him and make him confess, and I require your help."

"I'll do what I can."

I thought fast. "I'll ask Hermie to come and meet me somewhere private, get him talking, and then you might—I know, you could spring out of nowhere and startle him and tell him you know about this scandal with the French girl, and we'll get him to confess everything."

"Do you really think you can coerce Hermie into spilling the beans just like that? You're a gorgeous girl, don't get me wrong, but Hermie's more keen on poodles than girls, so—"

"I've got it—I'll tell him I'd like to talk about poodles. That ought to do it. I know. I'll have him meet me at my yacht in the Hare's Hollow Marina. It's not seaworthy, but that probably doesn't matter."

"What about my yacht?"

"You own a yacht?"

"Of course. And—here's a thought—I've discovered a beautiful little sandy cove up the coast a bit that seems quite unused by mankind. I'll ring up Hermie with an invitation, and I'll talk to the Hare's Hollow police and arrange for some of the boys to be hiding behind the rocks on that beach, ready to hear Hermie's confession and jump to it with handcuffs and whatnot. Simply meet me at my sailboat in, oh, two hours. Slip number five at the Hare's Hollow Marina."

"Oh, thank you, Raymond."

"Put on your bathing suit, motor over, and I'll see you soon."

36

....

I threw off the covers and went down the corridor to Lillian's bedroom. Lillian snored softly in her canopied bed. I crept into her closet and found the drawer where she kept her bathing suits. I chose a black one—black is slimming, correct?—with yellow stripes around the thighs. I also stole a summery dress, a pair of beige pumps, and a sun hat.

Next, I took a jar of Pond's Vanishing Cream from Mother's vanity table. I wouldn't expose my skin to the light of day without a thick protective coat of cream. I already had enough peril in my life without the risk of a sunburn.

I bathed quickly, did my hair and makeup, and put on Pond's and the bathing suit underneath the dress. Lillian is slimmer than I am, so the legs of the bathing suit produced a tourniquet effect at mid-thigh, and the dress hugged my hips. But the shoes and hat fit like a dream.

I dined on coffee, toast, and an omelet and then arranged for

Chauncey to look after Cedric and oversee the veterinarian's visit at one o'clock.

"Miss Lillian will suffer hives with a dog on the premises, madam," Chauncey said, trying to hide a malicious smile.

I kissed Cedric good-bye, found Mother's Rolls-Royce keys, and at last, I was off.

An hour and a half later, I walked along the dock at the Hare's Hollow Marina, searching for slip number 5. Overhead, the sky was still blue, but bruise-purple clouds seethed on the horizon. Raymond had said we'd sail along the coast, though, and anyway, the plan was that Hermie Inchbald would be locked in the back of a paddy wagon before that storm ever made landfall.

A majestic white sailboat with teak trim and a gleaming mast was anchored at slip number 5. The gangway was down.

I climbed aboard. "Ahoy?" I called. Everything on deck was neatly arranged: ropes coiled like baskets, snowy white sails, brass fittings winking in the sun.

Raymond's head poked up from the stairs. "Ahoy there, Lola." He stepped around me and smoothly pulled up the gangway.

"Is Hermie already here?" I whispered.

"Down below, changing into his bathing trunks." Raymond smiled. "Say, where's that Swedish dame you're forever toting about?"

"Berta? She's gone. Took a job in Massachusetts."

"Well, that's a relief."

"A relief?" Oh dear. "Raymond, I think you're just a peach, but, well, I'm a bit goofy about another fellow at the moment. I know my mother has given you the wrong impression about all this—and I shouldn't have kissed you yesterday—and all I can say is, I'm sorry."

Raymond stalked away from me. Men and their tender feelings. Jeepers.

"Listen," I said. "We can talk about all that—*What are you doing?*"

Raymond had given the boom a heave, and it was whizzing toward me. It hit me smack in the forehead, my feet flew up in front of me, and I went down like Raggedy Ann.

Throbby-red pain. Spiraling stars. My body wouldn't move. A white blob appeared over me, and when some of those stars got out of the way, I saw it was Raymond's face.

"That was not enough, Lola?" he asked.

Why did it sound like he had a stronger French accent all of a sudden? I tried to lift myself on my elbows, but the universe gyrated and I sagged back.

Raymond crouched beside me.

Oh no. Oh no no no no no.

He had a rope.

"Get away from me!" I tried to shout. A gurgle came out. The rope was around my neck, and he was squeezing it, squeezing it, and then all sensation just wiped away, and everything went black.

I couldn't seem to move my hands and feet. Everything was rocking. My *head*.

"You're a-w-w-wake," someone said.

I forced my eyes open. Darkness. Blue light shining through a porthole. Two small, shining circles—wait. Those were glasses. Whose glasses? "Who is there?" I said. The sickbed weakness of my own voice frightened me.

"Hermie Inchbald."

Fear zinged through me. But Hermie was rope-bound, too, and wedged diagonally across a folded sail. We were in a storage hold of some kind. Two eyes gleamed beside Hermie.

"Is that Bitsy?" I croaked.

"Poor th-thing. M-muzzled and t-t-tied. Sh-sh-she's terrif-f-f-ied."

"What is happening?"

"Isn't it obvious? That ins-s-sane R-Raymond Hath-th-thorne is sailing us out to deep waters, where he p-plans to toss us over. At l-l-least, that is what he t-told me. I have n-no reason to d-d-doubt him."

"But—but *why?*"

"You th-th-thought I did it, didn't you? That I m-m-murdered poor Muffy, and then Winfield? For th-the inheritance, is that what you th-th-thought?"

"Not exactly." Raymond must have impersonated Hermie and faked a stutter on the telephone with Ida Shanks. He certainly hadn't been lying when he said he was a good actor.

"It's the p-p-poodles, isn't it? My hobby makes m-me seem odd?"

"No!" This was not the time to tell Hermie that I thought he was a Grade A Weirdie.

"You have a d-d-dog, Mrs. Woodby. You know wh-what it's like when your d-dog is the only thing you h-h-have in the world."

Tears leaked from my eyes. "Actually, yes, I do."

A latch clattered and someone ducked into the storage hold. But it wasn't Raymond.

"Violet?" I breathed. Yes, that was Violet Wilbur, all right, wearing a chic sailing dress that was perhaps too youthful for her years. She'd bobbed her hair.

"Just popping in to make sure you two haven't soiled yourselves from fright. That's a nasty bump on your forehead, Mrs. Woodby. Not that it matters much anymore, since no one but the sharks will see your corpse. Of course, the sharks will be in such a tizzy over the storm that they probably won't really see you before they chomp down."

Bitsy growled, low and vibrating.

"Oh shut up, you little bitch," Violet said.

I pushed down panic. "Do you mind filling me in as to why I'm to be shark luncheon? Not, mind you, that I believe they'll bite, seeing as I'm coated in Pond's Vanishing Cream, which works simply wonderfully for the sun but has a rather sour taste."

"Isn't it obvious, Mrs. Woodby? You are a meddler—albeit a comical one—of the first order. You and that fat little Swedish woman are like a roving vaudeville act. My God, the problems you've caused for us."

"Us?"

"François and me. I have a nerve issue, you realize, and you've pushed me rather too close to the cliff for my liking. I couldn't sleep a wink last night!"

"François is . . . Raymond Hathorne?" I asked.

"Y-yes," Hermie whispered. "And he's m-m-mad."

Violet went on. "In fact, I'm really very angry with you, Mrs. Woodby." She stepped a little closer, and I saw she'd penciled her lips into a Cupid's bow. The bob, the lips, the seamed stockings . . .

"What's happened to you, Miss Wilbur?" I asked. But I already knew: Violet was drawn to baddies like I was drawn to the candy counter at Schrafft's. And Gil Morris wasn't her gentleman friend. Oh no. Raymond was. "When did you fall in love with Raymond—I mean, François? Did you meet him in France?"

"Of course not. I met him at Willow Acres, just like you did."

"But that was, what, a week ago? And you've gone and bobbed your hair for him? That'll take ages to grow back out, you know, with a rather awkward stage to endure when the fringe passes your eyebrows—"

"I'm not growing it back out," Violet snapped. "François says this hairstyle suits me, and that is all that I desire."

"But what about good taste? I distinctly remember you writing in *Tête-à-Tête* magazine that the craze for bobbed hair made you think of a herd of Shetland ponies."

"Did I?" Violet patted her hair.

My eyes fell on her feet. She wore small, pointy shoes, the very same shoes she'd worn while trampling my hand. "That was *you* at Coney Island! Why did you murder Muffy and Winfield Morris?"

"I didn't murder them, darling. François did."

"Don't you . . . mind?"

"Why, no. I find it rather exciting, actually. I could tell the very moment I met him that he was one of the few remaining true men, a man who lives by his own rules, a man with that old noble wildness in him like a Viking or a buccaneer." Violet's voice had gone a little breathy. "I've always worshipped men like that. I saw François come out of Muffy's room that night, and when I learned in the morning that she'd died, I knew he'd killed her. I decided I must speak with him alone, tell him that I knew, tell him that I was all his, body and soul, if he'd have me."

"And he said yes?"

"How could he turn me down? I knew what he'd done, and besides, men can't resist women who worship them. Toodle-oo." Violet left, shutting the door behind her.

"Why would Raymond—François—murder Muffy and Winfield?" I asked Hermie.

Hermie shrugged.

"Do you know how he killed Muffy?"

"He b-bragged about it while he was t-t-tying me up today. He g-got the n-night n-nurse drunk in his room—"

"Beaulah!"

"—yes, so he could replace Muffy's v-vial of m-m-medicine with a v-vial containing rat poison. I knew I'd heard a w-woman g-giggling in his room the night M-M-Muffy . . . Beaulah is to m-marry Father, you know. Cunning f-floozy."

When Beaulah said she wouldn't let anyone louse up her plans, she'd meant her plans to marry Obadiah Inchbald.

And Beaulah had been terrified of *Raymond*, not me, at the book signing and at the zoo. *Raymond* had been trying to kill Beaulah. She knew what Raymond had done, but she couldn't go to the police without admitting that she'd unwittingly abetted his crime by getting splifficated on the job.

"Is she all right?" I asked Hermie. "Beaulah, I mean? Have you seen her?"

"Oh yes. She was p-planning out how she's g-going to redecorate Inchbald H-Hall this m-m-morning. T-t-tart."

The sailboat leapt and surged through choppy waters. A motor vibrated. Raymond must have been using an outboard motor to take us out into deeper waters. No one could manage sails in such a storm.

The temperature dropped. Bitsy was restless and I caught a whiff of doggy anxiety-musk. Hermie was oddly lethargic. But then, who knew what kind of violence he'd been subjected to by Raymond in order to get him tied up in this hold. My own forehead pounded with pain, and a crushing headache was in the cards.

The motor cut off. The boat swung to and fro and the wind howled, but we were no longer moving forward.

I was running out of time.

37

I jerked my hands behind me, mostly out of desperation, but . . . something marvelous happened. The ropes about my wrists slipped easily up and down. I tried moving my wrists even more, with success. All that Pond's Vanishing Cream that I'd basted myself in! I squeezed my thumbs against my palms so my hands were like seal flippers, and pulled. With a couple of strategic corkscrews, my hands slid free of the ropes.

"Abracadabra," I said.

Hermie was silent.

"What's wrong with you?" I asked. "Just as soon as I untie my ankles—" I was already working on that. "—it's your turn."

"Need I remind you that w-we are in the m-m-middle of the high seas? During a st-storm, no less?"

"So you're simply going to sit there?"

"I'm sc-scared."

"You're a war hero!"

"That's what th-th-they s-s-say."

"Never mind all that, Hermie." I knelt beside him and picked at the knots that bound his ankles. "The first order of business is getting off this boat alive, and that means that you and I must work together to restrain Raymond and Violet, and then sail back to land." Hermie's feet were free. I went to work on the ropes around his wrists. "Do you know how to sail?"

"No. Father n-never allowed me to. He prefers to d-d-do it himself."

"Even now, at his age?"

"He says I t-tie knots like a g-girl."

"Well, we'll figure it out. There is a motor. It can't be terribly difficult to operate."

As soon as Hermie was free, he reached for Bitsy's muzzle.

"Wait," I said. "Not yet. If Bitsy barks, she'll blow our cover."

"L-let me at l-least untie her."

"All right, but hurry. The storm is getting worse." The yacht pitched from side to side. An unlit lantern arced through the air, screeching.

Hermie said good-bye to Bitsy and joined me by the door.

I braced myself against the wall. "Here's the plan," I whispered. "We'll find Raymond and Violet and we'll restrain them—"

"W-with what? Our bare h-hands?"

I squinted around the storeroom. "No. With the same ropes Raymond tied us with."

We both gathered up a length of rope and went down the hallway. The yacht was heaving so violently, I clonked into the wall twice. We stopped a pace shy of an open door. Voices inside. I plastered myself against the wall and peeked in.

Violet sat atop the tall galley table, legs crossed, holding an empty champagne flute. "Hurry up, darling," she said in a pouty voice. "I'm thirsty from all this crime and we must toast our success."

Raymond was crouched in front of a low cupboard, digging around. Looking for booze, I figured.

I turned to Hermie. "Ready?" I whispered.

He nodded.

I made a floppy open knot with my rope. I burst into the galley, and before Violet could do anything more than squeal, I looped my rope up around her knees. Her champagne flute crashed to the floor.

Raymond was on his feet. "*Sacrebleu!*"

"Get off!" Violet kicked at my midriff.

I managed to tighten the rope. Violet flopped sideways on the table, floundering.

Raymond lurched around the table toward me with a champagne bottle held high like a bludgeon.

"Hermie!" I yelled.

"That worm is loose, too?" Raymond's lip curled. "Where is he?"

Footsteps pounded beyond the galley door. Hermie was running away.

Raymond scoffed. "Always the coward, eh?" Keeping hold of the champagne bottle, he shoved past me and out of the galley.

"François!" Violet shrilled. "Come back here and help me!"

I dashed after Raymond. He would kill Hermie. I knew it in my gut.

In the hallway, I stumbled against one wall and then the other as I followed Raymond. Stinging-cold rain gusted down the stairs.

He went up. I followed.

I emerged behind Raymond on deck. A weird, wet glow lit the bucking yacht. Gray clouds churned, seawater slopped, and in the distance, thunder rumbled and lightning flashed.

Hermie clung to the mast. His soaked shoulders rose and fell.

Raymond had grabbed the boom, and he inched toward Hermie while the boom made crazy pendulum swings.

I clutched the side railing, trying to inch closer to Hermie, too.

We dipped to the side and I got a faceful of icy brine. My lungs seared and my feet slipped, but I didn't loose my grip on the railing.

Raymond was going to beat me to Hermie, but I'd be darned if I didn't get to learn the solution to the puzzle before I became tartare for octopi. "Why did you murder Muffy and Winfield Morris?" I shouted to Raymond over the gusts and crashes.

"Why don't *you* tell her why, Hermie?" Raymond yelled.

Streaks of water trembled across Hermie's glasses.

"Tell her, Hermie!" Raymond shouted.

"Hermie?" I called. "Was it about the girl in France?"

"I h-had no ch-choice!" Hermie called over the gush of the sea. "It was me or her. Anyone would have done it!"

"Tell Lola what happened!" Raymond shouted. "She deserves to know before she dies, after all the trouble she has gone to."

"I c-can't!" Hermie yelled, and burst into tears.

Raymond turned to me. "Hermie killed my sister Jeannette during the Great War."

"Killed?" My voice was lost at sea.

"Not on p-purpose!" Hermie yelped.

"Oh, shut up, you coward!" Raymond roared. To me he called, "And what happened when he came home? He was decorated with a medal for gallantry!"

"What happened to your sister?" I shouted.

Raymond swept sopping hair from his eyes. "The Germans were firing upon my village. Jeannette had taken refuge in our family chicken coop. Hermie—coward!—fled from the action and also attempted to hide in the chicken coop. But there was only enough room for one." Raymond drew a labored breath. "Hermie dragged Jeannette out of the coop, threw her to the ground, and climbed into the coop himself. Jeannette was shot by a German soldier moments later. I saw it all from the barn. It happened so quickly, but I never forgot Hermie's face before he fled later into the trees. Fat, red, foolish little face. Jeannette was my best friend, and this *worm* left her dead, facedown in the mud of a chicken yard."

There had been no bun in the oven, then. Only an act of cruel cowardice.

Hermie denied nothing. He merely whimpered and clung to the mast.

Raymond went on, still shouting over the gales, "For the rest of my days, I was haunted by nightmares of that scene. I went forward with my life. I was trained as an actor, but to support myself, I became a bartender at the Normandy Barrière hotel in Deauville. Then one day this spring, like a miracle . . . Hermie Inchbald walked into my bar. It was as though I had been sent a gift: the opportunity for revenge. I would not squander such a gift, oh no. I watched. I planned. I would invade Hermie's hometown as he had invaded mine. I would kill his beloved sister as he killed mine. I would watch him suffer and then, when I'd had my fill, I would kill him, too. As luck would have it, I found Grace Whiddle's diary in Muffy's room— she'd stolen it, I suppose—and that proved to be an effective means for destroying Hermie's little world. Daddy a war-profiteering criminal? Oh, I couldn't have planned that." Raymond smiled in a sizzle of lightning.

"You leased the mansion next door to Hermie in order to watch him," I cried.

"But, of course! Spent every last franc I'd saved on this ruse, but I think it was well worth it. I haven't had a single nightmare about Jeannette since I poisoned Muffy."

"You hit golf balls onto the Inchbald estate in order to go over and snoop." Realization sucker-punched me. "You overheard me talking to Beaulah in the hedge maze the day you shot Senator Morris!"

"Yes."

Dear sweet baby bejesus. "Is that where you got the notion to kill Senator Morris? From my conversation with Beaulah?"

"Oh yes. As soon as Beaulah dropped the hint that she'd told Senator Morris what she had done the night I poisoned Muffy— allowing me to get her so drunk that she passed out—well, I knew Senator Morris and Beaulah must die, too. The Coney Island pageant sounded like a wonderful place to shoot someone. Crowds of idiots to hide in. I decided to bring Hermie and stupid old Ulf along for the ride. Very spur of the moment—bringing them was Violet's idea, actually. We supposed that between Hermie and Ulf, well, someone besides me would take the blame. Did you hear Violet and me yell 'Anarchist!'? That was all it took for that crowd of fools to panic."

"Violet is mad, you know!"

"Isn't she, though? Suits me. She'll do anything for me, silly cow."

"How did you know Tibor Ulf's sons owned Luger Parabellum pistols?"

"I didn't. That was merely a happy accident. It all worked out rather seamlessly, don't you think? Of course, I acquired *my* Luger during the war, from the corpse of a German soldier in a field outside my village."

"And you meant to kill Beaulah?"

"Yes. She's slippery, of course, but she'll be next. Last night I almost had her. I pursued her all the way from the zoo to Inchbald Hall. She got through the gates just a moment too soon. Now. We must get down to business because I really do wish to sail out of this storm. Who wants to go first? Lola, I suppose, since Hermie is such an awful coward." Raymond pulled a pistol from somewhere and aimed it at my face.

The thrum of a motor—a different motor—cut through the gush of the water and wind. Then it was obliterated.

I had no choice but to tackle Raymond and risk getting shot. I went at him, head down, like a bull in high heels.

Raymond's gun fired just as the top of my head rammed into his belly. He fell back and I staggered. The pistol went sliding. I caught the boom and clung. The three of us watched as a wave slopped over the side and carried the pistol away with it.

Hermie sobbed like a child. Violet emerged from the stairs, a dark shape behind her. Bitsy.

"François, my love!" Violet shrieked. "We must turn toward shore! Set aside your mad plan or we will all die!"

Raymond crawled toward Hermie with murder written all over his face.

The motor-thrum sliced through the waves and wind again. I caught a whiff of gasoline.

"Mrs. Woodby!" someone cried.

Was that . . . *Berta?*

Without letting go of the boom, I turned my head. A motorboat bobbed on the waves only a few yards away. Berta was waving frantically, and another shape crouched beside the motor.

Ralph called, "Don't move! I'm coming!"

"No!" I cried. "I can do it! Try to come closer!" I let go of the boom and pitched and skidded over to the yacht rail. Ralph maneuvered the motorboat alongside the yacht, leaving an undulating two or three feet of water between.

"For God's sake," Violet screamed, "I'm not going to die!" She climbed over the railing, leapt, and thunked down onto the motorboat.

"Bitsy!" I cried. Bitsy was skittering around on the deck, searching for her master. "Come on, girl. Come!"

Bitsy skidded toward me.

"Good girl! Come on."

"What are you doing, Lola?" Ralph shouted up at me.

"I'm not leaving an innocent dog to drown!"

Bitsy was a big girl, but I managed to heave her—she kicked and bucked—over the railing. I dropped her onto Ralph. Then I slung my legs so I was sitting on the rail. I took a big breath. I jumped—and banged painfully on hands and knees inside the motorboat.

Ralph's hands were on me. "You all right, kid?"

"I think so." I sat up, dazed, and cupped my hands around my mouth. "Hermie!" I screamed. "Hermie, come on! Jump! He'll kill you! Hermie!"

Hermie's white face appeared over the railing.

Bitsy squealed and reared up.

"Come on," I called to Hermie, coaxing now.

Raymond appeared behind Hermie. Hermie scrambled up and over the rail—

Whack! A white dazzle of lightning hit the sailboat's mast. Wood splintered and cracked. I smelled burning.

"You've got to get off that boat!" Ralph yelled to Hermie and Raymond. "It's gonna go down!"

"My love!" Violet shrilled. "Hurry, my love!"

Hermie jumped. He disappeared beneath a foamy splash. Raymond jumped, too, and came up gasping next to Hermie. Hermie dog-paddled toward the motorboat. I clung to the edge and held out a hand. Just before Hermie's outstretched fingers met mine, Raymond slung his arms around Hermie's shoulders. He pushed him under. They both disappeared beneath a frothing wave.

"No!" I screamed.

The wind hissed. Waves dashed against the motorboat.

We waited—Ralph, Berta, Violet, and I—five, six, seven minutes, bobbing on the wild dark sea. Bitsy whined and circled, whined and circled. The yacht slipped, inch by inch, below the water.

Hermie and Raymond never surfaced.

I hunched over my knees and sobbed. Berta patted my shoulder. "There, there, Mrs. Woodby," she said. "There, there."

"Men are so *stupid*," Violet said. Her eyes were glassy.

Ralph turned the motorboat toward shore.

38

....

I was seen by the doctor at Hare's Hollow Hospital. I had suffered bruises, knee-scrapes, and a lump on my forehead; he gave me aspirins, a funny pink pill for shock, and a lecture to stay warm and get plenty of rest. I was grilled by the police, and then at long last, I was snug in a big plushy bed at—yes!—the Ocean Princess Hotel. The room was a business expense, Berta said so herself.

Only after pushing aside my room service tray—chicken soup, salmon sandwiches, chocolate mousse—did I think to ask Berta how she and Ralph had found me on the stormy sea.

I rang Berta's room from my bedside telephone.

"You ought to be asleep, Mrs. Woodby," she said. I thought I heard a man's gravelly voice in the background.

"Who's there with you?" I asked. "Mr. Demel?"

"No one is with me. You must have seawater in your ear. To answer your question, this morning I was at Penn Station awaiting my Boston train when I thought, since I had arrived so early, that I would telephone Ida Shanks and beg her one last time for a tip regarding her informant."

"But you'd quit the agency," I said. "And you told me you've always considered it beneath you to beg."

"It seems that my heart, Mrs. Woodby, was still with the case. And, well, I felt ashamed for having left you in the lurch."

"I deserved it."

"There is that. At any rate, I reached Ida just as she was leaving for Hare's Hollow, where Eugene Van Hoogenband had just been arrested for bribing Senator Morris. Miss Shanks informed me—with not a little triumph—that you had given her an interview and that she had turned over her pivotal tip, that her informant had a stutter. I guessed it was Hermie, of course, and I grew alarmed. I telephoned your parents' apartment, and the butler told me you had gone to meet someone on Long Island and that you meant to bathe or sun yourself because—the butler said—Miss Lillian complained of you having stolen one of her bathing suits. Knowing your dislike of bathing suits, Mrs. Woodby, I surmised that you meant to take drastic actions to trap Hermie."

"Yes, well, luckily the bathing suit never had an airing." I should've asked the doctor to treat the red dents in my thighs from that suit.

"But you were willing. To continue, after I spoke with your parents' butler, I hurried to the Long Island Railroad ticket counter. I arrived in Hare's Hollow and, not knowing where to look first, I went to Breakerhead, where, as I had hoped, Mr. Oliver was still speaking to newspaper reporters about his bust of Mr. Van Hoogenband. Together, Mr. Oliver and I went first to the swimming beach and then, in a stroke of insight on my part, to the marina. And indeed, a rather rough salty dog said he had seen someone matching your description board a sailboat that subsequently sailed off toward the storm. At this juncture, poor Mr. Oliver was most distressed."

"Then what?"

"Mr. Oliver started the engine of our borrowed motorboat by short-circuiting the ignition, and we were on our way. We had a dreadful time finding you in that storm—" Inexplicably, Berta giggled, and I heard a slapping sound and more of that gruff voice in the background.

"Berta?" I said.

"We will speak tomorrow, Mrs. Woodby—the, ah, the maid with the extra towels is rapping most persistently at the door." She rang off.

Something was suspicious. But it was, for a change, the good kind of suspicious. I scraped up the remnants of my chocolate mousse, curled up under my silky quilt, and fell back to sleep.

I slept for sixteen hours, breakfasted in bed, bathed luxuriously, and at eleven o'clock, I found myself in hell.

Scratch that. The beach in a bathing suit had once been my idea of hell, but I was finding it actually rather pleasant. The sky was Dresden blue with a few lamby clouds. No trace of yesterday's storm. The sand was yellow and hot. The surf crashed on a medium-low setting—nothing to stir up shell shock after yesterday—and a red-and-white umbrella shaded me. I wore tinted glasses, slathers of Pond's Vanishing Cream, and—listen to this—I wore a *bathing suit*. In public. Not Lillian's thigh-strangling number, but one I'd purchased at the dry goods emporium on Main Street. My legs were scraped and bruised, but other than that, well, they looked all right. Nothing at all like blocks of cheese.

I sipped the iced lemonade that Ralph, beside me, had brought in a canteen from the Foghorn, where he'd slept last night. We had both apologized for being jelly beans, and I had told him how I'd come clean to the world about . . . everything.

Not that we'd discussed hearts or cupids or coconut icing. I'd sworn off such topics.

Newspapers were spread out on our beach blankets, fluttering in the salty breeze. Cedric panted gently beside me. I scratched his ears.

When I telephoned my parents' apartment that morning, Mother had refused to speak with me. I spoke with Lillian instead, who couldn't contain her glee when she told me that Mother had disowned me—whatever that meant. Then Mother sent Chauncey and a doorman in the Daimler to fetch the Rolls-Royce I'd borrowed—and to deliver Cedric to me at the Ocean Princess Hotel.

"The Spratt's Puppy Biscuits people telephoned to say that they've given the advertising contract to a Yorkshire terrier named Benny," I told Ralph. "Some big cheese at Spratt's saw a photograph in the newspaper of Cedric wedged between the bars of the tiger's cage at the zoo." We had all made the newspapers. I supposed that meant we were famous.

Ralph petted Cedric. "Aw. But you know, Cedric's not cut out for the working life anyway, is he? And his pudge, well, it saved his life. Without this tummy of his, he would've slipped right into that cage like a coin into a slot."

"You're probably right," I said. Secretly, I was relieved that I'd be making more money than my dog. I do have my pride.

"Did I mention you look pretty swell in that getup?" Ralph said. He flicked a few grains of sand from my thigh.

Swell? As in, swollen? No, he hadn't meant it that way. I smiled. "You don't look half bad in your bathing trunks, Mr. Oliver. And I must say, I'm relieved you have that Irish skin and must stay out of the sun, because otherwise I'd feel a bit lonely under this umbrella."

"It's pretty cozy, isn't it?" Ralph leaned over Cedric to kiss me.

"I beg your pardon," Berta said from her canvas chair on the other side of me. "I am still here, you know."

"So am I," someone else said in a grinding-gears voice. Jimmy the Ant peered around Berta. His bandy legs were hairy and pale beneath his one-piece woolen bathing suit. His glass eye lolled.

"Sorry, Mrs. Lundgren," Ralph said. "Sorry, Jimmy."

"Sorry," I said.

Berta, wearing a modest blue bathing suit with bloomers, rustled her newspaper. "Mr. Oliver, *The Morning Chanticleer* says that you are—and I quote—a 'gumshoe par excellence.' I think Mr. Van Hoogenband's arrest will be very good for your business."

"I had two job offers over my eggs and toast this morning," Ralph said, leaning back on his elbows.

Berta folded *The Morning Chanticleer* and unfolded *The New York Evening Observer*.

I sighed. I hadn't yet had the heart to look at the Ida Shanks interview.

Berta said, "Ida's interview of Mrs. Woodby paints a picture of a mad, accident-prone, vampish woman who will do whatever it takes to collar her prey—"

"I need an ice cream cone," I said.

"—and who, along with—and again I quote—'her intrepid and resourceful former cook'—will be sure to crack many cases in the future."

I perked up. "She wrote that?"

"Indeed, she did."

Ralph said, "Well, I'll be. Ida threw you a bone."

"Do you know how cats keep mice alive just so they can torment them longer?" I said. "That's what Ida's up to."

"Probably," Berta said, "but regardless of her intentions, I believe this interview will bring us the work that our one-and-a-half-inch-square advertisement failed to."

"Fingers crossed." I stared out at the glittering sea. Raymond and Hermie's bodies hadn't been found. Not yet, anyway. Maybe it was poetic justice, the way they had gone down together. Their lives had been melded together years ago in that muddy chicken yard in France.

"Don't think about it, kid," Ralph said, brushing a strand of hair from my bruised forehead. "You need a little distance first. A little rest."

"If Mother hadn't lied about knowing Raymond's mother and all that, I would've been more suspicious of him. She lied simply to try to marry me off!"

"Don't beat yourself up," Ralph said. "You did all you could, and you did a hell of a job, too."

"Golly geebejabbers, am I roastin' in this suit!" Jimmy said. He stood and offered a hand to Berta. "Tomato, how's about a swim?"

"I would be delighted," Berta said.

Jimmy hoisted her to her feet, and together they walked down to the surf.

"What hole did he crawl out of?" Ralph asked, gesturing with his chin at Jimmy.

"I'm not sure. But evidently, it was Berta's photograph in the newspaper yesterday—of her competing in the Mermaid Queen Pageant, you know—that lured him out of hiding. He could no longer endure being apart from her, he said, and I guess the Feds aren't looking for him anymore." I poked Ralph's warm, hard chest. Which was . . . distracting. "Jimmy's lucky you're not a Fed."

"Well, actually," Ralph said, "after the Van Hoogenband bust yesterday, the Feds tried to recruit me."

I sat up and pushed my sunglasses to the top of my head. "What did you say?"

"I said no. I've got to be my own boss. I'd hate to be tied down to anything."

Anything?

"Aw, don't look at me like that," Ralph said. He leaned in till all I saw were his bright gray eyes. "I'm crazy about you, kid, all right? I—" He scratched his eyebrow. "—well, the funny thing is, I . . . this has never happened to me before, Lola, but I—aw, c'mon and just kiss me already."

Our lips were tickling-close, but I pulled away. Later, I knew there would be a warm, starry night in Ralph's arms, with hot jazz, hotter kisses, and—at long last!—cold highballs. But right now, just this once, I wanted to be the one with my hands on the steering wheel. I batted my eyelashes. "What is it, Ralph? What were you going to say?"

Ralph sighed. He sandwiched one of my hands between both of his. He frowned out at the sea. He turned to me and said, "I love you, kid. God help me, but I do."

I savored the moment, made it a long one, before saying, "Ditto, sweetheart." Then I kissed him.